"Unbelievably interesting and fast moving. The first business book that covers the 'how to' and holds your interest constantly. The common sense novel approach caught me living the story as it unfolded. We will be applying the valuable principles in our business."

> Don Kitzmiller
> Vice-President of Sales and Marketing
> Midmark Corporation

"If the most puzzling mystery you face is how to turn around sales, you'll be happy to discover that THE QUADRANT SOLUTION provides the answer."

> John Folkerth
> President and CEO
> Shopsmith, Inc.

"Selling in the 90s requires new ideas and approaches. THE QUADRANT SOLUTION offers fresh insights and a process to follow for success in this new age."

> Buck Blessing
> President
> Buck Blessing & Associates

"The challenging questions to successful sales in the 90s can be found within THE QUADRANT SOLUTION, an informative book of drama for all sales personnel to read."

> J. Michael Lancaster
> First Vice-President, Director of
> Franchise Development
> Coldwell Banker Residential Affiliates

THE QUADRANT SOLUTION

A BUSINESS NOVEL THAT SOLVES THE MYSTERY OF SALES SUCCESS

HOWARD STEVENS and JEFF COX

amacom
American Management Association

This book is available at a special
discount when ordered in bulk quantities.
For information, contact Special Sales Department,
AMACOM, a division of American Management Association,
135 West 50th Street, New York, NY 10020.

Library of Congress Cataloging-in-Publication Data

Stevens, Howard, 1941-
    The quadrant solution: a business novel that solves the mystery of
sales success / Howard Stevens and Jeff Cox.
        p.   cm.
    ISBN 0-8144-5986-2 (hardcover)
    I. Cox, Jeff, 1951-   .   II. Title.
PS3569.T45155Q34   1990   90-53217
813'.54--dc20   CIP

Printing number

10   9   8   7   6   5   4   3   2   1

To
all professional salespeople
who build sales, develop market share, and satisfy customers

Contents

Acknowledgments

A large number of salespeople, customers, and executives volunteered time and insights about sales and salespeople that aided in the development of this book. Our thanks go to all the truly professional salespeople who made possible the data on which this book is based. We especially wish to thank Keith Crutcher, Jim Grimm, and Robert Wright for their assistance.

We further wish to express our appreciation and gratitude to Weldon Rackley and Eva Weiss for their support throughout the project, and extend thanks to the AMACOM staff.

We also thank David Loynd for concepts and background pertaining to high-tech electronic communications systems.

I went to work for Elemenco at a time when few had a clue that this was a company stalled under the weight of its own success. To most people, including most of our own managers and employees, Elemenco was one of the glamour names in electronics and computers. We were solid yet exciting, a demi-celebrity of a company experiencing merely a brief lull, so everybody believed, before we collected our energies and grew to dizzying new heights of performance and profit. Well, it was because of the lull that I was hired. As months passed, Elemenco's president, Reed Morrison, began to doubt that the marketing plan in place could make it go away. We had worked together before, and he thought I could help. I didn't know all of this when I arrived, but I brought some new ideas with me. This is how I got my chance to make a difference.

    I arrived in mid-January at Elemenco's headquarters in Chicago. About a quarter past eight on a Thursday morning—I had been with the company since Monday—I was getting ready to go down to a meeting of all the regional sales managers when my phone rang. It was Gene Cherson, my new boss, telling me to come down to his office instead.

    As I walked in, Gene was sitting, cigarette in hand, at his desk. Behind him was the city in winter shades of gray, from Jackson Boulevard on south. He was talking to Jim Woller, the national sales manager, who was standing with his back to me.

"So go ahead and start the meeting without us," Gene was telling Woller. "David and I will be down as soon as we're done here."

Woller walked past me and left without any comment.

"What's up?" I asked Gene.

"I just found out I have to do an interview this morning," he said. "The *Journal* is writing a story on us. Morrison can't meet with the reporter until later, if at all, and he wants me to talk to her. I'd like it if you would sit in."

Being the new kid on the block, I had hoped to get to the meeting early and talk to some of the sales managers before the presentations started, but obviously that would have to wait.

"Fine," I said. "I'll be glad to sit in if you want me to, but I really don't know what kind of contribution I can make."

"Why not? We need to talk about new products. You're manager of product development. Why can't you make a contribution?"

"Well, I've only been here three days," I said.

That seemed to ignite something in Gene.

"Hey, David, how much time do you need? A month? A year? What the hell is this? I've got news for you. This is a fast-moving business. I don't know what it was like at your last job, but around here you've got to be able to think on your feet."

This was a great start. Maybe he was mad at Morrison, and the anger was being vented at me. But I didn't deserve this.

"Gene, wait a minute," I told him. "I said I'd do the interview with you, no problem. I just believe in getting my facts down before I start making public statements. Now would you mind telling me why it's so important for me to be in on this?"

He was a huge man in every physical dimension—height, width, and circumference. I stand about five feet ten, but Gene was half a head taller. He leaned forward, bringing his face down to my level, and said with forced calmness, "I want you here because we've got to give them some blue sky to look at."

Blue sky to look at? What did *that* mean?

"You know what I'm getting at?" Gene began to pace in front of the window, gesturing with his cigarette. "We're in a down cycle now, but I don't want the slump to be the focus of what's said about us. If this reporter starts harping about how

2

sales are off and how we're losing share, I want to be able to say, 'Now, wait, let's look at the future!' Right? Are you with me? Let's aim their attention at the new products we've got coming."

"Okay, such as?"

That set him off again.

"Come on, David, wake up!" he said.

He stepped over to his desk and crushed out the cigarette in a big, amber ashtray already soiled with four or five butts.

"What do you *think* we ought to talk about? Don't you even know the products by now? We got to talk about the new 720 Network. We got to talk about the new 486 machine we've got coming. Plus PowerCase and we ought to get in a word about PowerSeat for the airlines. Let's talk about the new retail chain, too, and how . . . Well, no, let's not talk about that unless it comes up."

He yanked open the top drawer of the desk and took out a roll of antacids, peeled back the foil, and put a pair of the white tablets in his mouth. His face was flushed.

"What about the new tracking software for Apogee?" I asked. "Should we mention that?"

"Sure, that's fine," said Gene. "Now, look, the main points I want to get across are about our increased selling efficiency, the new leaner sales organization, and . . . well, you know, implanting entrepreneurial vision, selling systems solutions, aggressive marketing posture, and all that blah, blah, blah. Okay?"

I didn't say anything.

"Look, I'll do most of the talking, maybe even all of it. But, just in case, you be ready to throw in some optimistic words about new developments. And don't be afraid to hype it up a little."

Then he gave me a weak little smile.

"I'm sure it'll be fine," he said. "And don't mind it if I sounded a little honked off. You'll find I'm just an intense kind of guy. Okay?"

"Don't worry about it," I said. "How soon is the interview?"

"Any minute," Gene said. "Our PR guy just called. They're on their way now."

"Well, I'll just stick around then."

"You want some coffee?" he asked.

"No thanks."

He went out, mug in hand. I stood looking out his window—his other window, the west one, which mostly offered a great view of the middle floors of the Sears Tower, plus my own reflection on the glass. Dark hair and dark eyes, dark suit, dark tie, white shirt, and white face. Pants a little tight from too many restaurants. The unexpected sight of myself gave me a sense of calm and confidence. I could handle this—both Gene Cherson and the reporter. I'd handled worse.

We've got to give them some blue sky to look at. With lines like that, no wonder the company was in trouble. It crossed my mind that maybe coming to Elemenco had been a mistake.

Reed Morrison had been after me for a couple of years to come to Chicago. We had worked together back in the 1970s in California at IJK, my—our—former employer. He'd been in charge of manufacturing and I had started as a product engineer. That was before my move to marketing. Anyway, Reed and I had developed a mutual respect. He had supported me in tackling some quality and design problems, and my team and I had turned out a line of winners.

Morrison went on to bigger challenges at Elemenco as head of operations. Time passed and one day I got a call from him just after he'd been named Elemenco's new president. He'd asked me then if I wanted to move, but I was comfortable so I'd turned him down. Two years went by. We met by accident at a trade show in Las Vegas, had dinner together, and he made the offer again. By then I thought I was ready for a change. So I flew to Chicago for a visit a month later and Gene interviewed me, but it was Morrison who really hired me (perhaps another reason for the friction with Gene). Well, that happened late in the fall; now it was winter and here I was.

Gene came back with his coffee, went behind his desk, and fired up another cigarette. It was cold and quiet, neither of us saying a word to each other. Then voices sounded from just outside in the hall, and knuckles tapped softly on the open door.

A young guy in a dark blue suit was the one knocking. Next to him was a woman in a well-tailored gray dress and

4

jacket. Her hair, cut to "professional" length, was a richly colored blond, and she wore glasses with big, clear lenses, behind which were big, clear gray eyes. She was in her late twenties, I figured, maybe early thirties. In one hand, she carried a satchel-style leather briefcase, and over her shoulder, her purse.

Gene immediately snapped into enthusiasm and said in a booming voice, "Hello, Brian, come on in!"

Brian began the introductions.

"Lynne, this is Gene Cherson, our vice-president of marketing and sales. Gene, meet Lynne Welsey of the *Journal*."

Gene shook hands with her, then said, "And this is David Kepler. He's our new manager of product development and I've asked him to sit in with us. David, do you know Brian, our PR manager?"

I had seen him a couple of times in the hall, but we hadn't met. I shook hands with both Brian and the reporter.

At one end of Gene's office was some visitors furniture—two armchairs, a coffee table, a sofa, lamps, and so on. We all sat down, Lynne and Brian on the sofa, Gene and I in the two armchairs next to it. Lynne took out a microcassette tape recorder and a yellow pad from her briefcase, and set the tape recorder on the coffee table.

We made some small talk about the weather while she was getting ready, then she looked up at Gene and said, "Let's make sure I have basics right. To start, Mr. Cherson, how would you define your business?"

Gene put a hand on his chin momentarily, as if pondering a reply, then said, "As you may know, Elemenco manufactures and markets electronic products, ranging from satellite dishes to cellular car phones to computer cable to software to . . . well, you name it. But I would define our business as selling systems solutions to the electronic communications needs of our customers."

Wow. Wasn't that smooth? And off he went in that direction, dispensing a speech that he might have given to a prospective customer. He was very good at it. He told her about Elemenco starting out in the 1950s making transistors and electronic circuitry, and about a couple of our "firsts" in the industry history book, about how all of that evolved into computers and data communications through the 1970s and into the 1980s.

And Lynne sat there, leaning forward, a pleasant look on her face, taking it in, pad on the top of her thigh, jotting a note now and then, and otherwise letting Gene's words flow passively into her tape recorder. No wedding ring, I noticed.

"So we really cover the spectrum," Gene said. "With annual sales of about a billion dollars, we're a mid-size giant of quality computer and electronic communications systems for everybody—from single users to multinational corporations."

"How would you describe your overall marketing strategy?" Lynne asked. "Or, to pose that familiar question, where would you like to see your company in, say, five years?"

"Well, frankly, we're striving for market leadership," he said. "Our plan, in fact, is to become a department store, if you will, of computers and communications for the next decade and beyond."

He got up from his chair and began to stroll about the office as he talked, gesturing fluidly, as if his energy would not allow him to stay still. As I said, he was a huge man, well over six feet tall and a good twenty or thirty pounds overweight. Walking around, he dominated the room.

". . . So our future will be characterized by maintaining the solid base we have built over the years and expansion into new areas of growth."

"Speaking of expansion," Lynne asked, "what about the purchase of that chain of retail computer outlets? How's that working out for you?"

"Just fine. It's a bold new direction for Elemenco," Gene said.

Bold? Come on, Gene.

"But don't those stores market computer systems for small businesses and home users? That's straying a bit from what you know, isn't it?" asked Lynne.

"Not really. It's still electronics, and that's our business," said Gene.

"Don't you find the needs of large corporate accounts differ considerably from those of smaller business, not to mention individual consumers?"

"Well, if we can satisfy the complex needs of a *Fortune* 500 customer, why can't we satisfy those of smaller customers as well?" said Gene. "In fact, if results match our optimism, we could grow strongly in the retail area. After all, what matters to all customers, be they large corporate accounts, small businesses, or individual consumers, is a quality product at a reasonable price. And that's what Elemenco is committed to providing in every market where we compete."

Lynne was still nodding, but I saw a downward twitch at the right corner of her mouth. She was getting skeptical, while Gene kept talking, trying to convince her.

"You see, no matter who they are, customers want value. . . ."

And he went on with some nice-sounding patter that glossed over the fact that the retail chain had gone from mediocrity to red ink at the end of last quarter. With every passing month, it was looking more and more like a big loser.

"So, getting back to your mainstay business," Lynne said, "tell me, what went wrong on the Northern Airline negotiation?"

She asked this in a casual tone, as if she were a friend who just wanted to know.

"What went wrong? I don't know that anything went wrong exactly," said Gene. "We were one of several suppliers considered for the contract."

"Insiders tell me it was worth $320 million over three years," she said. "Isn't it tough to miss the chance for that kind of business, assuming you want to grow?"

"Sure, it was one we would have liked to have had, but. . ."

"But it went to your largest competitor," she said.

"Largest in that product area, not our largest overall," he said.

"Regardless, the fact remains you didn't make the sale. It was a huge contract and it went to a competitor."

"True, but I don't feel too bad about that one. We were, after all, in the final running, and our technology really is superior—"

"Then it must have been heartbreaking," Lynne said, cutting him off. "I mean, knowing you're topnotch and still not getting the business. What could it be?"

"You'd have to ask the customer," Gene said.

"As a matter of fact, I did ask them, and they did indeed confirm that your technology was topnotch, your reputation for quality good, and all that. But my source there became vague when I asked him for a clear reason why they didn't go with you. He could only offer that his company's trust was stronger in your competitor, even though they weren't technically quite as good. Now how do you explain that?"

There was silence for a few seconds. Gene was looking pained and rather pale. As if retreating, he went behind his desk and took out his antacids again.

"If I may, Gene," I broke in, "I really don't think we can speak for our competition. Obviously, we don't know what was in their proposal or what they may have promised."

"And, anyway," Gene added, "who can say what goes through the mind of a customer when they make a buying decision?"

"That wasn't the only big contract you lost last year," responded Lynne. "Even before that was the National Motors contract, one of your oldest and best customers, lost to another competitor."

"Well, that happens. All I can say is you win some, you lose some," said Gene. "You know, we've had our successes, too." He rattled off half a dozen big-name companies for which we were doing business.

"Okay, but look at the last three years, Mr. Cherson. There has been no real growth in that time. Your reported third-quarter earnings were down considerably. And lately industry sources say that Elemenco has been losing share in almost every product category across the board. How much of a decline are we going to see in Elemenco's sales and income for the past year?"

This time Brian jumped to the rescue, saying that we couldn't comment on that because fourth-quarter earnings wouldn't be announced for another week or two. All the same, we were very much on the defensive. This was not going to be a friendly interview.

"But you have to be expecting a decline, don't you?" she persisted.

"Well, it's true that we've encountered some market soft-ness," said Gene.

"But even in a soft market, many of your competitors don't seem to have had the problems you've had."

"Well, in all honesty, there were complicating factors for us," said Gene. "For instance, we've been undergoing a substantial reorganization of our marketing and sales operations and this may have been a factor."

But Lynne was not backing down. "Something doesn't add up here, Mr. Cherson. You're telling me that you covet a market leadership position, that you have all this excellent technology and great quality, and you're looking toward expansion into new areas, and yet the record shows otherwise. If your products and technology really are superior, and nobody I've talked to doubts that they aren't at least highly competitive, why isn't this being demonstrated in sales?"

Gene was in trouble. The glib corporate clichés were not working. She was asking exactly the kind of questions that neither Gene nor anyone else at Elemenco had been able to answer. I looked at Gene and actually began to feel sorry for him. Had Morrison, not wanting to take the blame, deliberately shifted the interview to Gene to put him on the spot? Gene's earlier confidence had evaporated. He rubbed the fingers of his left hand and forced a laugh.

"You sound like the board of directors," Gene said. "Seri-ously, though . . ."

Gene glanced at Brian and then at me, desperate for one of us to come to his aid. Brian looked down at the floor and said nothing, so I jumped in.

"Let's look at the bright side."

"You mean there is one?" asked Lynne.

"Of course there is," I said, wondering if I was lying. "No matter how you cut it, we have a lot going for us."

I started blathering about the advances in product devel-opment, like the 720 Network, and PowerSeat, "which we expect to introduce very— well, sometime soon."

"What's PowerSeat?" she asked.

"PowerSeat has capabilities similar to our existing prod-uct, PowerCase—"

"Which are?"

"PowerCase is a briefcase with built-in fax, cellular telephone, and personal computer. Most of the circuitry is VLSI and built into the shell of the briefcase, which is made out of composite materials. It's lightweight, very strong, very powerful. We can show you a sample—"

"No, that's all right," she said. "A press release would be fine."

Brian made a note.

"And PowerSeat," I continued, "takes the same capabilities and builds them into a passenger seat on an airplane. At least, that's the concept."

"I see," she said.

"So with new technology and new products, we should achieve the market leadership position Gene was talking about."

"Wait a minute," said Lynne. "If the products you already have are so good, then why aren't they selling? And if you can't sell what you already have on the market, is it going to do you any good to introduce new products? Doesn't the problem of growth for your company pretty much rest on the doorstep of marketing and sales?"

I was about to respond—try to, anyway—when Gene stopped me.

"Okay," he said in a confessional tone, "I would say that any recent leveling off or decline—if that's what the actual numbers for the year finally show—was due largely to inefficiencies in our marketing and sales. There was a time, and it was not so long ago, when we had as many as four or five salespeople calling on the same customer. It was confusing to the customers, and it was not a cost-effective way for us to do business."

Lynne started scribbling.

"So we undertook a complete reorganization of marketing and sales operations. Last year, we consolidated offices and districts, trimmed the middle-management reporting tree, and introduced new systems, such as telemarketing, to help us generate leads in all our markets. As a result, we've gained some important cost and operational efficiencies."

Lynne was nodding. "And how do your salespeople feel about it?"

"Well, we did some things for them too," said Gene. "We introduced a brand-new compensation plan, which unifies the levels of pay and benefits all Elemenco salespeople receive. We also reoriented how the Elemenco salesperson will sell. Now all salespeople are responsible for selling *all* Elemenco products and services. This should create more professional challenges and opportunities for the salespeople, and enable greater sales effectiveness."

Gene took out a handkerchief from his back pocket and patted his brow. He was pacing by his desk now.

"So, to sum up, we have unified and improved a number of aspects of our marketing organization that may have been holding us back. We're working to develop an entrepreneurial vision throughout this new organization—"

"We call it Gene's Lean Mean Marketing Machine," said Brian.

"Really?" said Lynne, looking dubiously at Gene's enormous girth. "That's cute." She made a note on her pad.

"And," Gene continued, "we are now in a very aggressive posture for future growth through systems solutions and with our new marketing and sales organization."

Lynne frowned and said, "Still, Mr. Cherson, as I understand it your new organization has been in place for a while now, and it still doesn't seem to be producing results. How are you going to recover not only from some big contracts you've missed, but a general decline in sales that the industry analysts are expecting?"

"I really think it's just a question of time before we start hitting on all eight cylinders, so to speak. What you've been seeing, I think, is the, uh, aftermath of the . . . well, the confusion from the reorganization, which is now behind us. In the months ahead, I'm sure you'll see us fighting our way back."

"One of the things industry observers have been saying lately," said Lynne, "is that you've only been able to maintain what market share you do have by sharp discounting, and that a high proportion of your sales are volume for the sake of volume. What do you say to that?"

"I would say that, yes, some of our pricing is aggressive," Gene said. "In this day and age, it has to be, doesn't it? One of the other things we've done for our salespeople is to give them more leeway in making pricing decisions. That's just part of our commitment to compete in the electronics market with the highest efficiency."

Lynne was shaking her head. "Maybe I'm missing something, but I still don't get it. You keep talking about sales efficiency and yet how can you say that your new organization is more efficient if you're not producing more sales?"

A look of pure terror flashed over Gene's face. He didn't say anything at first, but began reaching for his tie. I wasn't sure if Gene wanted to loosen the tie or just straighten it. He seemed to be fighting for composure.

"Well, uh, we're more efficient because . . ."

He trailed off. His face became extremely distressed. And then I realized that his distress had nothing to do with her question.

"Gene, are you all right?" I asked.

Gene didn't answer. He was behind his desk now, reaching for his chair so that he could sit down. Instead he fell to the floor.

From the corner of my eye, I saw Lynne cover her mouth with her hands. Brian jumped to his feet but then stood there frozen. Then both their faces turned to me, as if I were in control, as if I had to do something. I rushed across the office and went behind the desk to where the big man was sprawled on the carpet, staring up.

"What's wrong with him?" asked Lynne.

I bent down over Gene, whose face was all twisted in panic and pain. I asked him a couple of questions and he couldn't even talk. His mouth kept opening, but he couldn't seem to get air.

"It looks like he's having a heart attack," I said.

I asked Brian and Lynne if either of them knew how to do CPR, because I didn't. Brian didn't either. Lynne said no, but she'd written a story about it once. Great. So, burying my own revulsion, I got down on my knees next to Cherson's head and gave him mouth-to-mouth.

I heard Brian behind me on the phone calling the paramedics as a throng of people gathered around. Feeling helpless, I watched Gene's skin take on a blue tinge. He was unconscious by now.

2

Years ago, when I was a teenager, my father began complaining of indigestion one evening after Mom made corned beef and cabbage for dinner. He tried the usual remedies, but his indigestion got worse. By morning he was dead. His indigestion was in fact a heart attack that went on and on for hours until it finally killed him.

Knowing that heart attacks are not necessarily sudden, I'm surprised I didn't recognize the symptoms sooner at that meeting. But, in any event, Gene Cherson did not die that morning. The paramedics must have arrived pretty soon after I started the mouth-to-mouth. They came with cases of gear and took over. A few minutes later Gene was on a stretcher and they were on the way to the hospital.

Just because I felt somebody should, I went after them, hailed a cab on the street, and followed the ambulance to the hospital. I sat in the waiting room off the intensive care ward, me and a bunch of dull green vinyl chairs, until Gene's wife got there. By then, the nurses said, Gene was stabilized and resting, and there was nothing for me to do except get back to work, trivial as that seemed in the scope of things.

It was early afternoon by the time I got to the sales managers' meeting, an all-day affair. I found the meeting room and as I walked in I was somewhat surprised to find none other than J. Reed Morrison himself sitting there at the table next to Jim Woller. After hearing about Gene, Morrison had apparently canceled his appointments to be there.

All faces around the table—Cherson's staff (who knew me) and the sales managers themselves (who didn't yet)—turned to me as I came in.

Morrison held up his hand to stop the meeting and asked, "How is Gene doing?"

I told them as much as I knew.

"Must have been a rough interview," somebody said.

"Rougher on some of us than others," I said.

Which won a chuckle around the table and relieved some of the tension, but left me feeling guilty, because it wasn't really funny.

"For those of you who haven't had the pleasure, this is David Kepler," said Morrison. "He comes to us from IJK, which is where I met him. Most recently, he was head of marketing at IJK, which was struggling until David came in and got sales back on track. I've asked David to manage our product development function, because I think he has some ideas and viewpoints that could help us. Anyway, I invite all of you to get to know him."

The meeting resumed. A typical agenda for these meetings, I've been told, opened with some low-key presentations in the morning to the sales managers. This was when engineering or the R&D folks would wheel in new products, the ad manager would talk about new campaigns, market research would be reviewed, that kind of thing. Then, in the afternoon, it would be the sales managers' turn and Gene Cherson would hold court while the managers presented results for the previous quarter and forecasts for the next.

So now, with Morrison at the head of the table, the sales managers one by one got up and gave their grim reports. It had been an absolutely terrible fourth quarter. Sales were off 24 percent from the same quarter of the previous year, and down 10 percent from the third quarter, which also had been abysmally low. Huge numbers, tens of millions off the mark.

It was a sad parade made all the more miserable by the sales managers' struggle to make the news sound not quite so bad in front of the boss of bosses. The worst report came from Ann Lansky, sales manager for the Central Region, who was last to present that afternoon. Not that I think this is automatically significant, but Lansky was the first (and at that time only) woman to be named an Elemenco regional sales manager. More noteworthy in this context, Ann and her salespeople had been doing well even when everybody else's performance had stagnated. Until the reorganization, that is. Sales for the year just ended were more than 35 percent below her own projections.

"Wait a minute," said Woller as Lansky was concluding a summary that tried to make the numbers look better than they were. "I seem to recall that as of last quarter you had something like $40 million in pending contracts and other negotiations."

"Well . . . I don't know if it was exactly $40 million," she said.

"All right, whatever it was, what the hell happened to those sales?" Woller asked.

Ann opened her mouth, but no words came.

"Your rate of successful closings is way, way off," said Woller. "And now you're telling me that for the first quarter of this year you only have $28 million pending. If your success rate on closings continues to be the same, how much of that $28 million are you going to bring home?"

Ann nervously put a finger to her temple and pushed back a strand of brown hair. Mostly brown, some gray. She was a woman in her early forties.

"Now wait a minute, Jim. If you look at what we all know is a very significant number, the sales dollar volume per salesperson ratio, you'll see we're not that bad," said Ann.

"Ann, less is still less!"

Ann hesitated for a few seconds, then said, "Yes, that's true. And I admit we've had a disappointing fourth quarter. But bear in mind, the rise in interest rates didn't help us any—"

Morrison cut in, saying, "Fine, Ann, I think that's all we need to hear. Thank you."

Getting up from the table, Morrison turned his back to the group for a moment. Morrison is a tall, fit, good-looking man with salt-and-pepper hair and the hard, narrow brow and eyes some of the advertising research folks say we subconsciously associate with dominance. When he turned back around his eyes drilled through everybody in the room.

"So this is where we begin," he said. "First of all, these results are totally unacceptable."

He looked directly at Ann.

"Some of you should be embarrassed by what you're turning in. All I can say is there had better not be another meeting in which we get a group of reports like these."

Ann was staring back defiantly, clearly very angry. Her look said, *don't you dare tell me it's all my fault.*

"I have to leave in a few minutes. But if anybody has any comments or suggestions I'd sure like to hear them," Morrison said. "Ann, you're looking straight at me. You got something to say?"

"Yes, I do, Mr. Morrison. With all due respect to Gene Cherson, I can't help but feel that some of the changes we made last year are at least partly responsible for what's happening. I'm not saying Gene's Lean Mean Marketing Machine wasn't a good idea, or that some trimming wasn't warranted. But maybe it's time we had a little more meat on the bones."

"What exactly *are* you saying?"

"I'm saying I need more resources, more good salespeople to get the job done."

"Bull," said Morrison. "You haven't even shown us you can be effective with what you have. Look at the numbers!"

"My salespeople have been working as many hours as ever," Ann argued. "And we're still not bringing in the sales."

"But that's exactly my point, said Morrison. "Nobody is questioning that you're all working hard. Nobody is questioning your dedication. But you're not selling effectively. Where are the results? Where are the sales? You've got to do better with what you've got."

But instead of backing off, Ann leaned forward. "Mr. Morrison, I had *three* good salespeople leave in the last six months. Not as a group. There was no conspiracy that I know of. They just were unhappy and they left."

"Then what are you doing as a sales manager that's causing these people to leave?" asked Morrison. "It's your job as a manager to keep your people satisfied and motivated so that they strive to reach the objectives of this organization."

With that, Ann sat back and kept quiet. Angry, but quiet.

"Are there any more questions or comments?" Morrison asked.

One brave soul asked, "Who's going to take over for Gene Cherson while he's in the hospital?"

"An interim manager will be announced shortly," said Morrison, not looking at Jim Woller, but in fact looking away from him.

Then Morrison glanced at his watch.

"All right, I have to leave," he said and turned to Jim Woller. "Jim, I want you and your people here to review your projections for the coming year. In my opinion, your sales targets need to be upwardly adjusted. I want you to come back to me by the end of the month with new, achievable targets *and* with strategies for how you are going to reach those targets. I do thank you all for your efforts. But it's going to take a lot more than ordinary effort to get this company growing again. We deserve to be in a leadership position, and it's your job to get us there. I expect more from all of you."

He began walking out of the room and Woller stood up to take charge. Just as Woller started to say something, I felt a hand on my shoulder.

On his way out, Morrison leaned down to whisper into my ear, "Come see me in my office after the meeting. I want to talk to you."

All eyes and ears were on Woller. He was a slim and smooth guy who had impressed me in our first meeting, because he seemed to know a lot about the electronics industry and about sales. But in our second meeting, it became obvious that he had told me most of what he knew about both in our first meeting. One of those kinds of guys. Still, he was energetic and personable, and not young, so maybe he had more to offer than he knew. I was hoping for that when he started his follow-up to Morrison's harangue.

"We all know that we have to get our salespeople to sell more product this year," said Woller. "But before we get down to discussing our actual sales targets, I've got something new on the agenda for you today. Fortunately, you're not going to have to go it alone when you get back to your offices. Because Gene Cherson, the marketing staff, and I have put together a program that can help us regain the initiative in the market," said Woller. "Will somebody get the lights, please."

Down went the lights and on came the slide projector. Woller started reading from a script. "I'd like to introduce to you a powerful new force that will be working with us in the future. It's a force that can help all of us attain new heights in sales revenue and profitability. I'd like to introduce . . . SAMMY!"

Up on the screen came a cute little cartoon figure with SAMMY on its chest. Across the table from me, Ann Lansky looked down at her lap and rubbed her forehead.

"And what does SAMMY mean?" Woller continued. "SAMMY means 'Sell All Markets to the Max this Year.' And that means new opportunities for sales growth for all of us. Most of your salespeople are accustomed to selling one or two types of product and service. We want to promote the idea that each of them is now capable of selling all Elemenco products to all customers."

That was Jim Woller's answer to the challenge. The sales managers were supposed to go back to the field with their SAMMY kits, fortified with their cartoon decals, a canned pep talk, and an incentive program, and just tell everybody to sell everything.

At first, I tried to listen noncritically, but I couldn't do it. Never mind that everything I'd learned at IJK told me this was an inadequate response, even *instinct* told me it was wrong. I suffered through most of the presentation with the rest of them, just to know what it was about. What made me feel worse was that a lot of hard work and a few dollars as well had gone into producing this. Finally, I decided I'd heard enough and sneaked out the door to find out what Morrison wanted.

I went up to 52, the Elemenco executive floor, and made my way back, past hardwood furniture and canvases of corporate art, to Morrison's office. The door was open. Morrison stood by the window in his shirt sleeves, looking out at Lake Michigan, which that afternoon looked gray and very cold.

"Don't jump," I said as I walked in.

Morrison turned and said, "Not even with a golden parachute. Come on in."

He gestured to the chair in front of the desk and we both sat down.

"How do you like it so far?" Morrison asked.

I tried to think of something clever to say, but the day had been so crazy that all I could do was wave my hands around vaguely in the air.

"Oh, that much?" said Morrison. "Well, at least you have your health."

He had talked to Cherson's wife and gave me the latest news, which was that Gene was awake and able to talk, and that he would probably make a reasonable recovery. But it would take time, a few months, maybe longer.

"Look, I'd like you to do me a favor," he said.

"What's that?"

"Check with Gene's wife every couple of days for the next week, will you, and then periodically after that. Find out how he's coming along, whether he needs anything, or if she or the family need anything we can help with. If they do, find a way to get whatever they need."

"Fine. I'll take care of it."

"Thanks," he said. "And I was also wondering if you would take over Gene's responsibilities for a while."

I'm sure my eyes blinked two or three times before I said anything.

"I can't say it'll be permanent," said Morrison, "but I'd like you to fill in either until Gene can return or until we can determine what to do about his position."

"This is unexpected," I said. "I'm flattered that you would ask me, and I'll be happy to accept, but aren't some of the other staff people more . . . well, you know what I mean. They probably know how things work around here a little better than I do."

"I'm finding that the way things work in the Elemenco marketing department isn't necessarily for the best," said Morrison. "You're right, though. Ordinarily, I'd ask Jim Woller to step in. But after last year's performance, there's no way I'd do anything that might be construed as a promotion to him. He's not solely to blame, of course, but that would just be the wrong message. No, I want you to step in for the moment, if you're willing. After all, I know you and I know I can count on you. You want to give it a go?"

"Sure. I'll do my best," I said.

"Good," said Morrison. "Now, there are two parts to this. First, I want you to handle the day-to-day. Run the meetings, field the phone calls, collect the reports, do the numbers, put out the fires. Delegate whatever you can, of course. But no changes in personnel or policy without my approval. And if you have to make any spending decisions over $25,000 I want you to talk to me first. Is that clear?"

So he wanted me to be a caretaker. I found that a little depressing, but I said, "Okay. What's the second part?"

"I want you to make an assessment of our marketing," Morrison said. "It's clear that we're not doing something right. So I'd like you to think about how the sales force can break through whatever it is that's holding us back. Maybe from the top seat in marketing you can get a better overview of what works and what doesn't."

I was nodding. This part I found exciting.

"I'm leaving tonight for Europe," Morrison said. "We're setting up some new operations over there, and I really need to be on hand. So I'll be out for two weeks. When I get back, what do you say we get together and talk?"

"Sounds fine."

He said that before he left he would send around a memo announcing me as the temporary replacement for Cherson.

Then Morrison stood up to shake my hand.

"Go to it," he said.

Allow me a brief flashback to the Sunday before the Monday when I came to work for this company. I was flying to Chicago and somewhere over the Rockies I was sipping coffee and making plans. What I'll do after I get there, I thought, is keep a low profile for a while. You know, look around, get to know the company, figure out what has to be done, gather some support, and start my push to make things happen after six months or so.

Well, that plan was out the window. When I walked out of Morrison's office, I suddenly was the boss. I already felt the urgency, but also the excitement. If I handled this right, a few months from now I could start to try some things that I otherwise might not be allowed to do for another year or more. Which was probably going to be a good thing, because after listening to what had been said in that meeting, I wasn't sure we could take another year like the one we'd just had.

I looked at my watch after I got on the elevator. It was past five o'clock, but I went back down to the sales managers' meeting anyway, hoping that Jim Woller's SAMMY presentation would be over and that I could catch some of the managers and talk to them before they left.

When I got to the meeting room, the only people left were Ann Lansky and Jim Woller; apparently they had lingered to talk something over.

"Is the meeting through?" I asked.

"All finished," said Jim.

"Morrison wanted to see me before he left town," I explained, hoping he wasn't insulted that I'd left in the middle of his presentation. Then to Ann, I said, "You know, I'd hoped to talk to you and some of the other sales managers before they left town, get an idea of what's going on out there."

"Well, my office is on the twenty-second floor and I'm usually in town. You can stop by any time. But we're going to meet most of the others across the street for a drink after we're done here, if you want to join us."

Jim poked Ann's forearm with his finger and winked at her. "Yeah, we're all going to drown our sorrows after being beaten up by Mr. Morrison. Right, Ann?"

Ann didn't seem to appreciate the humor, but Jim laughed for her. She looked tired and depressed. I could understand why.

"Why don't we meet you over there?" said Jim. "From the sound of it, you could probably use a drink as much as the rest of us, after the day you've had."

"'You're right. I could," I said. "Where are you going?"

"It's the old yuppie fern bar on the corner," said Jim. "Right across the street. You can't miss it."

I said I'd see them there.

I went up to my floor, 49, to pick up my phone messages and get my coat. Then it dawned on me that if I were to cover for Gene, I'd better find out what was on his calendar. So I passed my own office and walked to the southwest corner. Rose, his secretary, was gone for the day. All the secretaries were. Gene's office door was closed, but it was unlocked.

I had to let my eyes adjust, because the lights inside his office were off. The dim blue light of the late January afternoon came in from the two windows. Outside, it was already past sunset and it had begun to snow.

His desk was still in the middle of the floor. I had helped one of the paramedics move it so they could get the stretcher in. I had a vague sense that I shouldn't be in there, but I found the switch for the overheads and started looking for his calendar. It wasn't on top of his desk, so I opened the center drawer and there it was, behind the roll of antacids.

He'd been planning to take next week off. Probably needed the rest. Most everything else on the calendar was the normal stuff: a couple of meetings scheduled for the annual report, a big meeting with the ad agency, an appointment with his barber on the twenty-eighth, that kind of thing. So I went through his calendar, thinking about what I would cancel and what I would keep, and jotted down the important dates on a piece of paper.

I put back the calendar and was getting ready to leave when I happened to glance at the coffee table. Something shiny caught my eye. It was that reporter's little microcassette tape recorder. I picked it up from the coffee table. The tape had gone all the way to the end and stopped. She must have forgotten it in the panic and confusion after Gene hit the floor. On the back of it, taped above the battery compartment, was a label: *Please return to Lynne Welsey.* Below was her work address and phone number.

I switched off the lights and went back to my own office, taking the tape recorder with me. I called the number. When Lynne answered, I said who I was, and there was the briefest pause while she mentally placed me. I told her what she had forgotten and heard her riffling through her things, instinctively checking that it was gone.

"I really need to get that back as soon as possible," she said. "Could I stop by your office tonight?"

"I'm not going be here very much longer. I have to meet with some people for about an hour or so," I said.

"Maybe I could meet you someplace," she said.

I almost said she could meet me at the bar across the street, but I figured it was unwise to have a reporter show up. So I asked her to pick the place. She named a restaurant.

"The earliest I could be there is seven," I said. "Or you could stop by tomorrow."

"No, seven is good," she said.

"See you then."

One nice thing about being new on a job is that nobody knows to call you. I didn't have many phone messages, which meant I didn't stick around long. I got my coat, took the elevator down to the lobby, went across the street to the fern bar.

I found them at a long table in the back, segregated into two groups. On the near end were three of the five sales managers, one of them being Ann Lansky. On the other end was half of the marketing staff. The heads of marketing communications, human resources, administration, and research were there, along with some of their assistants, plus Brian, the PR guy. Missing from the group when I got there was Jim Woller.

As I walked toward the table, Ann Lansky called out, "Well, there's our hero now."

"Why am I a hero?"

"If putting your lips on Gene Cherson's mouth doesn't qualify you for hero status, I don't know what does," said Ann.

"Oh, you heard about that."

"Of course. We've been pumping Brian for all the gory details since we got here," said Ann.

She was holding a glass of white wine and her spirits seemed somewhat restored. I took the last available chair, the one at the head of the table, the position I've always called "Dad's chair," which put Ann on my left and the two other sales managers on my right.

"You know, in retrospect, he was a walking heart attack waiting to happen," Brian was saying. "Overweight. High-stress job. Loved his martinis. Golf once or twice a month was his only exercise. Smoked a couple packs a day."

"And he lived," Ann said. "Maybe there's hope for the rest of us."

Somebody nudged my arm.

"I don't think we know each other," the guy to my right said, his hand extended. "I'm Bud Bowman."

I knew him, of course, from listening to him in the meeting.

"Right, you manage the Southern Region," I said. "I'm David Kepler."

The man farther down was Greg Heindekker, who managed the Northwestern Region. He too introduced himself. I asked about the other managers; Greg said they had earlier planes to catch and were already on their way to the airport.

"What about Jim Woller? Isn't he coming?" I asked.

"He'd better show up," said Bud. "He said he was buying."

"He got tied up on the phone," said Ann. "But he'll be along."

This was my chance. They'd probably speak a little more freely without Woller around.

"So what did you think of the meeting?" I asked the three of them.

Bud shook his head, leaned in toward me, and said, "I'll be honest with you. I don't know what to think. But I'll tell you one thing, Morrison doesn't know what the story is if he thinks we're not out there pushing. Because we are. Every damn day my people—and these are solid people with experience—are out there knocking on doors, making calls, giving presentations, taking care of the customer."

Now Ann got into it. "That was exactly my point in the meeting. Where does Morrison get off telling me that I'm not a good manager when I've got situations imposed on me from outside that dictate how I run my region?"

"Well, what would you do differently?" I asked her. "I mean, obviously we've got a problem. We've got to build sales. If you had a free hand, what would you do?"

Ann sat back, thinking, while the other two looked at each other, neither sure he wanted to say anything. Then Bud jumped right in.

"I'll tell you what we need," he said. "We've got to build volume. That's the whole issue. That means we've got to drop the price on a lot of what we're selling. We need stronger discounting. We're just not competitive on half of what we've got in our line."

"Now wait a minute." said Greg. "You're not going to sell a complex, brand-new 720 Network by lowering the price."

"Why not? Price is always an issue," argued Bud.

"Price may be an issue, but it's not always the determining factor in a sale," said Greg.

"Yeah, well, tell me something. How many 386 machines and PC work stations do you have sitting in the warehouse out your way?" said Bud. "How many could you sell if you could give a little more on the rather stiff price we're listing?"

"I'll tell you this," said Greg, "you start bringing down prices and that's exactly the direction your business is going to go: straight downhill. I say that in this business, you keep your quality good, your technology high, your service first-rate, and your image topnotch. And you charge prices to match."

Bud was shaking his head the whole time Greg was talking.

"That's not what I hear from the customers," said Bud.

"Yeah? What customer doesn't want quality?"

"Sure they want quality. They want reliability. They want everything you mentioned *and* they want a discounted price."

Now Greg was shaking his head. "Can't be done, Bud. No way. Something has to give. I say that if you sell the right product to the right people, you don't have to discount."

"Come on, Greg, let's talk about the real world here."

"I *am* talking real world. You want an example? The 720 Network is a perfect example. We've sold three of them this year, and we didn't close a single one because of our price. You want to know how you sell them? First of all, you don't sell to the data processing department. Because if they didn't think of it first, they won't buy it. And even if they did think of a system like a 720, they probably believe they can put one together on their own with the PCs they already have. No, you sell a 720 to the customer's CEO and the operations managers. You show that you're offering them a competitive advantage. And you convince them that what you've got is state of the art."

"Oh, state-of-the-art, my foot!" said Bud. "Most of our customers don't want state of the art. You say 'state of the art' to them and they're afraid of it. They don't need it. They're tired of hearing about it. And come to think of it, so am I. Hey, Brian!"

Brian looked down the table.

"We need one of you wordsmiths to come up with another phrase for 'state of the art.' We're sick and tired of that one."

"Advanced technology," said Brian.

"No, I'm sick of that one too," said Bud. Then he turned to me (for what I thought for sure would be some concluding piece of wisdom) and asked, "What are you drinking, Dave?"

"I'll have a beer," I said.

"Yo, Emily!" Bud called.

"Now there's a salesman," said Brian. "He's from out of town, and already he's learned the waitress's name."

"Well, I'm here to tell you, my friend, I closed a lot of sales in my day by remembering people's names. Emily, give us another round here, would you please, and give my pal, Dave, a beer."

"Draft?" Emily asked.

"No, give him a _____," he named one of the expensive imports. "He deserves it. He's had a rough day."

"You see!" said Greg, "Why didn't you just tell her to bring him the cheapest swill they've got? No, you ask for the higher-priced, high-image brand."

"That's completely different," said Bud.

During all this, Ann had been listening, not saying anything. It wasn't that she was shy; speaking up to Morrison the way she had in the meeting proved she wasn't. She was, I suspect, still pondering the original question. I caught her eye.

"What do you think the problem is?" I asked her.

I was set to hear what she had to say when, from the far end of the table, a new voice chimed in, "*I'll* tell you what the problem is! The ad budgets aren't big enough!"

That was Nick Dominica, who managed avertising and sales promotion.

"This company has never committed the resources it should have to advertising and sales promotion," said Nick. "We need more space advertising, more presence at the conventions—"

"No, no, no, that's not the problem," Greg interrupted, voice at full volume now. "Advertising can expose the product. Advertising might generate a few leads. But advertising does not sell the product. *People* sell the product."

These and other platitudes began to fly back and forth wildly.

Jane O'Shea, who headed marketing research, complained that nobody took her customer surveys seriously enough, that of course they were expensive, but that we needed more of them.

Then Brian tried to make a point about trade publicity. But he was cut off by Clinton Jones, who managed human resources; he thought the real answer was in better selling-skills training for the salespeople.

Roger Newburg, who handled administration, waved all this away as nonsense. Roger thought they were paying the sales force too damn much, that they could weather a slight dip in sales if they could retain profitability.

"And I'll tell you another thing. They all ought to be on commission, every one of them," said Roger. He was chopping the table with the side of his hand.

Ann, who had long ago given up trying to make her point about what the problem was, said, "Roger, half my people couldn't live on commission."

On and on it went, everybody throwing in an opinion, all of them favoring their vested interests, none of them looking for (let alone seeing) a larger vision. I decided to stay out of it for now. Ann's eyes met mine, and I could tell she thought the discussion was as petty as I did.

"You never got a chance to say anything," I said to her.

"I probably said enough in the meeting. Too much, in fact."

"I'm sure everybody will forgive and forget if you turn in better numbers next time."

The frustrations of her day seemed about to boil over and spill out.

"How am I supposed to do that?" she asked. "I'm running my region exactly according to the new plan and look what's happening. And who has to stand up and take the blame?"

She caught herself before she went further. I felt bad for her. She seemed at wit's end. We sat silently at the table while the others jabbered away. The two of us had lost interest in what they had to say. Ann raised her glass, then looked at me again. She wanted to talk, but she also wanted to change the subject.

"So Morrison said you come from IJK. What did you do there?" she asked.

"I was marketing manager."

"Did you come up through sales?"

"No, I started as a product engineer and got into marketing almost by accident."

"Really? What happened?"

"The company was wasting a lot of money trying to sell customers what they didn't need. We were having trouble identifying market opportunities. Anyway, I got assigned to a task force to find a solution. I didn't know very much about marketing, so I did a lot of reading on the subject. One day I came across a concept that seemed to put everything about marketing into perspective. I made some calls, got back to the source, and we used that concept to refocus the company."

"Did it work?" she asked.

"I'd say so. A 50 percent increase in sales after one year. Plus healthy increases in profitability. And it wasn't just short-term. Sales were still increasing when I left."

"No wonder you have Morrison's stamp of approval."

"I didn't do it alone, of course. I was just the point man."

"Fifty percent is an incredible increase," she said.

"Well, it's been done. It's not impossible if you have the opportunity and you know what you're doing."

"IJK is a much smaller company than Elemenco. Do you think the same thing would work here?"

"That's what I'd like to find out," I said. "But I'm sure the same concept applies here, because it's valid for every business."

"What is it, a lot of strategic planning or something?"

"No, it's more than that. For instance, it could help you, as a sales manager, sort out what kinds of people you need on your sales force, the best way to generate leads, what you want new business presentations to be like, how to develop customer relations—all the important sales issues you've got to deal with. It also helps with corporate issues, like what kind of image you need to project."

"But what worked for IJK isn't necessarily going to work for Elemenco," she argued.

"The concept we used assumes that every business is different. That's one reason why it's valid."

"Even in my region?"

"Sure."

"Fifty percent, huh?"

"Well, I wouldn't get hung up on that figure," I said. "But it's a safe bet that using what we learned at IJK would give you better results than what you're getting now."

I definitely had piqued her interest. The others around the table were busy talking among themselves, but Ann had turned in her chair so that she was facing only me.

"So how did all this work at IJK?" she asked. "What did you do to get that kind of a gain?"

Well, it had been a hell of day. I'd been yelled at by my new boss, watched him have a heart attack, chased his ambulance, sat through an abysmal business meeting, and received a promotion. I was feeling a little tired. Ann was talking because she was at the end of her rope and curious about this possibility I'd raised. I'd gone this far, but I wasn't sure I really wanted to get into a heavy discussion of marketing. I tried to give her the simplest explanation I could think of.

"Basically we refocused our resources so that they addressed the customers' needs."

"I'm not sure what you mean by that," Ann said.

"Well, all customers have needs, right?"

"Right."

"But do they all have the same needs?"

"No, of course not."

"And if their needs are not the same, they must be different. Right?"

Ann thought about it.

"Maybe not the same, but all customers have *similar* needs," she said.

"No, not really. All customers do not have similar needs. Look, a lot of this is just common sense. If I want to eat, I have to go to a supermarket and buy food. But if I want to get rich, then maybe I have to buy an oil drilling rig or whatever tool will give me the means to make money. As a customer, what I need from the supermarket clerk and what I need from the drilling rig salesman are very different."

"Well, of course, if you put it that way," said Ann.

"Different products and services meet different needs for different customers. That creates different markets. And with that we need different styles of selling."

"Okay, but now how did that help you at IJK?"

Again, I tried to think of the briefest possible explanation. "Well, in a nutshell, we used a two-dimensional grid to sort out the differences and match our marketing with customer needs using common variables."

Ann stared at me for a second, then did a double take. "What was that? Come on, Dave. Speak English."

"It's complicated. I'll explain it to you some other time."

She grinned, reached out, and briefly gripped my fore-arm. "Oh, no, fella. You hooked me. You can't get out of it now. You're staying until I know what you're talking about. Unless it's just a bunch of corporate buzzwords."

"No, it's got substance."

Emily arrived with a new round of drinks. She put down cocktail napkins, another glass of wine for Ann, and a beer for me. I poured the beer and took a swallow.

"Really, I'm curious," said Ann.

"I have to give you some of the theory."

"I'm listening."

I took out a pen and pointed to one of the plain, white, square cocktail napkins on the table.

"Okay, let's say this is the marketing world. In this world, we've got every company, every salesperson, every product and service, every industry and every customer. Now how do we make sense of it all? How do we take the millions of different pieces, sort them, and match them so that we can see the whole picture?"

"I don't know," she said. "Maybe you can't."

"Well, we have to try, because we can't work in chaos. We have to find an order or create one. To find out where we are in this world, it helps to have a map. To make a map, we need a north and a south, an east and a west. Okay?

"Okay."

"Let's start with north to south. And let's call the variable that runs north and south *complexity*. Because complexity is something common to all purchases, but varies widely in degree. If I'm buying a supercomputer, it's likely to be a purchase of high complexity. If I'm just buying an adding machine, it's likely to be a purchase of low complexity. So in the middle of our

31

marketing world, I'm going to draw an equator, which divides north from south, high complexity from low.

| High complexity |
| Low complexity |

"Now let's say you're a customer buying a supercomputer. And I have one for sale that is technically acceptable. But you don't know me very well, I offer you only one design, give you no help ordering options, insist you make your own arrangements for delivery and installation, and never call on you unless I want you to buy another supercomputer. Would you do business with me?"

"No, not if I had a choice," said Ann.

"I knew you were smart. For us to do business together, what would you need from me so that we could deal with the complexity?"

"First of all, I'd need you to stay in touch with me."

"You said the magic word: *touch*. To be successful in the market, the degree of touch has to match the degree of complexity."

On the napkin, I added "high touch" and "low touch."

| High complexity
High touch |
| Low complexity
Low touch |

"When the customer is making a very complex purchase, with a lot of customized features and a lot of things that could go wrong, the seller has to do a lot of hand holding during the purchase and delivery. That's high touch. If it's a simple purchase—the customer takes the product out of the box, turns it on, and it works—then you don't need to hold hands. It's a low-touch sale. Are you with me?"

"Sure," she said.

But, for emphasis, I added, *"High touch* means the customer needs a lot of hand holding, and a longer, more secure relationship with a seller. *Low touch* means the customer is generally confident of handling matters on his own, and doesn't need or want a lot of hand holding. The relationship with the seller is relatively brief or temporary."

I flipped over the napkin and turned it ninety degrees so that I wasn't drawing over the same line on the other side.

"Now it's time to divide west from east on the map," I said. "Let's take something from science fiction and say I invent an anti-gravity device. And I'm marketing it to you. Would you know how to use it?"

"No, of course not."

"So you would be an *in*experienced buyer."

"Right."

"Would you consider my anti-gravity device to be high tech?"

"Sure," she said.

"Suppose twenty years have passed and there now are dozens of manufacturers of anti-gravity devices, everybody owns one and uses it daily, and you're now buying your fifth one. Would you be an inexperienced buyer or an experienced buyer?"

"Experienced."

"And would you still think of the anti-gravity device as high tech?"

"No, I guess you'd call it low tech," she said.

"I can see that you're picking this up."

I drew a vertical line on the napkin. On the left, I put "inexperienced customer" and "high tech." On the right, I wrote "experienced customer" and "low tech."

Inexperienced customer	Experienced customer
High tech	*Low tech*

"Kind of like our weather patterns flowing west to east," I said, "most of the market naturally enough moves from inexperience to experience over time. But it's an individual matter. If I'm a first-time buyer, I'm going to be inexperienced, even if the product has been around a long time. A purchase will be high tech for the inexperienced even if it's low tech for most of the market. As I'm using it here, tech has little to do with the behind-the-scenes technology that goes into providing it; it refers to the buyer's ability to understand and use the product without assistance from the seller."

I gave her the example of buying a sophisticated new stereo. If *I* were in the market to buy a stereo, I would know what to look for. Not only do I work in the electronics industry, but I've also bought three or four stereo systems since I was a teenager. I'm comfortable with the terminology, I can make sense out of watts per channel and percentage of harmonic distortion and so on. I could contact the component manufacturers, read the technical specs, then go to a discount store, specify what I needed, bring everything home, set it up myself, make the right wiring connections, work out any problems I had.

"And I'm confident I'd end up with a system that would meet my needs. For *me*, buying a stereo system would be a low-tech purchase because I have experience on my side," I said.

Ann nodded. "Well, I could too for that matter."

"Right. But on the other hand," I said, "let's say that my brother, who manages a restaurant and bar in Baltimore, wants a new stereo system for his business. First of all, my brother is less experienced in that kind of thing than I am. He knows food service, not electronics. And second, he's running a business. He doesn't have time to learn all the technical stuff. My brother is likely to call in an audio professional—someone who will come to the restaurant, check out the acoustics, design the system, tell my brother what he needs, and so on. Even though stereos are relatively old technology and low tech for most of us, buying one for the restaurant would be a relatively *high-tech* purchase for my brother."

"It's all relative to the individual customer," she said.

"Exactly the point," I said. "I may know stereos, but if I had to throw a party for a hundred people, I would be totally at a loss. I'd have to hire a caterer who could plan the menu, order enough food and drink, and prepare it all. My brother doesn't do catering, but if he had to hire a caterer, he has the experience to specify exactly what he needs. For me it would be high tech; for my brother, low tech."

"Okay."

"It's *high tech,* then, if the customer needs a high degree of technical and applications support," I continued. "It's low tech if the customer has the experience to handle those aspects on his own."

I took a new cocktail napkin, opened it up so that the creases gave me four quadrants on the square. I began scribbling in all the labels.

"Now we put the dimensions together—complexity and experience, touch and tech—and what we find is that the chaotic marketing world, pardon the phrase, can be rationally arranged into four quarters or quadrants," I said.

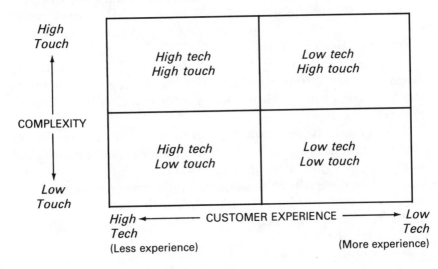

35

"And if you plot where your products and customers are on this map," I continued, "you have a fairly accurate way to know what you need to do. Because each of these quadrants defines a type of marketing and selling you need to do in order to be successful."

Ann's brow was lumpy. She was thinking it through.

"Let's go back to stereos," I said. "If you and I have a company that makes a state-of-the-art audio component years ahead of everybody else, we're in a high-tech market. If all we do is sell that component, we're in the high-tech, *low-touch* quadrant. If we also integrate that component into a complete system, tailored to each customer's situation, and we deliver the system, set it up for the customer, teach the customer how to use it, service it, and so on—that puts us in high tech, *high touch.* Because now we're dealing with both a complex purchase and an inexperienced customer."

"So that audio professional your brother called in would be in a high-tech, high-touch market if he not only sold advanced components, but also set up the system in the restaurant and taught your brother how to use it," said Ann.

"You really *are* quick." I'd been paying her compliments that were a bit tongue-in-cheek before, but I meant this one sincerely. "And I'm sure you can see that the audio professional would be using a very different kind of sell than the discount audio store down the street where I might go to buy my stereo."

Ann's eyes brightened as she finished putting the pieces together in her own mind.

"Let me see if I've got this," she said. "Take the catering example. Say we're in the catering business together. We'd be in a high-tech, low-touch market if we're offering some kind of nouvelle cuisine—"

"That only we know how to make," I said to qualify it. "It's a unique recipe, we're the only supplier, and we make the food, but we don't serve it at the party."

"But if we offer the same nouvelle cuisine or some gourmet menu and we do the whole party with French waiters and exclusive touches that only we can provide, we're in high tech, high touch. Right?"

"Right."

"If we're doing the party with a traditional menu, providing the waiters and bartenders—"

"And probably promoting our great service and reliability," I added.

"—we're in low tech, high touch," Ann said.

"That's it."

"And if we're selling cheese platters that anybody can buy in our store and take home for parties they do themselves, we're in low tech, low touch."

"Fantastic!" I said. "You've got it!"

She smiled. "But would you mind telling me what all that had to do with IJK?"

"Sure. When IJK was a start-up company back in the 1970s, at first—and only briefly—it was in a high-tech, low-touch market. Most of our products soon shifted to high tech, high touch. Which was our market for quite a while. As we got into the 1980s, the market for most of IJK's original products moved to low tech, high touch. That was when we started having trouble, and eventually we formed that task force I was on. I recognized that while our products mostly were low tech, high touch—like those of most industrial companies, by the way— our biggest opportunities were in high tech, high touch. That was where we had been successful for so long. So we refocused the company, went after those opportunities, and that's how we got the 50 percent first-year gain."

"I see. That's interesting," Ann said. "Now how does this apply to Elemenco? Where do you think we are?"

"*That's* what I plan to find out," I said. "As you mentioned, Elemenco is a much bigger company and much more diversified than IJK. I want to look the company over firsthand before I make any judgments. But if we can figure out where we stand on the map, we'll be able to do things like match the selling approach of most of our sales force with expectations of the majority of our customers."

I was about to believe that I'd won an ally when Ann shook her head and said, "We just made a lot of changes, as you know, and I think we'll be locked into this new system for quite some time. The one you'll have to convince is Gene Cherson or his replacement."

I was about to comment on that when Bud Bowman butted in. "What was that about a replacement? Did you hear who's going to take over for Gene while he's in the hospital?"

Before Ann could answer, Jane O'Shea said, "Bud, don't be so crass."

"What's crass about that? It's a question somebody's going to have to answer."

"It'll be Jim Woller, of course," said Greg. "At least that's my guess."

"Then why didn't Morrison just announce it at the meeting today?" asked Ann.

"But Woller is the logical choice," said Greg.

"No, he might name one of the other staff people," said Nick, "which would be . . . interesting."

"My guess is that he'll call in a headhunter," said Roger.

"I would think that human resources would be the first to know," said Clinton, "but Morrison hasn't talked to me about it yet."

I wondered whether I should say something or let them wait for Morrison's announcement memo. I had just about decided to spill it out when Jim Woller, as if on cue, walked in, pulled up a chair from an empty table, and sat down at the opposite end. He looked directly at me.

"Congratulations," he said loudly, but without much warmth.

"Thanks," I said, "but it's really nothing to be congratulated about."

"What's this?" asked Greg.

"Mr. Kepler will be taking over for Gene," Woller announced. "I just talked to Reed Morrison. And he said there would be an announcement tomorrow."

All faces turned immediately to me.

"You? You're going to be Gene's replacement?" asked Bud.

"Temporarily at least," I said.

The whole table went quiet as it began to sink in. I could feel the stares.

"Gee, I'm glad you're here then," said Ann, leaning toward me. "This is probably the right time to talk to you about my raise."

Everyone at the table burst out laughing. But nobody wanted to say much after that. Jim Woller ordered a drink. Bud and Greg downed theirs and agreed to share a cab to O'Hare. Woller started telling jokes, but his heart wasn't in it. Though he was trying to cover it up, he was angry. Every so often I could see the hardness in his eyes when he looked my way. Which was not often.

One by one, the staff people tactfully finished their drinks, got up, and left. Before long, only Jim Woller and Ann and I were left.

"Well, I have to get going," said Ann.

"I'd like to talk to you again. There are a lot of things I'd like to know about the sales situation," I said. "What about lunch sometime?"

"Sure," she said. "I think I'm even free tomorrow."

"I'll call you," I said.

And then there were two. Jim and I sat at opposite ends of the table. Emily came over and asked if we wanted another round. I said no, I had to leave, and Jim didn't argue the point. But as we were waiting for the check, he came down to my end of the table.

"You know, Dave, if we're going to be working together, we should get to know each other better."

"You're right, we should."

"How long have you worked in sales?"

"I've never worked in sales."

"Oh. I see. You've *never* worked in sales. Well, I've been in sales all my life. Thirty years of professional sales experience. Been with Elemenco for fifteen years. Wonder why Morrison picked you to take over for Gene Cherson instead of me?"

"You'd have to ask him," I said.

Jim became stone-faced. "I understand you two worked together years ago."

"That's how we met, right."

"You must be real good friends."

"Not that good."

"Uh-huh. Well, then, Dave, tell me something. Just what is it that you're bringing to the party here?" asked Jim.

"Well, I have, I guess, a special understanding of marketing."

"What's that? A *special* understanding?" he said. "So that's it. Well, that's wonderful. Excuse me."

Then he walked away. I saw him head for the door.

About five seconds later, Emily brought the check. Of course, nobody had left any money on the table; I suppose they expected it to be on the company. What the hell. The bill was under $25,000 and I was the boss. Wasn't that what bosses were for? I took out a credit card.

Outside, snow was falling in the dark. Traffic was all but stopped, cabs and cars and buses all pumping out clouds of vapor into the cold air as they idled in front of jammed intersections. Snowflakes blew against my face and each time I looked down at the navy topcoat I was wearing it had more crystals of white clinging to it. I shuffled along through the slush toward the restaurant, moving faster on foot than anybody on wheels, Lynne's tape recorder in a pocket of my suit jacket.

When I found the restaurant, she was sitting at a table near the door and waved as I came in. She didn't get up as she said hello, but sat composed with every golden hair in place, a glass of wine, which she seemed to have been nursing, in front of her. I came over, windblown and dripping, brushed off the snow, reached under my coat, and brought out the tape recorder, which she took and immediately put away in her purse.

"Thank you for finding it," she said. "Would you like to sit down?"

"Don't mind if I do," I said. "It's a blizzard out there."

A waiter came by and I asked for brandy. Lynne ordered another chardonnay.

"How is Gene Cherson doing?" she asked.

"Looks like he'll recover," I said.

"Good. I'm glad to hear that," she said.

"Tell me," I said, "how is what happened this morning going to affect the story you're doing about us?"

"I talked to my editor and we've decided to hold off on the story for a while," she said. "Not just because of what happened, but some other things, like the release of fourth-quarter earnings."

"I see."

Nice to know that sentiment had nothing to do with it, I thought.

"You had some good questions this morning," I said.

"Thank you. I wish you guys had had better answers."

"We may have some in a few months," I said.

"Why? What's going to change in a few months?"

"Not much in terms of results; that'll take a year or more. But we may have a whole new marketing strategy," I said.

A look of intense skepticism crossed her face: *Right, big deal.* Then she softened. "I'll stay in touch with you, just to see how things are coming along," she said.

"I'd like it if you would," I said.

I found myself feeling a bit warm, but it wasn't just the brandy. She was nice. Maybe I should ask her to dinner. But asking her seemed to be crossing a line. This was business, after all. Or was it? I could have just left the tape recorder with the building security guard; she could have suggested something like that herself. Instead she wanted to meet me here. She seemed to like me. Maybe if I phrased the idea just right . . .

"Where were you before Elemenco?" she was asking me.

"A little company in California," I said. "Well, not exactly tiny. About $100 million in sales. Morrison made his mark there in the late 1970s, before he came to Elemenco."

"Why did you leave?"

"Walking across town tonight, I asked myself the same question," I said. "We never had weather like this in San Jose."

"Seriously, why did you leave? If you don't mind my asking, that is."

"Because I wanted to be with Elemenco."

"They must have offered you a lot of money," she said, almost teasing.

"Enough," I said. "But I really didn't come here for the money. Not for the money alone, anyway."

"What else then?" she asked.

"The chance to turn Elemenco into a great company."

She froze for half a second, not really believing that I'd said that. "You're kidding, aren't you?"

"No, that's really why I came here."

"Is that your life goal or something?"

"It's my goal for right now," I said.

She laughed. "How noble of you. And of course the money means nothing."

"Okay," I said, "why did you go into journalism? Was it for the money?"

"Well, I needed a job," she said.

"But there are lots of ways to make a living," I said. "My point is that you've got idealists who want to make the world a better place, and so they go into journalism or government or maybe join the Red Cross. And those are all worthwhile. But, in its own way, business is one of the strongest forces for positive change in the world. I want to be in a company that makes great products and does great things. I want to be part of making that happen. Which is why I'm here."

"You really believe that," she said.

"Yes, I do," I said. "And I like being in a business that makes things. To tell you the truth, I'm tired of seeing American industry retreat from manufacturing. I think Elemenco can be one of the companies that stops retreating and starts advancing."

She gave me a look I couldn't quite interpret, and we started talking about other things. I had just about made up my mind to ask her about dinner when a tall, handsome man came up to the table and stopped just behind my right elbow. His sandy hair had that styled look, short on the sides and long in back, *muy* cool.

"There you are!" said Lynne. "This is my friend, Kurt. Kurt, this is David Kepler, the guy I said I had to meet."

"Good to meet you, Kurt," I said.

"Same."

They kissed. He took a seat next to her and immediately moved his chair very close and put his arm across her shoulders. It wasn't affectionate. It was possessive, definitely first-person possessive. He didn't look at her, he looked at me.

43

"Where were you?" she asked him. "I thought you'd be here an hour ago."

He shrugged. "Had some clients who just wouldn't leave."

"Kurt has an art gallery," she said.

"Interesting business," I said.

"I'll sell it to you," he said. It was supposed to be funny; he laughed.

Fantasies of dinner and whatever else dissolved to nothing. I endured a couple of minutes of polite conversation, then said, "I'd better be going. Take me a while to get home."

I tried to pay for the drinks, buy Lynne insisted they were on her, as a favor for returning her tape recorder.

I woke up in total darkness. I rolled out of bed, still half asleep, took two steps and turned left, the way I had for years, and walked into a wall. Which woke me up sufficiently to make me realize I was not in my old house in San Jose, but in one of the Elemenco company condos on the Near North of Chicago.

The company had bought three or four of these condos, because somebody had said they'd be good investments that would save us money on lodging. The really plush ones were reserved for our customers' executives and our own very top brass. The one they had given me until I could find my own place had a tiny kitchen, bathroom, living room, and small bedroom. It was furnished like a glorified motel room. But, in one way, it was already like home: It was a total mess.

I found the clock under yesterday's shirt and saw that it was four in the morning, about two hours before the alarm was set to go off. So I got back in bed, but couldn't get back to sleep. My mind had engaged. Memories of the day before were playing in my head.

I saw Lynne sitting on the sofa in Gene's office and saying, "Tell me, what went wrong on the Northern Airline negotiation?" And, "If your products and technology really are superior, and nobody I've talked to doubts that they aren't at least highly competitive, why isn't this being demonstrated in sales?"

I heard Greg and Bud arguing about the price issue, about whether to pursue new technology or push the industry standards. Interesting, wasn't it? Two veteran pros of the same company with nearly opposite points of view about what was best.

Since I was already at work in my mind, I decided around five o'clock that I might as well be there physically. So I got up and took a shower and headed downtown.

I arrived at the office just after sunrise. There is always something spooky about being in a normally busy place when it's empty. I could hear my own footsteps on the carpet.

My office was on the eastern side of the building and I could see Lake Michigan beyond the other downtown buildings. The storm had passed and the early sun cast cold pinks on the snow. I switched on my computer and went to make some coffee. A few minutes later, the coffee brewing, I was calling up a spreadsheet I'd been working on for the past few days in an attempt to understand the company.

Since Monday, just after I signed the W-4 forms, I'd been poking around in the various company data bases and pulling out numbers. By now, I had pretty well satisfied myself that the problem did not lie with anything except marketing. I had ruled out any likely technology gap, lack of manufacturing capacity, quality problems, and so on. The constraint to growth was marketing's ability to sell.

Because Elemenco was in the computer and data communications business, we had some fairly good internal systems. I could bring up not only numbers, but text from key documents going back three or four years—the minutes from important meetings, executive speeches, product reports, strategy papers, market research, and so on. That Friday morning, I started seeking causes of the current malaise. One thing about Gene Cherson, he was thorough. He documented everything. I had a lot to work with.

Around nine o'clock the interruptions began to increase. My secretary, Sylvia, had received a copy of the announcement naming me as Gene's replacement, and wanted to know if I'd be changing offices.

"Hell no," I said, "I haven't had enough time to clutter up this one."

"But you're entitled to a bigger office."

"Forget it," I said.

As Morrison had requested, I called Gene's wife and offered assistance. She said he was already talking about coming back to work. Terrific. I asked Sylvia to arrange for flowers.

Then a few of the staff people started dropping by to brief me on projects they had going. Which ordinarily would have been fine, except that I felt I was close to something on this analysis and I wanted to finish it. So I scheduled a staff meeting for midafternoon.

Meanwhile, in the material I was pulling from the marketing data base, I had begun to see a pattern emerge in our decision making. Years ago, a basic policy had been set up: if a customer wanted a product and if Elemenco could make it at a competitive cost, Elemenco would market that product. It was the "department store" approach, something for anybody who would buy from us. And Elemenco could do it, because it had significant resources at its command; it didn't necessarily have to focus its capital on a small group of products the way a smaller company might.

I turned away from the computer for a moment and started thumbing through a product catalog for Elemenco. On the cover, the artist had put pictures—stunning photographs—of a satellite dish, one of the newer 386 personal computers, a boxlike piece of network hardware, a woman talking on a cellular car phone, and a cable split open to reveal the rainbow of colorful wires inside.

Inside the catalog were descriptions of every product and special codes the sales force could use to get current pricing, inventory levels, and so on. What a job it must have been to put that catalog together. At my last company, we didn't have even a quarter of the products. And the products in the Elemenco catalog were only part of the story; many of them were constituents of larger systems. The systems weren't even in the catalog, but had their own brochures. And then there were the services Elemenco offered—software, maintenance, engineering projects.

Who was it who bought all these products and systems and services from us? I found some research on that. The customers were almost as diverse as what we sold. Everybody from self-employed professionals—lawyers and doctors, for instance—to some of the largest corporations in the world. One of the largest segments was customers involved in some aspect of transportation—railroads, airlines and air express companies, trucking companies, automobile manufacturers. But there were also insurance agencies, banks, chemical companies, you name it. Something for everybody.

There was a very interesting section in the research on customer suggestions and other feedback on what Elemenco could do to improve itself. Most of it was so contradictory it was practically useless. Like 42 percent of our customers wanted more technical service, another 38 percent didn't, and 20 percent thought what we offered was fine. So which way were we supposed to go? While 72 percent wanted us to offer more features, 28 percent thought our products were too complicated. Great, huh? We want your stuff to do everything including walk the dog, but keep it simple.

Gene Cherson had been head of Elemenco's marketing for five years. As I looked back through minutes of meetings he had run and memos he had authored, I saw that much of what Gene had done through the years was what I would term "standardizing" the company's marketing. Confronted with this many-headed beast called the Elemenco product line, he had year by year been constructing a framework in which to contain it.

Little by little, I pieced together a chronology of what had happened. It had begun shortly after he came in as marketing VP, with standardizing all the graphics—the logos, where the logo should appear on the product, what color combinations were acceptable for Elemenco products, package design. Pretty soon, all the product brochures were standardized and the ads began to take on the same look. This had been a big deal and had taken a while to accomplish. Then certain pricing and servicing policies were standardized. Sales costs were adjusted to make them uniform for the whole company and all products. Internal procedures were changed so they all conformed with one another. Staff jobs were refocused to become, well, less focused, broadened to cover functions rather than groups of products or customers. The crowning achievement was the Lean Mean Marketing Machine, with its consolidation of sales forces, standardized compensation, new emphasis on efficiency and system-ization, and all the rest.

On one hand, I sympathized with Gene and what he had tried to do. The growth-by-marketing-everything-we-can-make strategy had made things quite complex. Plus there had been acquisitions, and each of the little companies Elemenco bought had its own way of doing things. Clearly, he'd had to do some-thing, or it would have been a total hodgepodge. And yet, what had he accomplished by attempting to create uniformity?

I went back to my spreadsheet and made it do a bar chart. Neat glowing columns grew from the bottom of the screen. The columns went up and up and up, like steps—$445 million, $572 million, $791 million. Then three years ago, things changed. The numbers leveled off at just over $1 billion, hovered there, and last year stepped down to $988 million. Just like the top of a roller coaster. I added in comparisons of net income. In absolute numbers it too went up and up, but as a percentage it became squeezed. The year before last it was down around 4 percent; not too good, folks.

It dawned on me that all those numbers and reports and so on might not be letting me see the true picture. What if, to support his own framework, Gene Cherson and his staff had altered the way reports were written and numbers collected?

The one undeniable fact through all of this was the drop in sales and net income. And the real shift away from growth seemed to accelerate when Cherson had started mucking around with the sales force.

A few minutes before noon, Ann Lansky called. I had forgotten all about her.

"You'd mentioned lunch yesterday," she said. "Are you still interested?"

"Yeah, let's do it."

"Should I come up?"

"No, stay put. I've never been to the twenty-second floor. It'll be a new experience for me," I said. "See you in your office in a few minutes."

I grabbed my coat and took the elevator to 22. Through a pair of doors marked "Elemenco Central Region Sales" was your average open office with fabric-covered partitions done in boring beige. I looked in some of the cubicles. There was a guy on the phone. Here were a couple of others getting coffee. A woman walked by with a file in her hand. It all looked very normal. And yet there was a certain energy here that you didn't feel in, say, accounting.

I didn't know where her office was, but I wandered around until I found it. She was waiting for me.

"Ready to go?" I asked.

"Sure. What are you hungry for?"

"Corned beef."

"I've got just the place," she said. "Wait a minute. I thought IJK was in California."

"It is."

"And you want corned beef? What are all your health-nut California friends going to think?"

"Let 'em eat kiwi."

Outside, we started walking to a deli on North Michigan that Ann said was her favorite. Side by side with her, I suddenly couldn't think of anything to say. Just as the silence was becoming embarrassing, she spoke up.

"So how do you like Chicago?"

"I don't know the city very well," I said. "But I like Chicago. It's been fine. . . . Well, a little cold so far."

"Does your wife like it here?" she asked.

"My wife? I'm not married."

"Oh, I don't know why, but I just thought you were married."

"What about you?" I asked.

"Divorced,"

"Was it recent?"

She laughed. "No. Sixteen years."

It seemed we were getting too personal, so I asked her another question I thought would take us to more neutral territory, not knowing it would do the opposite.

"How did you get into sales?" I asked.

"Actually, it was because of the breakup," she said. "I was twenty-three years old. I had two kids. I was on my own. I had dropped out of college to get married, so I didn't have a degree. We weren't going to make it on the little bit of child support we were getting, which he wasn't paying anyway. My dad had died of cancer, and I couldn't burden my mother. I didn't have much choice. My dad had owned a television repair business, and I had helped him in the shop while I was growing up. So I knew something about electronics. I talked my way into a job in sales here at Elemenco, which was a fast-growing company in those days, and they couldn't add salespeople fast enough. My mother stayed with my kids and I went to work."

"That must have been very tough on you," I said.

"At first. But in two years I was making $50,000. I found out I was good. And I liked it. The only thing that was bad was the traveling and the hours. It was hard on my kids. Which was why I finished my degree and moved into management when I got the chance. I actually make less money in management than I would selling, but more than enough to live well, and the hours are better."

The more I heard, the more I liked Ann. I suspected she had earned every one of those gray hairs showing in the brown. But the good life was showing on her. She was about ten pounds and a few years past voluptuous, yet one of those women who might have been considered beautiful enough to be an artist's model about a century ago. She was kind of Greek or Italian looking, smooth skin, nice hands.

"You never remarried?" I asked her.

"Almost. One time. I wanted a man in the house for the sake of the kids while they were growing up. But it was a good thing we broke it off, because . . . well, it probably would have been another disaster. No, between my kids and my job and getting my degree, there hasn't been a lot of time left."

"How many kids do you have?"

"Two. Both boys. The older one, Adam, has always been the perfect kid. He's a junior at Notre Dame studying business. The other one, Patrick . . . well, he's a good kid, too, but he's the one I worry about."

"Why?"

"He likes things that go fast, especially cars. I offered to put him through college, but he doesn't want to go. He wants to drive race cars. Right now, he and a friend are in Daytona working as waiters so they can go to the winter races down there."

Ann rolled her eyes as if she just couldn't understand it.

"He's always been competitive," she said. "Like his mom, I guess."

We reached the deli on North Michigan and were able to get the last available booth before the lunch line started forming. It was time to get down to business, and I started by asking her to tell me about her region—how many people, that kind of thing.

She told me that, aside from the clerical staff, she had nineteen salespeople in the office, about half of Central's total sales force. The rest were in smaller offices across the Midwest, from Minneapolis to St. Louis and from Omaha to Cleveland. Some were in two- and three-person offices, some worked out of their homes. But Chicago was the hub and most of the major customer accounts were handled from here.

"What do you think is going on out there?" I asked her. "You never got much of a chance yesterday to say what you thought the problem was, what you'd do differently."

She said, "I don't know what to tell you on that score, except that I'm doing the best I can right now and it doesn't seem to be making any difference. Anyway, you folks on the marketing staff are the ones who are supposed to have all the answers, aren't you?"

"Gene Cherson must have had you brainwashed," I said. "Actually, I don't know that I want answers right now. I'd just like your help finding out what the real story is."

She thought for a second and then said, "Don't ask me to write a research paper on this, because I don't know what the reasons are, but I get a sense that half the problem is we've taken all these salespeople and thrown them together in the same pot."

"The same pot?"

"Before Gene's Lean Whatever Machine, we had a separate sales force for each group of products. We had a computer systems sales force. We had a telecommunications sales force. And we had a specialty electronics sales force. The reorganization took everybody and made them into one big sales force. I'll be the first to admit that the old way had its problems, but Gene's

Lean Mean, or Mean Lean, or Whatever Machine isn't the answer either."

"I'm inclined to agree with you," I said. "But what makes it look like it's not working? What are the symptoms you're seeing?"

"The people I've got don't work together very well," she said. "Time and again I see opportunities slip away. Even my top performers have been dropping the ball, leaving sales on the table, letting competitors in the door. We just can't seem to get the job done."

The sandwiches arrived, brought by a dumpy waitress who was probably my age and looked twenty years older. It was good corned beef, lean and tasty, but I was more interested in what Ann was saying than in the food.

"At first I thought that it was just a learning curve we had to put up with. I thought maybe they just didn't know all the products well enough. But we put everybody through seminars and product training. By now, they ought to know what they're selling, or at least know where they can get the right information. No, it's something else. And I don't know if anybody has figured this out yet, but this company has a turnover problem in sales. I get along pretty good with most of my people. Without me, some of the better salespeople would have left by now. And if you don't believe that, you can talk to them. Frankly, I don't know how long I can keep the top performers on board."

"I'm not pointing any fingers at you," I said. "But what's making them leave?"

"I hate to say it, but it seems like it's motivation. I'll tell you, only a few of the salespeople I've got are happy about the compensation program, and the ones who are happy are generally not the best performers. Now, it's true that our average sales rep makes $55,000. That's *average*. Yet some of them could make a lot more than that under the old plan, and it's really got them upset."

We ate quietly for a minute or so while I thought over what she had told me. An idea began forming in my head. Despite all that analysis I'd been doing for the past few days, I still didn't feel I had a good handle on how this company was really selling its products. The information on the computer, extensive as it was, couldn't tell me everything I needed to know. There were numbers and numbers and more numbers—any kind I wanted. There were millions of words of text. Yet I couldn't get a picture of what was happening when one of our salespeople came face to face with a customer. Even talking to Ann, it was still secondhand information.

"I'll tell you what I'd like to do, and I'd like your help making it happen," I said to Ann.

"What's that?"

"Starting Monday, I want to work alongside your sales force as much as possible for the next couple of weeks."

"All right. But why?"

"I want to see for myself what's really going on. I want to go out with them on calls, meet their customers, listen to them on the phone, have them show me exactly what they do. I want to know how we're selling, and why we're not selling."

"Well, okay, but I frankly don't know if that's the best use of your time," Ann said. "I mean, if there's anything you need to know, I can either tell you or find out for you."

"Thanks, but I think it's important to see it for myself."

"Fine," she said. "You're the boss."

"Good," I said. "I'll come down Monday morning and we'll get it going."

In the back of my mind, I didn't know if spending time with the sales force would teach me anything. It might be invaluable or it might be a total waste. I would have to see. But, right or wrong, I was going to delegate everything I could at the staff meeting that afternoon and make time for it.

I talked to Reed Morrison early Monday morning. He called from Dublin and asked how things were going. I told him that everything was under control and that I was going to spend time with the sales force and meet with some customers. He thought that was wise, as long as I didn't lose hold of the administrative end of it.

"Do you know Aaron Abbott?" Morrison asked me.

I knew *of* him. I'd even met him once at a conference about three years before. He was a name in the industry, not a huge name, but well known, well connected. He had a reputation for being something of a visionary, a champion of innovation. Around the time I'd met him at that conference, he'd started his own company.

"He's coming to work for us," said Morrison.

"You're kidding? How'd you pull that one off?"

"He sold his company a couple months ago, and now he's bored," said Morrison. "I met him in Boston on my way to Europe and we came to an agreement. He starts next week and he'll be working out of Chicago."

"What's his position with us supposed to be?" I asked.

"We came up with a title, something like 'executive director of advanced systems,'" said Morrison. "Functionally speaking, he'll be kind of a grand salesman-at-large."

"You sound excited."

"I am. He could be our rainmaker," said Morrison. "Just what we need right now."

After we hung up, I wondered if I agreed with that.

Even though I'd delegated everything I reasonably could, between my own job and Gene Cherson's there was still an abundance of details and decisions to be dealt with. It was mid-morning before I was able to get down to Ann Lansky's office.

She asked about my weekend, and I told her I'd spent most of it looking for a place to live. She told me about a play she'd seen Saturday night.

"Which theater?" I asked.

"Oh, it was on television," she said. "Anyway, I guess you're here because you want to work with some of my sales-people."

"Right."

"Did you have anybody specific in mind? How would you like to do this?"

"Well, who are your best people?" I asked her. "I'd like to work with two or three of your best, and perhaps meet some of the others as we go along."

She thought for a moment. "Why don't we try Charlie Summers. He'd be my first choice. Charlie's a great guy for you to start with, because he's been around for quite a while. His customers love him."

So we went to see Charlie, but Charlie was out.

"Let's see. Well, maybe Jennifer Hone. She's one of the best I've seen at presentations."

But Jennifer, too, was out on the road.

"Okay," said Ann. "I know. Kevin Duttz is the one for you. He's in most of the time. Kevin has adapted the best of anyone to the telemarketing systems that Gene Cherson and Jim Woller had us install."

I followed Ann down the hall and made a left into one of the cubicles. Kevin was on the telephone. At his left hand was a product catalog. With his right hand, he was tapping the keys of the computer terminal in front of him. We stood just inside his cubicle, next to his desk, as he finished his call. Then Ann introduced us.

Kevin stood up to shake hands. He was a big guy in his early thirties, looked as if he might have been a football player in high school—not the quarterback, but a lineman. Ann explained that I wanted to observe some salespeople in action and that I was to work with Kevin, and he was to give me his cooperation.

"So, ah, where do we go from here?" Kevin asked after Ann had left. He didn't seem to have a clear idea of what this was all about. I didn't blame him; I wasn't sure I did either. To some extent, I was making this up as I went along, figuring I would know what I wanted to see when I saw it.

"I'd like it if you would just do what you would ordinarily do," I told him. "Ann picked you out as one of the better performers here in the Chicago office. As you know, our sales could be a lot better than they are and I want to watch some good people in action to see if maybe there are things that you do that our other salespeople across the country can apply."

That was more or less the truth.

"Oh," said Kevin, warming considerably. "Well, normally what I do right now is make my phone calls. Then if I have appointments, I use the middle of the day to go see people."

Not exactly an original approach, but I told him just to go right ahead and try to ignore me, that I wasn't here to criticize or judge, but just to learn. So he picked up the phone and went to it.

"May I speak to Ron Campbell? Hi, this is Kevin Duttz with Elemenco. How's it going today? Not bad. What's the weather like down there in Terre Haute? Still snowing? Come on up to Chicago. We've got sunshine today. But the reason I called, Ron, was that we've got a good deal for you right now on all our cable products. Fifteen percent off list. And I see on the computer it's been about two months now since we made our last shipment to you. How's your supply of twisted pair holding up?"

Next call:

"Hello, is this Urbana Systems? May I speak to Doris Krebb? Hi, Doris. This is Kevin Duttz with Elemenco. How's it going today? Not bad. What's the weather like down there in Urbana? Snow let up yet? Come on up to Chicago . . ."

And that's pretty much the way it went, call after call. Kevin took it nice and steady, always friendly, but plowing ahead.

"You know, this is probably going to get pretty boring for you," he said at one point. "Maybe I've got a magazine you could read."

"No, I'm fine," I said.

In fact, I did sort of tune out after a while. But I know from experience that to get value from observation you often have to endure a lot of seemingly insignificant details before larger patterns emerge. So I stuck with it.

Then I noticed the nature of the calls had switched. Instead of making a pitch over the phone, he was calling people and confirming orders, reading from sheets of paper. I asked him about it.

"Oh, yeah, I should have mentioned this. Maybe you'd want this idea for the other offices," said Kevin. "See, this is something I came up with."

And he held up a photocopied sheet of paper that said: "FAX YOUR ORDER TO ELEMENCO!" Below that was the office fax number.

"I sent copies of this flier to all my accounts along with our catalog and one of my business cards. Then a couple times a day I check the fax machine to see if any orders have come in. I always give the customer a call to confirm everything and let them know the order is being processed and when they might look for it."

"Does it work?" I asked.

"Sure it does," said Kevin. "Well, some of the other sales reps here don't think that much of it. But, heck, I get four or five orders a day on the fax. A lot of them aren't very big, but a sale is a sale. And it's business we wouldn't be likely to get otherwise."

I told him I thought he was probably right, but on the other hand, we weren't going to sell any big systems that way.

"Oh, I don't know," said Kevin. "I've even had some orders for our 386 PCs come in this way."

I didn't want to tell him that a 386 PC hardly qualified as "a big system." These days, despite the lingering technical aura, personal computers were almost in the category of commodities.

After the fax confirmations, he started on a new set of calls. "These are my follow-ups on inquiries routed to me on the 800 line."

"The 800 line? Tell me, what do you think of that? Is it very worthwhile?"

"Yeah, I think so," he said. "I mean, it doesn't hurt. Anything I can do to develop leads is to my advantage. Plus it's more convenient for the customer."

"Uh-huh. Well, don't let me slow you down."

He worked energetically, moving right along from one call to the next, not wasting any time. And I didn't get a sense that he was acting diligent just because I was there. By eleven-thirty, he had finished his phone work, stood up, and stretched.

"How well did you do this morning?" I asked.

Kevin tapped a few keys on the computer, which kept a tally of his orders.

"Not bad. A little above average," he said.

He had his computer print a summary of the morning's activity and, son of a gun, the guy had racked up sales of more than $6,000 while I was sitting there. It wasn't glamorous, but not too shabby for a guy sitting at a desk making phone calls.

We went to lunch together. I let Kevin pick the place, because I wanted to see what was usual for him. We walked a couple of blocks, Kevin's gait being just a bit faster than mine—he definitely had a store of physical energy—and arrived at an old-fashioned lunch counter. Kevin led the way through the door, saying something about how he ate there two or three times a week. We sat on stools at the counter.

"You know, you can drop a lot of money in this town just buying lunch," said Kevin. "I like good food, but I'd rather spend my money after work, go have a good time on Saturday night with my wife."

Okay, the food *was* quite reasonable in price, and not bad, if you like to eat at diners. I'd rate it about a fork and a half. I had the cheeseburger deluxe, extra pickles, hold the chips; Kevin opted for the tuna-salad special on rye, no onion. Not really your power lunch, but that was all right, because we started talking and Kevin began to open up. I found out he was in his late thirties, married, two kids, had a house in the suburbs. What we think of as an average, normal guy.

"How long have you been in sales?" I asked him.

"About ten years."

"Do you like it?"

"Sure. I mean it's okay," he said. "The money is nice. And I like the people. Most of the time anyway. I can't see myself in a job where I was like maybe just running a machine all day, where I couldn't talk to anyone. That would drive me nuts. It just isn't me."

"Seems like you have an established routine," I said, actually not knowing if he did or not.

"Sort of. But I change it now and then. Depends on what kind of mood I'm in. You know, in sales there's always another call you can make, something you can be doing. I like that. I like being busy. Makes the time go fast."

I noticed he was getting bored just talking about work. Sports is usually good for conversation, so I asked him if he'd watched any of the basketball games over the weekend. That brightened him up. I soon found out his real passion was football; he had season tickets to the Chicago Bears.

"You ever take any customers to the games?"

He got a tense expression on his face.

Right away, I said, "I'm not saying that's good or bad if you do or if you don't. I just wondered if you did it."

"Well, no, not too much, unless we're already friends or something. I mean, my weekends are my time. I give a hundred percent at the office, but after work . . ."

He started talking about what else he did in his spare time, about the radial-arm saw he had just bought. I found out he was into home remodeling. He seemed comfortable with his life and did not want much to change. He had his saw, his Monte Carlo, his Bears tickets, and all the other comforts and diversions he wanted.

"We'd better get going," he said. "I've got a customer appointment scheduled for one-thirty at a plant over in Indiana. Are you going to come with me?"

"Absolutely."

We had to stop back at the office so that Kevin could pick up a few things, including his sample PowerCase, the electronic briefcase with the phone, computer, fax machine, and a few other whistles all in one.

"Ann is on me to try to sell PowerCase. But I haven't had much luck with it yet," said Kevin.

"Is that why we're going to see this customer?"

"Nah, I just thought I'd take it along and show it to them," he said. "You never know. Maybe they'll have a need for one. No, these guys make automated controls and they want a price on some AD510s."

I knew the part. It's an analog-to-digital board we offered. Pretty standard stuff.

"I talked to the guy over the phone a couple days ago," Kevin was saying. "I've already got an estimate worked out for him. Figured I'd go down and deliver it myself since it's a big order."

We got in Kevin's car and headed south on the Dan Ryan toward Hammond and East Chicago. Traffic was crazed as usual, but Kevin handled it without much trepidation. I sat back and tried to ignore the various brushes with death.

"You think we'll get the business?" I asked.

"To be honest with you, I don't know. We're a little pricey compared to some others who make basically the same product."

"Do you know this guy? You've had orders from him before?"

"This guy? No, not from him personally, but from the company," said Kevin.

We arrived at a smallish industrial building with a drab, brick office building next to it. The sign read "Lakeside Electronic Controls." Kevin led the way across the parking lot to a pair of 1950s-style institutional doors marked "Vendors' Entrance." Inside there was a small counter and a window with one of those circles cut in the glass so you can talk to the receptionist, a woman who looked at us and said nothing. Kevin spoke to her, and she responded in a nasal monotone.

"Have a seat."

The waiting room had a couple dozen molded plastic chairs. The walls were barren except for a three-dimensional representation of the company logo. We sat there for about fifteen minutes, and then were directed into the bowels of the purchasing department. We met with a little bald guy behind a small gray desk. The placard next to his in-basket designated him as "Mr. Macy."

There were quick, almost cold introductions, no coffee ritual. Mr. Macy was not at all impressed that I was on hand. In fact, he seemed a little put off by two people showing up for the meeting. As we sat down, Kevin reached into his suit jacket and pulled out an envelope, the prepared price quote. Mr. Macy raised his chin to look through the bottoms of his bifocals.

"Delivery within thirty days?" he asked.

"No problem. I've already checked with our inventory people," said Kevin.

Mr. Macy continued reading. When he got to the price, he put the quote down on his desk.

"Elemenco is an established company. We've purchased from you before with satisfactory results," said Mr. Macy. "I'd be inclined to give you the order, but I already have a bid from another vendor with a lower price."

"Tell me what it is and maybe we can match it," said Kevin.

"You'll have to do better than just match it," said Mr. Macy.

He opened a file, wrote down a number on a piece of paper, and handed it across the desk. Kevin studied the number.

"We can meet that price and give you an additional 2 percent discount," said Kevin.

Mr. Macy swiveled toward his adding machine. His fingers tapped the keypad—Chk, chk, chk, chk, chk, chk, *brrrm!* Chk, chk, chk, chk, *brrrm!* He looked at the total with no more expression on his face than your average lamppost, then reached for a form and started filling in the blanks.

Kevin looked at me and gave me the barest of nods. We were getting the order. Mr. Macy went *scribble scribble* on the bottom of the form.

"The other supplier already indicated their bid was final, so I'm awarding the order to you. Take this form to Mrs. Ashneyer, second desk on the left, and she will issue your purchase order."

"Thank you, Mr. Macy, and, by the way, have you seen one of these yet?" asked Kevin. "This is PowerCase. It's a complete portable communications center. Got a fax machine, cellular phone, and personal computer integrated into one unit. Runs off its own batteries, the cigarette lighter in your car, or regular AC power."

Mr. Macy was amused, but we might as well have shown him the space shuttle. What use did he have for a $20,000 briefcase?

Finally, as Kevin was about to demonstrate the fax machine, Macy said, "If you're trying to sell me one of these to impress your boss here or something, you're wasting your time. I only buy what the engineers tell me to buy. If it isn't on the components lists, I don't get involved in it."

Kevin said he thought Mr. Macy might just want to know about PowerCase, maybe pass the information along, but it was clear he wasn't getting anywhere. Macy was just an administrator. In fact, the whole preceding transaction had been like one administrator dealing with another. Kevin really had not sold the product; he had taken the order. Since it was convenient, we waited for the purchase order and left.

Outside in the car, I said, "You know, that price break you gave in there shaved off a lot of our margin."

"We should still make a few bucks. I mean, that was a pretty big order," said Kevin. "Anyway, how else am I supposed to get the business? We're up against competition—Korean, Taiwanese—that's all making the same basic product. What else do I have to work with?"

"Sorry, I didn't mean to be critical, but I just wanted to point that out to you," I said.

"Ann gets on me from time to time about that, but I figure, what the hell, it's better for us to get the order than someone else—even if we do have to come down a little on the price."

To change the subject, I asked him what he would do to improve sales. He talked about telemarketing, about dumping the distributors, going directly to the customers, doing more pullthrough kinds of marketing. He thought we should be doing more advertising, particularly the lead-generating kind. I let him talk, didn't argue with him or agree with him on any of it.

Kevin had another appointment that afternoon, this time with a new prospect, a president at a big trucking company.

"What are we going to talk to him about?" I asked.

"He wants to know about our satellite communications and tracking systems," said Kevin.

"Oh yeah?"

This was big-ticket, big-bucks stuff. You could be talking $2 million and up for these kinds of systems from Elemenco.

We drove out the interstate, farther into Indiana. Kevin got off at one of the interchanges, and drove down into an industrial park with a four-lane highway. We drove along looking for address numbers among the warehouses, offices, factories. Kevin didn't know where the place was, but we didn't have any trouble finding it, because we came upon an expansive parking lot with a hundred or so tractor-trailers lined up, most of them with "All-Points Express" on the side. Down the road, past the dispatcher's building and the maintenance shops, was the company's headquarters, a four-story building with a lawn and trees around it. Rather nice landscaping, actually. And on the corner of the lawn was an expensive sign with the company name, spotlights in the grass to illuminate it by night.

No vendors' entrance here. We walked up a broad sidewalk across the lawn, up some steps, into a carpeted lobby with mahogany paneling. A receptionist smiled and greeted us, called up to the president's office, then directed us to the elevator. On the top floor, the president's secretary offered us coffee or soft drinks.

This was more than some little trucking company run by a guy and his brother-in-law. Although it was not exactly *Fortune* 500 either, it was a company with some stature. We waited about five minutes, then she said, "Mr. Sternholtz will see you now."

Arnold Sternholtz came around his desk to shake hands with us. He was heavyset but vigorous. He had well-trimmed black hair and a hell of a grip. I guessed that he had worked on the loading docks in earlier years, though those times were clearly behind him now. Unlike Mr. Macy, Sternholtz seemed impressed that I was in the meeting. Little did he know it was only by happenstance that I was there.

Kevin got down to business fairly quickly. "Your inquiry indicated you were interested in our Apogee satellite communications network."

"Well, I don't know if we're interested or not," said Sternholtz. "I know that one of our competitors is putting in a similar system for its fleet, so I thought I'd see what it was all about."

"Then let me show you our brochure." said Kevin.

He pushed the brochure across the desk to Sternholtz and started explaining how the system worked. He was doing a fairly good job of it, telling Sternholtz about its various capabilities and benefits and so on. But I was watching Sternholtz's face and I could tell something wasn't right.

"Tell me," Sternholtz said, "what kind of investment would we be talking about for this kind of system and what kind of payback could we expect?"

From the look on Kevin's face, he might as well have asked how high the sky is.

"This sort of system doesn't have a list price," said Kevin. "It depends on a lot of factors."

"Like what?"

"Well, how many trucks you want equipped, what sorts of features you want in the system, any customizing of the software we have to do, that kind of thing," said Kevin. "I'd have to check."

"But, ballpark, what are we talking? I assume this kind of system can't be cheap. Are we talking $100,000, $1 million, $5 million, what?" asked Sternholtz.

Kevin didn't know what to say. He looked over at me. I had seen some figures in a report the other day and tried to remember them.

"I think our average installed cost per company is about $2 million," I said.

While Sternholtz didn't jump out of his chair, he did get a quizzical look on his face. He didn't know how to take a number like that.

"Of course, as Kevin says, an exact price would depend on the extent of the system," I added.

"I'm sure that we can configure a system that would be within your budget," said Kevin.

Sternholtz didn't like the sound of that. To his credit, though, he didn't throw us out of his office either. He started firing some questions.

"Seriously, what kind of bottom-line improvement could I expect if I went with this kind of system? And how and when would this start to pay for itself?" he asked.

Sternholtz was directing most of his attention to me, because, I began to suspect, I outranked Kevin. I was a manger; Kevin was the sales rep. Maybe he thought he could talk to me more easily. But this became rather awkward and made me uncomfortable because I had mentally cast myself in the role of observer. I wasn't even prepared to answer his questions.

It soon became apparent, however, that Kevin wasn't sure how to sell to this guy either. He'd done fine with Mr. Macy, but here he seemed ill at ease. He kept hedging on Sternholtz's questions, saying, in effect, it depends.

Opportunity was rapidly slipping away here. I could read it on Sternholtz's face. He was not impressed with us. We were not giving him what he expected, what he needed from us. Kevin seemed to sense it too, but he wasn't doing anything to save us.

Sure enough, about thirty seconds later, Sternholtz said, "Well, let me read through your materials here and think it over. If we're interested, I'll have somebody get back to you."

We went through the formalities of leaving, the shaking of hands, the smiles, the comments of appreciation. As we were walking out, I wondered if anybody from Elemenco would ever get in the door again.

At the elevator, Kevin turned to me. "That went pretty well, didn't it?"

Was he kidding? He had totally blown it in there. But Kevin seemed oblivious to whatever missteps may have been taken. I was very disturbed about the way things had gone.

It had been our first meeting with that company, yet Kevin had done virtually nothing to start building an image that would increase the customer's confidence in Elemenco. He had said nothing about how Elemenco was the best in the business, why we were the best, or why Sternholtz and his company should buy from us. He had done nothing to try to build a rapport with the president. He had done nothing to try to understand the company or what it might need from us, and hadn't asked any significant questions. All he had done was shown the brochure and explained the product. Yet I wasn't upset at Kevin so much as at the management that had put him in the situation.

As we drove back to Chicago, I wondered how many other Kevins there were in Elemenco sales who were expected to sell turnkey communication systems when they really belonged on the phone selling cable.

The next morning, I cleared some time and went down to the twenty-second floor. On the way to Ann Lansky's office, I passed Kevin sitting at his desk, phone at his ear, hands on the computer keyboard.

"May I speak to Larry O'Toole? Hi, Larry. Kevin Duttz here with Elemenco. How's it going today? Great. What's the weather like in Danville?"

Another day, another dollar for Kevin.

Ann was waiting for me in her office. "How did things go yesterday with Kevin?" she asked.

"I learned a lot," I said. "Tell me, is he really one of your *best* salespeople?"

Ann turned, took a computer printout off a shelf behind her desk, picked up a pen, and underlined a row on the sheet.

"Here. Numbers don't lie," she said.

She tossed the printout to me. She was right. For the previous four quarters, Kevin had been the third best sales rep in the office in terms of volume.

"Why do you ask? Did he screw up or something?" she said.

I really didn't want to get Kevin in trouble with his boss, so I worded my reply carefully. "I thought he could have been more effective on one of his calls."

And I explained a little about what I meant. Ann said something about everybody having an off day. I allowed that was certainly true, but then I asked, "Just how is it that Kevin was given Sternholtz and his trucking company as a prospect?"

"Simple. All-Points Express is in Kevin's territory. Dave, I have organized this office exactly the way that Gene Cherson directed all of us to do, and that's how we operate," said Ann.

"I see. Well, I'd like to work with one of the other people you mentioned yesterday. Can you set that up for me?"

"Sure, no problem," she said. "In fact, Jennifer Hone is here today and I already talked to her about you. Why don't we go meet her."

Jennifer was at her desk reading a presentation proposal that was probably fifty pages long. A stack of other copies sat on the corner of her desk. In another corner, Beethoven played softly on a portable CD player.

She was a woman I'd call handsome: clear-skinned, high cheeks, dark hair cut short, gray eyes, not much makeup, fairly tall. Overall, she looked like she had walked out of a page from *Dress for Success*. She wore a good-quality navy blue suit, hemline just below the knee, and a high-necked white blouse. I guessed she was in her late twenties or early thirties. Ann introduced us.

"Glad to meet you," Jennifer said. "Have a seat. I read the announcement that you're filling in for Gene Cherson. Is that right?"

"That's right," I said.

"Gee, that was terrible what happened to Mr. Cherson, wasn't it? Did you know him very well?" she asked.

"Yes, it was. And, no, not really."

"Have you been with the company long?"

"Just came in last week."

"Oh. Where did you work before?"

There were five or six more questions like that, all rapid-fire, but pleasant, as if she were just making conversation. I went along with it, and in a couple of minutes, she had learned that I had worked closely with Morrison, that I had worked in California at IJK, that I had started out in engineering, then had gone on to business. I suddenly realized that she knew a heck of a lot more about me than I knew about her.

"What about yourself?" I finally asked. "Have you been with the company long?"

"Oh, about five years now," she said, and then deftly resumed her own questioning. "So Ann tells me you want to work with some salespeople. Is there anything in particular you'd like to accomplish?"

"Just want to get a firsthand impression of how we're dealing with our customers," I said.

"It so happens that I have a customer presentation this morning about half an hour from now," she said. "You're welcome to sit in if you'd like. In fact, the customer will probably enjoy meeting you."

Ann left us then, but said she'd rejoin us for the presentation. Jennifer handed me a copy of the presentation proposal.

"Who's the customer?" I asked.

"MorrMart," she said. "I've got them interested in a 720 Network."

I had read about MorrMart in one of the business magazines. It was an expanding department-store chain that had made a name for itself by offering service that was a cut above the rest. They had store employees whose only job was to help you find the right merchandise, in-store displays that explained product features, faster checkout, a supervised play area for kids, those kinds of "little" things.

"They'd sure look good on our customer list, if they keep on growing the way they have in the past few years," she said.

"Who's coming from their side?" I asked.

"There will be three men from MorrMart," she said. "Richard Newlberg, Fred Carver, and John Joplin. Richard is president of MorrMart. Fred is vice-president of store operations. And John is head of technical services, what passes for management information systems in their organization."

Richard and Fred, she explained, knew their own business, but didn't know very much about telecommunications or computer systems—and didn't care to. So far, they had built their chain by emphasizing the human element, and had cut corners on technology. Now that they were getting big, inadequate systems were costing them. They were smart enough to know they needed a much more sophisticated system than what they had, but didn't understand what it meant to be sophisticated.

"I've been talking to them for a couple of months and I've heard all kinds of horror stories," Jennifer said. "Like merchandise gathering dust in the warehouses while store shelves are empty. And discovering that their store in Minneapolis has a two-year stock of suntan products while the Miami store is sold out. Things like that. When they only had a dozen stores all in one region, they could see and correct those kind of things fairly quickly, but now that they have a hundred stores, the mistakes are covered up easier and they cost a lot more. And I think we can help them, but they need somebody to educate and lead them through this. I've had to spend a lot of time with them just explaining the basic concepts they need to understand."

"What are they using now?" I asked her.

"A Bridely Star System."

I knew immediately why they were unhappy. Bridely was a big competitor of Elemenco, even though technically Elemenco was superior in most areas. Bridely had been strong back in the 1970s and early 1980s, especially in word processing and data base management. They offered licensed software that was easy for secretaries and clerks to learn and use. But their Star System was anything but a star in terms of performance—slow, menu-driven, inflexible, awkward for anything but routine tasks, designed for bureaucrats and people who were afraid of computers. True, it was reliable and simple to use, but not what you'd pick if you had some technical savvy and wanted the best performer.

"I happen to know," said Jennifer, "because I saw a new proposal on Fred Carver's filing cabinet, that Bridely is still courting them. But I think they may be leaning toward us."

"Good. What do you think will win them over?"

"Bridely doesn't have anything to compete with a 720 Network. I think that once they really understand the capabilities of the 720, they'll sign up with us. Now, of the three, Fred Carver is the hottest on Elemenco. Fred wants a system that will give them a competitive edge. He wants to use it for everything from picking locations for new stores, to making merchandise decisions, to planning and forecasting. But Richard is the one who has to be sold."

"What about the other guy, John?"

"John's opinion has to be considered, but he's the one who's been recommending Bridely, so he's not real popular right now. I've talked to John at length, and he's coming around, but he still seems to be down here someplace."

She waved her hand about waist level.

"He just can't seem to grasp why they should dump their Star System, and he's very loyal to Bridely. So I'm not sure he won't try to swing them away from us. But Richard and Fred are really the ones who will make the decision."

About then I noticed that I was actually getting excited. For one thing, a 720 Network, to me, is a heck of a lot more interesting than the computer cable and such that Kevin had been selling most of yesterday. For another, this was a potentially big sale to a big customer, and that in itself was exciting.

Jennifer looked at her watch and decided it was about time for us to get ready. We walked down the hall to the conference room. Inside was a long, oval, polished wood table and about a dozen padded chairs. Color monitors were set up in the corners and there was a podium to one side. Two guys were in the room, both of them engineers as it turned out, one at a computer terminal in a back corner and one seated at the table, looking over some schematics.

"We were in here at seven o'clock this morning rehearsing everything," Jennifer said.

A phone by the door rang. It was the receptionist calling to tell Jennifer that the customer was here. Jennifer went out to greet them. Ann arrived a few seconds later and the two of us, along with the two engineers, made an impromptu reception line by the door for the MorrMart people.

Richard, the president, was tall and tanned. He wore a crisp, perfectly tailored dark suit and a silk tie. He had a serious, no-nonsense look on his face.

Fred was more folksy looking. Rounded shoulders. Bald spot on the top of his head. Fairly short. Suit a bit rumpled. But very energetic, excitable. Big grin when he shook hands.

John was a skinny, rather nerdy-looking guy. Brown suit with a brown and gray tie. Pants loose around his skinny hips. Slick black hair a little too long in the back, receding hairline. Wire-rimmed glasses sitting on a big nose.

Richard and Fred sat together, John took a seat opposite them, and the rest of us filled in around them, with Jennifer taking the seat at the head of the table, next to Richard.

The first thing John did was open his proposal and flip to the back to see if there was a price list. (Which there was not. Jennifer had that on a separate sheet.) John tried to make a joke about it—"Guess it all must be free; they don't have any prices in here"—which Jennifer ignored.

She was directing most of her attention to Richard, chatting and smiling. I noticed that she was doing with Richard what she had done with me. In a casual, inoffensive way, she was asking questions to garner information that might be useful later on. Ann and I joined in the conversation.

"Well, we have quite a few things to show you this morning, so why don't we get started," Jennifer said finally.

She went to the podium and one of the engineers went back to the computer terminal. The lights dimmed. Up came the MorrMart logo on the monitors and, with some slick animation, the Elemenco logo joined it on the screens.

Jennifer didn't even talk about the 720 Network for the first ten or fifteen minutes. She talked about MorrMart, about inventory control, about the national expansion, about all the things MorrMart needed to grow. She worked in a couple of case histories, mentioned the other big-name customers we had, reminded them of things she had no doubt said in earlier meetings. *Then* she talked about the 720 Network—not as a product by itself, but as the key element of "the Elemenco Team Solution."

Her manner was knowledgeable, competent, professional. She had shapely, attractive hands and she used them effectively, gesturing for emphasis, pointing out specific things on the computer monitor.

"One of the most powerful things about a 720 Network is its GIS features," she told them. "What is GIS? Well, GIS can combine maps and other geographic information with marketing and inventory data to enable better management decision making. Let me show you."

Up came a map of the United States on the computer monitor.

"We've taken data that you at MorrMart gave us a few days ago and entered it into the system," she said. "Which means we can give you a picture of MorrMart's current operations."

Pop. There were all of MorrMart's stores on the map.

"Now we can add data to give you different perspectives on MorrMart's performance," she said. "For instance, let's take a look at each store's operating profit per square foot."

At that, the size of each store on the map then either increased or decreased relative to its profitability compared with all the other stores.

"We can zoom in to look at a particular region in detail."

And that's what happened on the screen; we were now looking at the greater Chicago area and the central Midwest.

"Let's say you want to know if you should adjust your inventories," she said.

Behind us, some clicking of the keys on the keyboard.

"Let's take a particular product, like televisions."

Up came a little TV icon next to each store, and next to each icon, a number representing how many days' supply of televisions the store had.

"As you can see, your Madison store has about an eight-month supply, while your Springfield store is—or was—nearly out of stock," she said.

Fred sat up. "Is that accurate?"

"Well, as I said, this is based on data you gave us a couple of days ago. But if you have this kind of system, we can add satellite telecommunication features that would give you up-to-the-minute data on every store," said Jennifer. "Your information at headquarters would be as current as the store manager's."

Fred had already started jotting down a note on the pad in front of him.

"You're going to check Springfield on that?" asked Richard.

"Damn right I am," said Fred.

He tore off the note and put it in his shirt pocket.

"Well, you just saw one of the advantages of the 720 Network's graphics," said Jennifer. "The meaning of the data is more obvious than it would be as just a column of numbers. Fewer things slip through the cracks. Now let's say you want to build a new store in the Chicago area. We can add demographic data."

Clicking keys. The map broke into colored sections of bright red, magenta, yellow, green.

"This shows you average household income by municipality." Jennifer went on, showing them overlays of interstate highways, commercial real estate, and property prices (simulated, of course, but it got the idea across).

Well, they were impressed. You could see it on their faces. Hell, *I* was impressed. I'd heard and read about this kind of thing, but this was the first time I'd seen it done with my own eyes.

"That's great to be able to have it all combined like that," said Richard.

The lights came up, and Jennifer sat down. Now it was time for questions. First to jump in was John. He began asking a bunch of questions. Our technical guys fielded them one by one. It was soon clear that John didn't know very much about this kind of system, but he was intrigued by the possibilities. He was not trying to trick us with his questions; he was trying to learn—and yet not appear too ignorant in front of his bosses.

Fred asked Jennifer if it was possible to combine such-and-such information with some other kind of data.

"We can customize the system to give you whatever you need," she said. "Elemenco is the only company that can provide satellite telecommunication with this combination of geographic and market data features. You'll get these kinds of capabilities only with us."

Jennifer was good. She made us sound like the experts, like competent professionals. But what impressed me the most was that there was no aspect of this presentation that she had not choreographed. As much as any human being could know, she already knew what every person on the customer's side wanted and didn't want, what each was afraid of, what each welcomed. She had made a special effort to customize it to their interests. How different Jennifer's style was from Kevin's, who seemed to use much the same approach with everybody.

"Okay, what's all this going to cost us?" asked Richard.

"I thought you'd want to know that," said Jennifer, "so I prepared this for you."

From a folder, she took out some sets of paper on which I could see a list of items and numbers.

But before passing the price sheets around, she said, "When I tell them about the 720, some of our clients ask me, 'How is this system going to save us money?' My answer is that a 720 Network will not save you a dime. If all you want to do is *save* money, this is the wrong system for you. Now I can give you a good price on machines that will let you do what everybody else has been doing for the past five years. If, on the other hand, you want a competitive edge to help your business to *grow*, if you want a capability that will enable you to do things you can't do now, things that only a handful of other companies can do at present, then this is the right system for you."

Which, it seemed to me, was exactly the right thing to say to Fred and Richard, though possibly the wrong thing to say to John. Now she passed out the price sheets. I took a peek at the copy she gave me. The bottom line was about $5 million.

She went over what the price covered and didn't cover.

"Well, what about teaching people how to use the system? If we go with this, are we going to have to retrain everybody?" asked Fred.

"Your in-store systems should stay more or less the same," said Jennifer. "We will provide on-site training for all the people who are going to use the system, plus continuing technical support. It's covered in the price you see here and we'll be with you every step of the way."

That seemed to satisfy him, but he turned to John and asked, "What do you think?"

John clearly was nervous about the price. "It's a good system. No doubt about that. But I just don't know that we really need to go to these measures to accomplish the benefit," he said.

"How else would you do it?"

John said something about talking to Bridely about some additional bells and whistles for the existing system, but Fred cut him off.

"We've already seen their best, and they don't have anything like what we just saw," said Fred.

Jennifer was still mainly talking to Fred and Richard. "If this system saves you from putting one store in the wrong location, if it keeps you from making even one bad decision, think about what kind of return that is for you."

By now, John knew which way the wind was blowing and he relented. In fact, he was starting to get excited about this new technology he was going to get to play with.

Finally, Fred asked, "How much of an interruption are we going to have to our current systems in order to get this installed?"

From that point on, I knew we were going to get the go-ahead. Richard was sold. Fred and John were talking about logistics: how they would get certain parts of the system off line so the work could be done without interrupting operations, that kind of thing.

"What about a timetable?" asked Richard.

"Elemenco can start just as soon as you sign this," said Jennifer.

Out of her briefcase came a letter of agreement.

Richard grinned at Fred. "Looks like she's got all the answers."

Richard read it over, stroked his chin for about three seconds, then said, "Let's go with it."

"Very good," said Jennifer.

She handed him her pen. Richard signed. Ann Lansky signed for us. And Elemenco's revenues went up five million bucks. I felt the hair on the back of my neck stand up.

A day later, I went out with Jennifer on a couple of her afternoon customer calls. Her territory was in the western suburbs of the city and she drove us in one of the company cars.

I managed to turn the tables a bit and found out more about her as we drove. She had a computer science degree from Cal Tech and an MBA from Stanford. We talked about California wines and San Francisco restaurants for a while. Her father was a dentist in Sacramento, so she got back that way once or twice a year. I saw she was relaxing, getting more comfortable around me.

"By the way, I thought you were great yesterday with MorrMart," I told her.

"Thank you. I just hope I can give them enough of my time to make sure everything goes right."

"Is there any question that you won't?"

"Well, like everybody else, I've got a fairly big territory to serve and we only have so many hours in a day," Jennifer said. "According to policy, after I get the sale, I'm supposed to fade into the background and let the technical service people take over. I've tried to do that, but too many times I've seen it get . . . well, you know. I mean, after all, they're technicians and they're coming in after I've already spent a lot of time with the customer. They don't necessarily understand all the issues. Things get lost in the translation. There are misunderstandings. Sometimes we drop the ball. Sometimes the customer expects too much. I'll get called back to straighten things out, but by then there are hard feelings. Plus cost overruns and wasted money. I just feel it would be a lot better if one person stayed in charge from start to finish."

"You don't mind getting involved in the installation and the technical issues and all that stuff?" I asked.

"No, not at all," she said. "I'd even prefer it, in a case like MorrMart, if I had total control over the whole project. I don't know why, but I'm just the kind of person who likes to see things through to the end. Once we've got the system installed and everybody's happy, then I'm satisfied to move on. After all, I want to keep growing in my career; I don't want to be married to the same customers forever. At the same time, I see my job as being more than just getting a signature on a contract. I feel it's my professional responsibility to be managing the total interaction between Elemenco and the customer. Only that's not the way the management policy or the incentives are set up."

"Do you like sales?" I asked her.

"Yes, basically I do," she said, "though, eventually, I want to move into management."

"Oh? Not a bad career plan. More than one CEO has done it that way."

"I'm all right with doing this for a few more years, but then I'd like to move up into either sales management, engineering management, or maybe a corporate staff position."

"Okay, you know we've got a problem in sales growth. Aside from what you've just said, what kinds of things do you think we ought to be doing?"

"Teams," she said without hesitation. "I'd set up teams to handle the big customer accounts. Give the salespeople more access to the technical side. I'd start stressing the superiority in our technology. In fact, that's what I try to do in most of my sales calls."

"What do you think of the 800 line?" I asked her as she drove.

"Let me put it this way: Can you imagine Fred or Richard calling an 800 number when they want to buy a better system? I get my share from the 800 line. But they're usually a waste of my time. I feel they are, anyway."

"How have your sales been on some of our other products?" I asked her.

"Like what?"

"Well, take computer cable for instance."

"To tell you the truth," she said, "I don't get that many orders for it. I know it means income, and every little bit helps, but there are other products I feel we should push. I'll sell it if someone asks for it, but I really don't know why we bother with that kind of business. You've got to sell a lot of cable to make any real money."

"That's true," I said.

She got off the expressway, we went down a two-lane street, and she made a turn into an unpaved, gravel parking lot. In front of us was a huge concrete-block building with loading docks and a sign reading Midcontinent Warehouse Electronics.

"Well, here we are," she said. "If you wanted to see a routine sales call, this is it."

"One of your better accounts?"

She just sighed and shook her head. "They're in my territory, so I have to call on them. Besides, they've bought from us in the past."

"What are you going to sell them today? Another 720 Network?" I asked.

"No, they're a mail-order house. They carry our 386 machines, our modems, stock some types of our cable. And cellular car phones," she said. "They're always haggling with me over the price."

Under the sign was a windowless steel door. As she went in, I watched her expensive high heels step onto the dirty linoleum floor. Here was the same woman who closed a multimillion-dollar deal the day before, now walking into a warehouse. I guess that's what they mean by "comes with the territory."

Jennifer asked the receptionist for Mr. Antonelli, and the receptionist paged him on the loudspeaker. There was a window that enabled us to look out into the warehouse, with its racks and cartons of electronic merchandise stacked to the ceiling. Way down the aisle, a man in a white shirt, no tie, beltless slacks started walking toward us.

Antonelli took us into his office, which was lined with brown wood paneling and had dirty wall-to-wall carpet. Jennifer introduced me.

"What, they figure there's strength in numbers, they're sending two of you out to see me?" said Antonelli. "Well, it won't make no difference."

"What do you mean?" asked Jennifer.

"I've got to discontinue Elemenco," he said.

"When did you reach that decision?" she asked.

"Yesterday morning when I signed as a Mitsugami distributor. I tried to reach you by phone, save you a trip, but you were in a meeting or something," said Antonelli. "Look, your stuff is quality, no doubt about it, but it's got Elemenco prices on it. Mitsugami offers the same products, which perform the same as yours or better, and they're lower cost. I get a better margin. So what do you expect me to do?"

"Now, Mr. Antonelli, you have to remember that in Elemenco prices you're getting the benefit of our research and development, plus you're getting our technical support—"

This was not winning him.

"Look, Jenny, you're a nice lady and I like you, and it's all very nice for your boss here to stop by. But my customers are shopping for a low price, fast delivery, no hassles. We've got our own technical hotline in-house. Now, if you can knock 30 percent off your prices, maybe we can talk. Maybe. But I'll tell you something else, same thing I told you the last time we talked."

He started waving a finger.

"Elemenco really honked me off when you went ahead and bought that retail electronics chain. That plus the telephone sales you've been doing—you're taking customers away from me and every other distributor out there."

Jennifer tried to argue that we were aiming for a totally different market, but Antonelli still was not buying. Finally, she looked at me.

I said, "I'm sure Jennifer has already given you the best deal we can afford. As for the rest, I'm sorry, but those are corporate decisions that we really can't change just for your benefit."

Antonelli threw up his hands. "There you have it then," he said. And we were out.

She had another call to make, at a company about ten miles away called Bennet Insurance. The contact was the computer services manager, a guy named Gary Bopoth. She told me while we were waiting for him to see us that she had delivered a proposal two weeks ago for a new interdepartmental computer network, to replace and greatly expand the network they already had. Good old Gary apparently had taken most of the meeting to prove to her that he knew more about computer networks than she did. Just when she thought she had finally got his ego massaged—irksome as that apparently was to her—his technical objections overcome, and was trying to close, Gary had insisted on thinking it over and talking to some other vendors.

"But I'm hoping I'll be able to close today," she said.

I could see trouble as soon as we got to his office. He was not smiling. His face was long, and he seemed bored and a little irritated. He also seemed confused and not at all impressed that I had come along. Jennifer went into her casual chat mode, trying to warm him up, but as soon as we sat down he cut her off.

"You'll have to excuse me, but I have a staff meeting in about twenty minutes, so we'll have to make this short and to the point," he said.

"Okay," said Jennifer. "What was your reaction to our proposal?"

"Not to be blunt or anything, but we're not going to go with your proposal. I've talked it over with my staff, and we think we can handle this in-house pretty well. So what we're going to do, instead of going one-stop shopping, is split things up and go with the best suppliers for each major component of the new system," said Gary.

This seemed to come as a surprise to Jennifer.

"Now we do like your 386 machines, because they've got a lot of features built in," Gary continued. "Even Bridely admits they're good machines. So we'd like to order eighteen of those. Here, I wrote up the specs for you."

He handed her a sheet of paper. Jennifer was remaining calm, but under the skin, she was furious.

"You're going with Bridely?" she asked.

"For the core system we'll be using," Gary said.

"Which one, may I ask?"

"We settled on the Bridely SuperStar Network."

Jennifer started shaking her head. "Gary, the system I specified for you will outperform SuperStar by any benchmark."

"Well, yes and no. Bridely supports all the industry standards. You have a lot of advanced features, but I know that could mean months of mucking around before you get everything running right. Plus a whole new learning curve for the users."

"We're offering training in the package," she said.

"It's still lost productive time. Besides, I don't need that aggravation," said Gary. "And from what I've been hearing, your network software has some significant bugs in it."

"We have a new version of that software coming out very soon, certainly by the time your hardware would come in," she said.

"Jennifer, I realize you put a lot of time and effort into our proposal, and I appreciate that. But I have to look at what's best for this company. The bottom line is I think we'll get better value doing most of it in-house and using Bridely as our primary supplier."

"But how could you judge their system to be superior?" she asked.

"Look, I know this company and I know its computer needs. To tell you the truth, your proposal outlined a system that, in my opinion, is overkill for us. It's got features we're not going to use—"

"I thought we agreed you'd need those features down the road," she said.

"After I thought it over, it just seemed that your proposal was like reinventing the wheel."

"Gary, I felt we didn't have any other choice," she said. "What you have in place here is outmoded even by today's standards."

"Jennifer, *I* specified the systems we have in this company," he said. "They're good systems."

I thought the battle of professional egos was about to flare anew, but Jennifer was smart enough to retreat.

"Of course, they're good, functional systems for today. But I was thinking about your future needs," she said. "I was thinking about what you need in order to grow."

Gary sat back, folded his arms.

"I think I know what we need," he said. "And what I need from you, or *want* from you, are eighteen of your 386 machines, which we will configure on-site here in this department. Do you want the order or not?"

"Very well . . ."

"Now you're going to have to give me a unit price—"

"What I gave you was a system price," she said.

"You'll have to break it out then and get back to me," he said, "because that's all I'm really interested in buying from you."

It was clear the guy had made up his mind.

"All right," said Jennifer. "I'll get back to you tomorrow on that price. Is it okay if I just call it in to you?"

"I'd prefer it that way. Why don't you just fax it to me, in fact. We're very busy around here right now."

He stood up and we left. No handshakes, no smiles.

When we got to the car, Jennifer closed her door a little more loudly than she needed to. She was angry, but after she started the engine, she took a deep breath and made herself calm down.

"I'm sorry you had to see that," she said.

"So it goes."

"I put *so much* work into that proposal. It was a good proposal. And I know damn well what he did. He took our design, went to Bridely, and got them to give him a better price. I should have told him it was all or nothing."

She needed to let off steam, so I didn't voice any judgments.

"Bridely's been courting them for a long time. So in a way it doesn't surprise me," she said. "I know how Bridely operates."

"Yeah?"

"I started out with Bridely, trained with them. I'd probably still be there if I thought I could have the opportunities there that I have with Elemenco. Anyway, I know how they work. They do a lot of customer entertainment. They wine and dine their customers, take them golfing, treat them like gold. And they're never threatening."

"What do you mean?"

"They all act like a bunch of good ole boys. All buddy-buddy. I was told not to try to act like an expert, but just defer to the customer's judgment. You know, the customer is always right, so don't argue. Always play it safe. But their systems are really mediocre. Our stuff will run rings around all of it."

"That didn't seem to be what mattered to Gary," I said.

She sighed again. "Maybe I should have stroked his ego more. Done it the way Bridely taught me. But I don't know. That just isn't me. I mean, they're using 4.77 megahertz XTs, for God's sake, that are too slow . . ."

And she went on with all the dumb things that Gary and his people insisted on doing, things that Bridely no doubt would have agreed were just fine, as long as he bought their equipment. I let her talk.

Finally, when it had gone quiet between us, she said, almost to herself, "You know, it's funny, but I always do better with upper management than with the computer guys. It's like the computer guys always want to prove they know more than I do."

"Sounds like you ran smack into the not-invented-here syndrome," I said.

"That's exactly it," she said. "That's exactly it."

But that didn't change the fact that we had gained one customer and lost two others. One step forward, two steps back.

8

Don't get the idea that all I did every day was go around with salespeople. During this period, my days were long and full. I was handling two jobs, Gene's and my own. (And my own was getting the back burner.) I met the account team at our advertising agency. I sat down with the firm that handled our market research. I took calls from customers who were angry at us for whatever offenses, petty or serious. I even took one call from somebody who liked us and bothered to say so. I did all the normal stuff—*and* I got to know a few of the salespeople.

All work and no play is not my idea of a good time. My personal goal generally has been to get all my work done in something close to 50 to 60 hours. A lot of times I don't make it, but I'm not hanging out at the office for glory points.

At this point, twelve- to fourteen-hour days were the norm. I didn't like it one bit, but I still thought getting to see the sales effort firsthand was important. So the following week I cleared some more time and went down to see Ann again.

"You know, one of the people I thought you ought to work with is Charlie Summers," she said.

"Yeah? How come?"

"Well, Charlie has been around a long time. He's a pro at keeping accounts. Might take him a while to bring in new business, but once he's got the contract, he really takes care of his customers. In fact, sometimes I wish he wouldn't take such good care of them."

"What do you mean by that?"

"Oh, you know, if one of his customers needs something, Charlie will find a way to get it for them, even if he has to bend a few policies to do it. Sometimes I wonder if he's really working for Elemenco or for the customer," said Ann. "Of course, if I were a customer, I'd sure want him handling my business."

She told me that late last year, right after the reorganization of the sales force, some of Charlie's customers found out that he wouldn't be handling their accounts any more. Well, they got on the phone and threatened to stop doing business with us.

"I had to do a little gerrymandering of the territories to keep everybody happy," said Ann. "Even some of the customers who couldn't fit in will still call Charlie instead of their assigned rep when they have a problem. Just can't break them of the habit. They're very loyal. Some of them will change jobs and Charlie will get their business at the new company, even though we might lose business at the old company."

"All right," I said. "I'd like to meet this guy."

So Ann took me down the hall to Charlie's office, but Charlie wasn't there.

"I know he's in today," said Ann. "Let's have a look around."

We walked through the corridors until Ann said, "There he is."

She pointed toward the coffee machine, where four or five guys were standing around talking, cups in hand. From what Ann had said, I was expecting some dynamic super-hero. As we walked up to the group my eyes automatically went to a couple of tall, handsome, athletic-looking guys wearing new suits fresh from the tailor, figuring one of them would be Charlie. But the group parted, those guys backed away, and there was the real Charlie Summers: a slim, nondescript man in his mid-fifties dressed in a drab suit with a neutral tie, a guy who just plain blended in.

The group broke up and Charlie and I went back to his office, where I did my now-familiar explanation about meeting customers and working with the sales force.

"Right now, I'm expecting a phone call," Charlie said. "Then I've got to go see someone. Do you want to come along?"

"Sure."

Waiting for the call, we talked. It was easy-going conversation with Charlie. I didn't get the feeling, as I did with Jennifer Hone, that there was any agenda. With Charlie, it was just a loosening-up kind of talk. The main topic, I think, was the construction taking place on the Dan Ryan Expressway. We were in the middle of talking about commuting times when the phone rang.

"You're sure that'll fix it for them?" he asked the caller. "Okay, I'll be right down."

He got his briefcase and we were on our way, walking fast toward the elevators.

"I've got to pick something up on 9," he told me.

We stopped on the ninth floor, where we've got our software services department. Next to the elevators, there is a receptionist who is supposed to be there for security, since we have a lot of proprietary code inside. But Charlie just smiled and walked past her, saying, "How's it going today, Linda."

"Fine, Charlie. Can I help you with something?"

"Just got to pick something up. Only be a minute," said Charlie.

Then she looked at me.

"I'm with him," I said, not wanting to explain who I was.

She almost didn't believe me until Charlie said over his shoulder, "He's okay."

Back we went, through an open-office arrangement with its fabric-covered cubicles. In the cubicles were programmers at their computers. Toward the far end, Charlie made a hard left into one of the cubicles. A young guy in a sweater stood up and handed Charlie some diskettes and some photocopied documentation.

"Don't tell anybody where you got it, because Rick will have a fit if he finds out I gave you this," he said.

"I won't even tell the customer where I got it," said Charlie. "And thanks, buddy, I owe you one."

"Well, I hope it solves their problem," said the young guy. "We should have issued an update months ago."

We were almost to the door when another guy, older and bigger and wearing a suit, came around the corner right in front of us. He nearly passed us by when he saw what Charlie was holding, and then his eyes got big.

"All right, hold it, Charlie. Is that the new update I told you this morning you couldn't have?"

"Excuse me, Rick. I've got to deliver this to a customer," said Charlie.

"No, you don't," said Rick, and he grabbed the diskettes away from Charlie.

"Rick, I've got a customer who's got a problem, and this will solve it for him. Now what's wrong with that?"

Rick wasn't even listening, was just shaking his head no.

"I told you this morning. John hasn't signed off on this yet, he's not due back until the end of next week, and that's aside from the fact that the documentation hasn't come in yet from the printer."

"My customer has the problem *now*. I want his problem to be gone by next week," said Charlie.

"This is not to leave the company until the official release date," said Rick. "If I do it for you, I'll have to do it for everybody else."

"Well, Rick, you *should* do it for everybody else," Charlie argued.

Rick just laughed at him. "No, Charlie, it's against policy. If you want to talk to John when he gets back from his conference next week, be my guest. But I'm sure he'll back me up on this."

Then Charlie slowly turned to me.

"Rick, have you met Mr. Kepler?" asked Charlie. "Reed Morrison just appointed Mr. Kepler our new head of marketing."

Well, that put Rick into pause mode.

I summoned up my best manager's don't-mess-with-me voice and said, "I don't think the customer cares about our internal policies. Give Mr. Summers the software."

The diskettes went back to Charlie's hands. We were turning for the door when Rick, thinking quickly, came up with another obstacle.

"But somebody has to sign a release for that."

"Send it up to Reed Morrison's office," I said. "I'm sure he'll sign it."

We got on the elevator again to go down to the parking garage.

"Thanks for helping me out in there," said Charlie.

"Don't mention it," I said. "I like your style."

We got into Charlie's car, another of the leased company cars, and drove out of the garage.

"So what was really going on back there?" I asked.

"I didn't want to say too much out loud in the office," said Charlie, "because strictly speaking this guy we're going to go see isn't even my customer."

"Yeah? Well, why are you doing this then?"

"He's an old customer of mine. They assigned Kevin Duttz to his account. Nothing against Kevin, but this guy is having a problem and, well, he called me at home last night."

"How come he called you?"

"He's frustrated as hell, because he's been having this problem off and on for about six months now. He's got one of our networks, and every so often, when one too many people with a certain kind of terminal get on the system, the whole network goes down. So he gets hold of Kevin yesterday. And Kevin follows the procedures he's supposed to follow, which are to have the customer call software services. That's supposed to give Kevin more time for professional selling, even though in practice it may lose us an old and trusted friend. But anyway that's what Kevin does. Or tries to do, because the guy isn't having any of it. He's done that before and he's been given the runaround, but he can't get anywhere with Kevin. So finally he calls me. I get him calmed down, we figure out what the problem is. This morning, first thing, I call down to software services and talk to Rick. Unbeknownst to the world at large, they have a patch in the new software that fixes the problem, but Rick won't release the software, because of—well, you heard his reasons. Well, luckily, I happen to know Bill, the guy in the sweater, because Bill used to be a sales trainee with us. And you know the rest."

"Who is this customer?" I asked him.

"It's a railroad," said Charlie. "The Chicago and Midwest. Not a huge customer for us, but not a small one either."

A few minutes later we were driving past an enormous railroad yard. We parked in front of a three-story utilitarian building of 1930s vintage and went inside.

The information systems manager, a guy named Bob Lilly, came out and greeted us.

"This had better not just be a social call to try to make me feel better, Charlie," he said. "Because I want some answers."

Charlie didn't say a word, just held up the diskettes.

"What's that?"

"Your answers, I hope," said Charlie.

"And who's this?" he asked, looking at me. "If it's the guy who wrote this software, I'm going to kill him."

"No, this is Mr. Kepler," said Charlie. He explained who I was and then added, "Mr. Kepler happened to be in my office this morning and decided to come along."

As Charlie sat down at a computer and began installing the new software, Mr. Lilly proceeded to dump on me all his frustrations. I got the full load. But as I listened to what he was and was not saying, it sounded to me as though he *liked* our network; it was just that he hadn't been able to get us to respond to his problems until he called Charlie.

After a while, Charlie came to my rescue. To get Bob's mind off his aggravations, Charlie launched into a litany of jokes, most of which were as screamingly funny as they were offensive. Finally, Charlie got up from the computer and Bob spent the next twenty minutes doing everything he could to crash the system.

You could hear his attitude toward us changing by the comments he was making as the minutes went by.

He started out saying things like "Now you watch, Charlie, this is what always happens . . . No, it's not doing it any more."

And "Just last week we were trying to send a big file and we got this error message and—oh, how about that. It's working now."

Then he started saying things like "Hey, you fixed that one, too? That's great!"

And finally, "I got to hand it to you, Charlie, I think it's bulletproof."

Charlie took a few more minutes to explain some of the new features, but we weren't there more than an hour. I'm not kidding you, Bob's attitude toward us swung nearly 180 degrees. He walked us to the door.

"This will not be forgotten," he said, clasping Charlie's hand in both of his, then pumping my hand in turn. "You folks are okay."

It was an emotional moment. A bond of trust between his company and ours had been reestablished. There actually were traces of tears at the edges of Bob Lilly's eyes. Outside in the car, the true impact of what Charlie had accomplished hit me.

"That was amazing," I said. "You turned that guy from an enemy into an ally."

"You don't get opportunities like that very often," said Charlie.

Opportunities. I had to smile, but he was serious.

"It's true," said Charlie. "A lot of customers, if they get upset with you, you're history before you even know what's going on. So it's an opportunity when you know the customer has a problem and you can do something about it. Doesn't happen very often. Sometimes only once or twice a year. You've got to watch and act fast when it does."

We went up the entrance ramp to the interstate, heading back toward downtown. Charlie kept talking.

"See, I could have just referred it to back to Kevin or talked to Ann Lansky about it. Or I could have just had one of our service technicians pay him a call when the new software was released. But that wasn't what Bob needed. Bob needed someone he knew and trusted to come out today, in person, and pay attention to him."

"Yeah, but you say Bob wasn't your customer."

"Details, details," said Charlie. "I've known Bob for years. I'm probably the reason he's stuck with us for so long. That might sound like ego talking, but it's true. Anyway, you can be sure I'm going to let Ann Lansky know what happened. And

I'm going to ask Ann for the account back. A good word from you wouldn't hurt either."

"Well, I'll tell Ann what I really think."

Charlie said, "Well, even if Kevin keeps the account, these things have a way of coming around. If Bob keeps calling me, I'm not going to ignore him. One way or another . . ."

We made one more call that morning. His name was Paul Ozlo, manager of a small company called Uniritz Mobile Telephone. They carried the cellular telephones we manufactured. Paul and Charlie had been doing business for three or four years—a reasonably long time, given the nature of our business. Charlie met with him the same time once a month, every third Wednesday.

Ozlo gave us his regular order, and all Charlie did was make a note of it. No purchase orders, no letters of agreement (maybe there were some on file, but nothing was signed on this occasion), just the guy's word, which was good enough for Charlie. In parting, Charlie offered lunch, which was customary between the two of them, but (maybe because I was along, an alien who was not part of the ritual) Ozlo declined. So Charlie delivered several of his newer jokes, left the customer laughing, and then Charlie and I went to lunch.

It was a place where almost everybody knew almost everybody else. Charlie had lunch there two or three times a week. Today we both had a drink before lunch. We both relaxed. I asked him some personal questions. Did he have a family? Oh, yeah, he had a solid marriage, had been married some thirty years to Doris. They had two kids, boy and a girl, both grown. He was active in the community, belonged to this organization and that. He was a deacon at his church. I'm not sure what a deacon does, but it sounded solid and respectable to me.

"What do you think we ought to be doing to get more business?" I asked him.

Charlie grinned, took a sip of his drink, sat back. "If you'll indulge me, I'll give you my dollar-seventy-five lecture on marketing and sales. It's very short. That's why it's only a dollar-seventy-five. As far as I'm concerned, there are only two important questions to be answered."

"Which are?"

"One, who is the customer? And, two, what does the customer want? Now sometimes those questions are easy to answer and sometimes they're not. But if you answer those questions, that's all you really need to know. Everything else follows. You know what to do and the rest is a matter of execution."

"Yeah, okay, but what specifically do you think we ought to be doing?"

"We ought be doing things to get to know the customer better. If you want my opinion, we ought to be spending more on trade shows. We ought to be spending more on customer entertainment so that we can build relationships with these people. We ought to be doing all the other kinds of things that get us closer to the customer. Because, let's face it, we have good products and services, but so does the competition. Knowing the customers and taking care of them—that added value of personal contact—is what makes the difference."

I told him I had asked Jennifer Hone the same question and she'd had different ideas.

"Well, Jennifer is good," said Charlie. "I don't mean to put her down. Not at all. From what I've heard she did a hell of a job bringing in MorrMart. But it seems to me like she's always trying to reinvent the wheel, coming up with the most elegant solution. She's always talking about *design*. Most of the products we sell don't need to be reinvented. You've just got to get out and sell them."

"Aside from what happened with Bob Lilly this morning, what do you think of Kevin Duttz?" I asked him.

"I like Kevin, but he doesn't get personally involved with the customer. I'd say the problem with Kevin is he spends way too much time on the phone. You can't get to know people over the phone. Not really. And you can't sell most of our products by phone. He's always talking about us getting better systems for handling orders and complaints and so on. Well, systems are fine, but they don't solve all your problems. I mean, we sell computer equipment. Computers are interesting machines. But how is a computer ever going to hold hands with a customer?" Charlie asked.

"I think I know what you mean," I said. "On the other hand, he does sell a lot of product."

"Yeah, but take a look where that volume comes from," said Charlie. "Cable, connectors, modems, boards, PCs. It's all off-the-shelf kinds of products. I don't think he's sold a network the entire time he's been with us. The kinds of products Kevin likes to sell are very price sensitive. As soon as somebody gives those customers a better price, away they go."

He leaned forward, lowered his voice.

"When people do business with me, believe it or not, they'll pay *more*. They'll pay more than they'll pay the other guy, because they know me and they trust me. That's added value for them," he said and then sat back again.

"No, I'm not going to give them a rock-bottom price, but I'm going to take care of them. They know I'm going to bird-dog their orders for them. I'm going to be there if they have a problem. And what the hell, I also tell jokes, I take them to the ball game, I make it fun for them to do business with me. Now, I have my limits. I won't cheat or break the law to make a sale, for instance. And I won't lie, either. Stretch the truth once in a while, sure, and sometimes it pays big to keep your mouth shut. I mean, I may go to church, but I'm not a choirboy. But overall, you've got to be honest. Any relationship worth having has to be based on honesty for it to last. That's my whole sales philosophy: you build relationships and you win accounts. You can't do it just with big projects, the way Jennifer does. And you don't just go for volume, the way Kevin does. Build relationships and you build your market share. Simple as that."

It was nice to be in that simple world with Charlie for a while. It was a place where people knew each other, trusted each other, did business together, made money together, even had a good time together. Love your customers and they will love you back. That was the moral and motto of Charlie's way.

"But what do you do when it takes more than a relation-ship to get or sustain a piece of business?" I asked him.

He didn't understand me.

"I mean, for instance, what do you do with an inexperi-enced customer?" I asked him. "What do you do when there's new technology? How do you get business from someone who doesn't understand all that they need?"

"Well, I'll tell you, Dave, the customers I get along with best already know their way around a computer, most of them. Used to be, as I was getting into this business, you had to do a lot of educating the customer. Any more, my better customers pretty much understand the technology. Not every little wire or chip in the machine—not any more than someone who drives a car knows why the car is designed the way it is. But they at least know what the machine is supposed to do. They know the standards. My customers understand what a LAN is and what it does. We know each other's jargon. We speak each other's language. I don't have to do much education with them. Frankly, some of them know more than I do," he admitted.

"Really? Does that embarrass you?"

"No, not usually. In fact, I play on that sometimes. I compliment them on their technical understanding. Most of the time it doesn't matter if they technically know more than I do. Because my job is to help them get things done. And that doesn't necessarily require a rocket scientist. My job, as much as anything, is to listen, because most of my customers already know what they need. It's up to me to deliver it to them."

He was right. Everything he said was right. As long as you were talking about *his* customers.

We finished lunch and got back in the car again. I asked him what was next on the agenda.

"Got a three o'clock meeting with a prospect up in Rockford," he said as we got into the car. "First, though, we've got to pick up the translator."

"Translator?"

"The meeting is with Haikkyu Manufacturing," he said.

"The Japanese car maker?"

"That's right. I've hired a translator so that we can talk to the Japanese managers in their native tongue."

"Nice touch," I said.

"Here," said Charlie. "Here's something else I did on my own."

He pulled a card out of his shirt pocket and handed it to me. On one side, it was a typical Elemenco business card, but the other side was printed in Japanese. Rather impressive, considering that we were in the middle of Illinois.

"Did our corporate marketing help you with this?" I asked.

"No, I started doing this on my own. I noticed from reading the paper that there were a number of foreign-owned businesses starting up. Some Japanese, some German, and so on. I did some digging, targeted the ones I might like to have as customers, did some research on the cultural differences, and started calling on them. Of course, then we reorganized the territories, which set me back, but it's looking up now."

"Have you gotten any business from Haikkyu?"

"Not yet, but this is only my fifth or sixth meeting with them," he said, "and you've probably heard how careful the Japanese are about choosing suppliers. You've got to hang in there. The first few meetings, I didn't even try to sell them anything. Just went in, told them who we were, what we did, what kinds of things we might do for them, got to know them. Finally about the fourth meeting, I found out they liked our cellular phones, but they wanted some features added. So I talked to engineering and manufacturing people, got it worked out. Today we'll see what happens—if anything."

We picked up the translator on a street corner in the Near North and then drove west, out of the city. The translator was a graduate student at Northwestern who had grown up in Tokyo. Charlie paid him a fee for each meeting.

The Haikkyu assembly plant was new and rose out of the cornfields surrounding it. We met with about a dozen people—managers, engineers, and other workers—in a conference room close to the assembly line. Through a window, we could see the Haikkyu automobiles going by. They made a luxury sedan here. The cellular telephones Charlie was offering would be installed as an option.

Only about three of the people in the meeting were from Japan, and everybody spoke English. Still, they seemed to appreciate that Charlie had gone to the trouble of bringing the translator. The most senior Japanese manager there, a Mr. Toshimine Shushita, seemed especially pleased that Charlie had brought me along.

Early in the meeting, Mr. Shushita made a rather formal statement. "We are pleased to announce that Haikkyu will be awarding our contract for cellular telephones to Elemenco. The reason we have selected Elemenco as our preferred supplier is that you are the only American company in this market to demonstrate attention to the values we at Haikkyu most appreciate, such as quality and the willingness to modify your design to conform to our standards. We hope this is the beginning of a long and productive relationship between our two companies."

After that, who wouldn't think of Charlie Summers as our hero? I told that story to Reed Morrison the next time he called in.

"Geez, this guy's the answer to our problems!" said Reed. "Why don't you talk to R&D and see if we can clone him. Seriously, if we could train all our sales force to work with customers the way he does, they'd love us!"

"He's very good," I agreed. "I'm sure that Charlie and people like him are part of the solution. But I'm not sure he's the total answer."

"Why do you say that?"

"We'll talk when you get back."

I worked with Charlie off and on over a couple of days and got to know him a little better. Charlie was a people lover. He liked taking customers out to lunch, taking them to ball games, buying a round of drinks at the end of a day. One morning, I walked into his office and found Charlie reading the paper. He saw that one of the assistant data processing managers at a company he called on had just been promoted. By that afternoon, there was a basket of fruit on the guy's desk. He treated customers—the good customers at least, the ones who stayed loyal to him—almost like family. Place an order with Charlie and you become part of the family. On his calendar, Charlie even had the birthdays and anniversaries of some of his better customers, inked in right along with the birthdays of his own wife and kids. Anything good happened to you at work and Charlie would be there knocking on your office door, pumping your hand, patting you on the back, maybe dropping off a bottle of champagne or scotch or flowers or whatever he knew you liked. That was Charlie.

I went along on another morning call with him. The customer was a restaurant service company called Santlinni and the main contact was a woman named Martha Beckley. She was a part of the Charlie Summers family. Back in the mid 1970s, when Elemenco was making dedicated word processors, Charlie had sold Martha a complete system, and he'd been calling on her periodically ever since, sometimes selling her supplies and upgrades and replacements, sometimes just staying in touch. He'd sent her Christmas cards, was known to have dropped off a rose on her birthday, took her out to lunch once or twice a year, gave her calendars and premiums. He'd stayed in touch all this time, and she'd stayed loyal, paying the higher price for printer ribbons and diskettes and memory boards from Elemenco. Now, finally, they were ready to scrap all that old dedicated equipment and buy an integrated system of work stations.

"She asked for an estimate a couple of weeks ago," said Charlie. "I'm almost 100 percent positive she's going to go with us. You'll see."

When we got to Martha's office there were two women waiting to see us. Martha was a chunky and smiling woman about Charlie's age. The other was introduced as Petrina Yarkovic, a much younger woman, who stood about five feet tall and wore too much makeup.

After the pleasantries were exchanged, Martha said, "Petrina is my new administrative assistant."

"Congratulations," said Charlie, turning to Petrina.

"Since my own responsibilities have expanded considerably, Petrina will be handling all of the office-equipment purchasing from now on," said Martha. "So I wanted to introduce you two, and I've told her how you've taken care of us through the years."

A few minutes later, Petrina Yarkovic took us down the hall past the typists and the secretaries to her own ten-by-ten cubicle and sat behind her own desk. Oh, my, the cool look of administrative power that came across that small desk.

"I've gone over your prices," Petrina said. "And I think they're awfully high."

Charlie, I must say, was magnificent. Did she realize the added value contained in those prices? Was she aware of the years of reliability and dependable service, the track record Elemenco had established with Santlinni?

"That may be," said Petrina, "but you've certainly charged us enough for all of that. According to my calculations, we could have saved nearly $18,000 in the past five years just by purchasing our equipment and supplies independently."

Charlie took issue with the figure—a tactical mistake, I think, when he might have pushed his claim to first-rate service. But never mind, I could tell already she was against us. I was wondering whether this had been a setup by Martha or whether Petrina was just asserting her new authority and independence.

"Furthermore, I think we can get by with PC clones and some new printers," she said. "So I called Midcontinent Warehouse Electronics, which isn't even very far from us, and they gave me a price on this Mitsugami equipment that will do everything yours will for about 25 percent less."

"But who is going to stand behind that equipment?" asked Charlie. "Who's going to service it for you?"

"Well, look, they're also offering a year's free on-site maintenance," Petrina said, shoving the estimate in front of him.

"All right, then," said Charlie, "you've been a good customer for a lot of years, so to keep your account, we'll match the Mitsugami price."

At that point, I put my hand on Charlie's shoulder and said to Petrina, "Will you excuse us for a minute, please?"

We stepped outside into the corridor.

"Charlie," I said, "it's no use getting the business if we can't make money on it."

"Dave, I've been doing business with these people for close to fifteen years. I feel I've got to at least offer to match the price, or we're going to lose them."

I had a sense this was a lost cause anyway, so against better judgment, I told him to do what he wanted. I didn't think it would make any difference.

Little Petrina was tough. She got Charlie to match the Mitsugami price, then beat it by a little bit, plus throw in free installation and maintenance for up to a year. They shook hands on the deal. Charlie went to look for Martha, but she was out. Wonder why.

When we got back to the office, I sat down at a computer and pulled up some figures. If we were lucky, and nothing serious went wrong on the servicing of the equipment, we were going to make a 2 percent net on the sale to Santlinni. I printed the statement and took it down the hall to show Charlie.

Two steps from his office door, I heard Charlie explode with a string of profanity. He got control again as soon as I walked in, but he wouldn't look at me.

"You know what she did?" he said. "As soon as we left, she called up Midcontinent and wheedled some discount software out of them! Even after we agreed the deal was final! Now she's going with the Mitsugami equipment!"

It was as if he had been betrayed. He grabbed for the phone again, but I put my hand down hard on the top of the receiver to keep him from dialing.

"Wait a minute, Charlie. What are you doing?"

"I'm calling Martha and I'm going to have a long talk with her."

I shook my head. "Forget it, Charlie, let them go. It's better that we *don't* get the order. Look at this."

I showed him the figures and went over them to make sure he understood. He slumped down into his seat and sighed.

"Fifteen years," he said. "Doesn't it count for anything?"

"You're not going to keep them," I said. "It's a shame, in one sense, but you're not."

"I'm still going to call Martha," said Charlie. "Not to give her a piece of my mind or anything. I'll take it easy. I'm just going to stay in touch. You know why?"

"Why?"

"Because you just wait. I'll bet you any money that equipment they're putting in isn't going to be up to the task for very long. There's going to be trouble sooner or later. And if she doesn't have someone on the supplier side taking care of her, she's going to be in it up to her eyebrows. And she's going to call me."

The odds were against him, but I let him have the fantasy. Before I left, he took a call from Haikkyu. They wanted a meeting to talk about a change on the electrical power leads for their cellular phones. Charlie opened his calendar.

The Friday before Reed Morrison came back from Europe, a snowstorm that was maybe one or two flakes short of a blizzard was heading across the northern plains toward Chicago. We had let the clerical staff go home a little early in anticipation of massive traffic jams.

I was in my own office late that afternoon talking to Ann Lansky, who had brought a listing of all the salespeople in the Chicago office, what customers they were working with, and what kinds of products those customers had bought in the last six months. We were going over the list when we were interrupted by a knock on the door.

Jim Woller was standing in the doorway and with him—in front of him, actually—was another man I didn't know.

"David," said Woller, "I thought you'd like to meet Aaron Abbott."

Aaron walked toward me, hand extended. He was in maybe his early fifties, long face, hair a distinguished silver shade. Even now, seeing him through memory, I can sense the energy he projected in that first meeting. He had a manner, an aura, that said he was a success. The subtle flash of gold cuff links, the manicure, the London suit and the handsewn shirt (I'm guessing here; they seemed fine and expensive, whatever the details of their manufacture), the immaculate silk tie, the perfect haircut—he had all the nuances that quietly elevate ordinary, already expensive business attire to the exclusive.

"Actually, we met a couple of years ago," I said.

"You're right, we did," said Aaron.

To my amazement, he named the conference we'd both attended—Aaron as a speaker and me as a member of the audience. Jim Woller, meanwhile, had come into the office and was hovering about as Ann and I were shaking hands with Aaron.

Jim Woller was clearly excited. "Aaron has got some absolutely terrific news to tell you. Really great news for us! Wait 'til you hear this!"

Aaron took a seat and leaned toward us. He, too, seemed excited by what he was about to tell us.

"I just got in," Aaron said, "and I wanted to give you the news in person that I closed a contract last night on PowerSeat."

"On *PowerSeat?*"

"Correct. You're familiar with PowerSeat? You know, it's the same basic technology as PowerCase. Except you build it into an airline seat so that a passenger, way up there over Kansas or anyplace, can use it to communicate with the rest of the world and get work done while he's traveling."

I said, "Right, right, I know what it is, but that's still in development, isn't it? I'm surprised you could sell PowerSeat because I don't think we even have a prototype ready yet, do we?"

"The arrangement I've lined up will give us that prototype. It will not cost Elemenco a cent. And we will earn half a million dollars on the arrangement, plus a $3 million initial sale if the prototype units perform successfully," said Aaron.

Ann's face said that she was impressed. I was too.

"That is good news," I said. "So how is this going to take place?"

"I sold the concept to Eddie Matt," said Aaron.

Eddie Matt, in case you haven't heard of him, is the maverick of the airline industry. While just about everybody else in the airline business has been going for volume with low fares, Eddie Matt, who started out running an airplane charter service, has gone the other way—by developing a new luxury airline called Diamond Skies.

Instead of an airborne cattle car, you fly in the equivalent of a Pullman with wings. Instead of rows of seats with everybody all jammed together, you're in an environment more like a living room or a cocktail lounge. Some of the seats convert into beds so that if you're flying cross-country or overseas you can actually get a decent night's sleep. The meals are gourmet quality. Half the plane is set up to provide some privacy for those who need to work. The other half is like a cocktail party. I've heard you can also meet some interesting people on board, from rock stars to corporate executives, and that it's not a bad way to make high-level business contacts. The flight attendants will radio ahead a few minutes before landing and have a limo or a cab waiting for you. It's the next best thing to having your own corporate plane. You pay for all this, of course. Fares are high, but if you or your company can afford the prices, it's a great airline.

"I happen to know Eddie from past dealings," Aaron was saying. "Last night I booked a seat on one of his planes, the same one I knew he would be on. He flies once or twice a week on his own planes, you know."

"I'd heard that," I said. "How did you know which plane?"

"Some discreet inquiries," Aaron said. "In any event, I had a sample of PowerCase with me—I sold Eddie one of those, too, for his personal use, by the way—and started talking to him about its capabilities. I said, Eddie, what if the seats on your planes had the same capabilities as PowerCase? A luxury seat with sophisticated telecomputing electronics built in so a traveling business executive can make phone calls, send faxes, tap into data bases, compose letters, and, in short, turn wasted hours into productive time. I told him, you would give your business passengers an additional incentive to fly with you. You add prestige to your airline by being the first to offer this technology. And the seats would pay for themselves because, initially at least, you would offer only six or eight on every flight and charge a premium for them."

"And he liked the idea?" I asked.

"He loved it! He went for it like *that*," said Aaron, snapping his fingers. "We hammered out a basic agreement—your legal people are looking it over now—and I used PowerCase to print it out, which impressed the hell out of him. I had his signature by the time we passed over Denver. I stayed over in

Los Angeles and flew back first thing this morning. But we got the sale!"

"Isn't that fantastic!" Woller chimed in.

"Yeah, it sure is," I said. "Not bad at all. What does Diamond Skies get out of this . . . arrangement?"

"They get ten prototype demonstration units to install, plus exclusive purchasing rights to the product for eighteen months," said Aaron.

"You say we get half a million to use for development? Can we do it for that much?"

"I'm told that we can, because we already have the essential technology," he said.

Hoping this was right, I said, "Then that's great. Does Reed Morrison know about this yet?"

"I tried reaching him from Los Angeles, but he couldn't take the call. You see, if the airlines had PowerSeat, he'd know by now!" Aaron said. "Anyway, there are a couple of things that have to be lined up right away, so you'll need to get someone hopping on this. Here are the contacts inside Eddie Matt's organization so that you can work out delivery dates and installation and so on and so on."

He took out a sheet of paper with some handwritten notes of names and numbers and handed it to me, efficiently dumping all the details of followup and execution into my lap. It seemed as if he were saying, *I did the spectacular; now it's up to you to do the rest.*

"So what's next for you?" I asked Aaron. "Do you have any other prospects lined up?"

Before Aaron could answer, Jim Woller jumped in. "Well, I've got a lead for you, if you're interested."

"Sure, I'm always interested in new leads," Aaron said.

"My wife and I were at a dinner party last night and the assistant controller from Hurley Commercial Services was there—"

"I know Hurley Commercial," said Aaron. "In fact, I know Sheldon Hurley, the founder. When I had my own company, Hurley and I did some business together."

"This is perfect then!" said Jim. "Because this guy was saying that he thought Hurley had pretty much outgrown the interoffice network they have. I was going to pass this along to you, Ann, because technically it's in that region, and have someone call their data processing manager, but maybe Aaron would be a better choice."

Aaron hesitated, and I started to intercede, but then, with just a touch of reluctance, Aaron said, "All right, I'll call Sheldon on Monday and see what I can get out of him."

"Thanks," said Jim. "That could be a good one for us, if we can bring it in."

Aaron looked at me next. "I'll tell you one of the things I'd like to do fairly soon. I'd like to talk to your R&D people and find out what's in development."

"That's a good idea," I said. "In fact, why don't we go together some time next week?"

We agreed on next Thursday morning. I wasn't free then, but I agreed to it anyway, because Aaron was and I knew if this got put off, it might be months before we could both go together.

Aaron then pulled up the sleeve of his shirt to check his watch—a Baume & Mercier, one of those thin gold Swiss numbers that cost as much as a sports car.

"Well, got to run. I've got another plane to catch," he said.

"Where to?" asked Woller. "Going back to Boston for the weekend?"

"Palm Beach," he said. "I invited some friends down and we're all going sailing on my boat."

His eyes became like those of someone watching an accident about to happen.

"Will you look at that," Aaron said, pointing toward the window.

We all looked, but there was nothing to see. The window was almost entirely masked by dark gray snow. We couldn't see anything outside except a trillion whirling flakes.

"Well, anybody want to come along?" asked Aaron.

Jim, for a second, seemed tempted, but then said, "Well, I'd love to, but . . ."

Aaron turned to Ann. "All you have to do is buy a bathing suit when we get there."

"No, thanks," said Ann. "Are you sure you don't want to stay?"

"Positive," said Aaron.

"The way things are going, you're liable to end up sleeping in some airport lounge all weekend," she warned him.

"I'll make it to my sailboat if I have to buy the plane and fly it myself," said Aaron.

"Well, have a good time," I said.

With a wave to us all, Aaron was off. The window glass rattled with the force of the storm.

10

As soon as Aaron was out the door, Jim Woller turned to me and said, "Now *that* is a salesman. Isn't he incredible? Do you believe the deal he put together?"

"That's our new rainmaker," I said.

Ann nodded her head and said, "Yeah, you've got to hand it to the guy. I mean, I don't know who in my office would have had the guts, the contacts, the resourcefulness, the whatever to pull off a deal like the one he just talked about."

She was right. Not Charlie. Certainly not Kevin. Not Jennifer, though she was more likely than the others. Not one in a hundred salespeople—and probably none of the people working for Ann, good as they were—would last very long in Aaron Abbott's brand of selling.

"That's exactly the kind of guy we need selling for us," said Woller. "If we could just get five hundred Aaron Abbotts out there in the field, selling the way he does, this company would be out of its sales slump in no time. Hey, David, I want to bounce an idea off of you."

"Sure, go ahead."

"This just occurred to me. What if we ask Aaron to set up an internal seminar to teach our salespeople some of those high-power closes he uses? You know, we'll bring people in from the field in groups for a day or two, get Aaron to share his knowledge, work with them personally, maybe do some role playing. That kind of thing. What the heck, we've got him on the payroll now. Why not have Aaron teach the rest of the sales force his formula for success? Huh? You with me? What do you think of that?"

I didn't want to tell him directly that I thought it was a lousy idea, so I said, "Well, I like the idea of improving the selling skills of the sales force."

"But with Aaron Abbott teaching everybody, getting them to be like him," said Woller. "What about that?"

"I appreciate the idea, Jim, but you're not going to turn the sales force into a bunch of Aaron Abbotts," I said.

Woller laughed and said, "I don't mean we try to clone him or anything. But if we could get everybody to sell the way Aaron does . . . I mean, think about it, Dave! Think of the potential if everybody could sell like that!"

"If you could successfully teach everybody to sell *exactly* the way Aaron Abbott does—and I don't believe you could— Elemenco would be bankrupt in a year," I said. "Maybe less."

"But why?"

"A variety of reasons. For starters, a good many of our customers would soon come to hate us, because of Aaron's style of selling, which doesn't deliver some of the values they need. We'd have problems with believability. Most of our products wouldn't sell very well. We also couldn't afford to compensate a whole sales force made up of people like Aaron. Reasons like that."

"But look at Eddie Matt and PowerCase! How can you argue with success?" Woller said.

"Aaron Abbott is what's known as a super-closer."

"Yeah, well, that's what we need: super-closers."

"No, we don't. And, anyway, super-closers are *found*, not made," I said. "It takes someone with a special kind of personality to be a super-closer. Aaron is the kind of salesman who is perfect for a certain type of product and a specific type of market. For most of what we sell, there are better people and better styles of selling."

"Such as?"

"Such as the three people in Ann's region I've been working with the past few weeks," I said.

Ann said, "You mean Charlie—"

"Right. Charlie, Jennifer and Kevin," I said. "Although I could say the same thing about each of them as I said about Aaron."

"You'd better explain that," said Ann.

"Yeah, I'm not following you either," said Woller.

But that was when my phone rang. It was Robb Jamison, the account manager at our ad agency, and after thirty seconds on the phone with him, I knew it was going to be a long conversation. I covered the mouthpiece.

"This is going to take a while, so you two ought to take off before you get snowed in," I said.

Ann waved good-bye and left. Before Jim walked out, I added, "Next week, I'm going to have a meeting with Reed Morrison to talk about how the sales force could be more effective. I'd like you to be there if you can."

Woller said, "Sure, I'll make the time."

I wished him good luck fighting the weather and got back to Robb.

The conversation lasted half an hour. While we talked on the phone, I looked out at the snow on the other side of the glass. It was falling fast. I could just make out the lights in the next building.

I'd been the one to turn on the lights that morning; now I was the one to turn them off as I left. I was going "home" to that sterile condo the company owned, because I hadn't found my own place to live yet, because I'd been working too many damn hours to go out and find one. There was nobody and nothing in my life except work. A stupid way to live. Why was I doing it?

The elevator came and I got on, felt the pull in my stomach as it dropped, and then felt it slowing down. It was going to stop on another floor, and it ticked me off, frankly, because I just wanted to get out with no delays. I glanced up at the round floor numbers and 22 was lighting up. The doors opened, and Ann Lansky got on.

"Well, fancy meeting you here," she said.

"You decided to bail out, too?"

"It's looking even worse than I thought," she said. "Anyway, something in me does rebel at working late on a Friday night."

"I know what you mean."

She stood on the opposite side of the car as we went down, facing forward, but once I thought I felt her watching me. Then she spoke up. "I have a serious question to ask you."

"What's that?" I said.

"Are you hungry?" she asked.

Ann and I decided to go to dinner, but we never made it. We stepped into the building lobby talking about where to go—the old yuppie fern bar, or what about the new place up the street?—but stopped dead when we looked outside through the doors. A couple feet of snow was piled against them. On Jackson Boulevard, an old Chevy wallowed in it, back wheels going round and round, while the rest of the car occasionally trembled but moved not an inch.

"You folks bring your sleeping bags?" It was the security guard. "Unless you got four-wheel drive or a snowplow you ain't going no place tonight," he said.

"Well, we can't stay here," said Ann.

"Oh, you can go out there," said the guard. "It's a free country, after all. But you'll be lucky to make it to the corner."

Ann turned to me. "What do you think?"

The snow was nearly horizontal as it blew past on the other side of the doors. The light poles were shaking in the wind.

"To tell you the truth, I think we might be stranded," I said.

"I'd at least like to try for some dinner," said Ann.

"You think any place is even going to be open?"

"It would take more than a blizzard to shut down Chicago. If we're going to be stranded, I'd rather be stranded at a good restaurant."

"There's merit in that line of thinking," I said. "Let's go."

The guard shook his head like we were crazy, but helped us push open one of the doors. We slipped out into the blizzard. The snow stung our faces, the wind blew it so hard against us. Three steps into it and we were bending forward to make any progress. We made it almost to the curb, when I felt Ann tugging on my sleeve.

"Let's go back!" she screamed in my ear.

I turned my back to the snow and saw the old Chevy still spinning its wheels. The driver was a kid and I could see the helplessness on his face. Well, as long as I had come out there to be snow-covered and frozen, I figured I'd at least try to make it count for something.

"Go on back," I said to Ann. "I'm going to give this guy a hand."

I waved to the kid, got behind his Chevy, and started pushing. Maybe if I got him moving, I thought, he could keep up his momentum. But it didn't do any good. His car would move forward a foot or so and bog down again. The best we could do was get his car to the side of the street.

The kid rolled down his window. "Hey, thanks anyway," he yelled out. "You want a pizza?"

On the front seat were half a dozen flat white boxes. He was a delivery boy.

"Yeah, sure," I said.

He gave me three. "Here. You might as well. I can't deliver 'em and I can't eat 'em all myself."

I waded back to the building, boxes in hand, feeling the warmth being sucked through the cardboard to my icy hands. One of them nearly blew off the stack and I caught it just as it took off like a Frisbee. The guard saw me coming and opened the door. Ann was behind him, dripping on the marble floor.

"You were right," I said to the guard. "I guess we're staying for a while."

"Will you sign the register please."

Blizzards don't stop Chicago and they don't stop bureaucracy either. I gave the guard one of the pizzas, the one that nearly blew away down Jackson.

11

We went upstairs to 49, but decided to go to Gene Cherson's office instead of mine. At least Gene had a sofa where we could sit back and relax. I was opening the pizza boxes when Ann spotted the little refrigerator in the corner. I'd never noticed it before.

The refrigerator was empty except for a moldy orange and two magnums of champagne, chilled in readiness for some celebration that never came. I opened one. Ann favored the mushroom and pepperoni; I ate most of the sausage with extra cheese. We drank champagne from coffee mugs while the storm continued outside.

"Well, now that we certainly have the time," she said, "what was it you were going to say about our sales force and why we don't want them all to be just like Aaron Abbott?"

I didn't answer her for a moment. I wanted to forget about business and sales and just enjoy the snowstorm, the pizza and champagne, and of course the company. But I said to her, "All right. I'll lay it out for you. In fact, maybe telling it to you will be a good trial run for telling it to Morrison. See if you think this is right, because you know even better than I do, dealing with it every day."

I poured more champagne into my mug, which had the Elemenco logo on it.

"Look at your own people—not as *sales*people, but just as *people*," I said. "Look at Kevin Duttz, for instance. Here's an average guy out to make a living in sales. What's he got, a basic degree from a community college? Yet he's making good money. He's the kind of guy who gets bored easily. He's a little impulsive. He likes to stay busy. He likes to interact with people. He enjoys them. He's got a lot of energy. But he doesn't care about being vice-president of anything. He's not some highly analytical, tightly focused, ambitious career achiever. He likes sales because it keeps him occupied and gives him money to buy Bears tickets and power tools for his home shop and a nice car and lots of other toys for himself and his family. His life is nice; why should he advance to a position of greater responsibility? It might screw up his weekends. That's Kevin, am I right?"

"I'd say so, more or less," she said.

"Now Jennifer Hone, on the other hand, very much wants more than just a nice living. She *is* analytical. She *is* ambitious. She *is* an achiever. She's a professional career woman. She told me how she grew up, where she went to school. I mean, she comes from a culture of professionalism. She's got a high-powered education. She's self-confident. She's *not* impulsive. She's careful; she's patient, not a big risk taker. She likes to be organized and prepared. This is not your average drone. Not at all. Jennifer wants—expects—a corporate title with prestige. She expects to have management responsibility someday. She wants a window office, preferably one in the corner. To her, working in sales is a means to an end, a faster path to the top."

"That's true," said Ann. "I'm well aware Jennifer isn't going to stay happy if we keep her in sales. At least, not at her current level. She wants to move up and I'm afraid she's going to move out, too, if that path isn't open to her."

"The point is that her personality and drives are very different from Kevin Duttz's, even though they're both quite capable in different ways. Now compare the two of them with Charlie Summers. What kind of guy would you say Charlie is?"

"Charlie? Oh, I don't know," Ann said. "I'd say he's pretty conservative. You can tell by his suits. Strong work ethic. He told me one time he actually feels guilty if he doesn't have something to do. Which I suppose is what helps him keep on plugging away, looking after the details, staying on top of things the way he does. I think he grew up in Wisconsin, but he kind of reminds me of a southern good ole boy. You know, a traditional kind of guy with traditional values. It took a long time for him to accept me, being a woman, as his manager. He's just old-fashioned. He believes in family, honesty, honor, the American way."

"And if you compare Charlie with, say, Jennifer . . . ?" I asked.

"Charlie, I'd say, is less open-minded than Jennifer. More rigid in a lot of ways. He doesn't accept new ideas as fast, new ideas in the industry or new social or political ideas. Charlie just likes things to stay the same. Of course, Jennifer is conservative, too, in her own way."

"Right, but her conservatism is different from Charlie's," I said.

"Jennifer is more status conscious than either Charlie or Kevin," said Ann. "Hers is an establishment kind of conservatism—a belief in proper references and credentials, the right kind of schools and blue-chip corporations. Jennifer is more trendy in her tastes. She likes to keep up on things, I think so that she can get the edge. She's just competitive in a lot of ways. Charlie is more folksy. He's a warm, giving kind of person, the kind of guy whose first instinct would be to give you the shirt off his back. Jennifer would help you with a generous tax-deductible contribution."

"Why do you think Charlie is in sales?" I asked.

"I'd say Charlie is in sales because he loves it," she said. "For the money, too. I mean, I'm sure that's a factor. Let's be honest."

"Exactly. Charlie likes what he does and wants to be a success, but he's not especially interested in running the corporation."

"Right. In fact, he's been offered management positions and he's turned them down," said Ann. "He told me he tried management once years ago, and once was enough. He'd rather be where the action is, I think is how he put it. In a way, though, Charlie is his own boss. He's very independent. If I look over his shoulder too often, or try to keep close tabs on him, he gets defensive."

"Okay," I said, "so we've got Kevin, the average guy out to make a decent living. We've got Jennifer, the focused career professional aiming for the top. We've got Charlie, who's in it because this is what he loves to do. Now here comes Aaron Abbott into the picture, and he's as different from the other three as they are from each other. But whatever his politics might be, Aaron is not a conservative in spirit. He does not want things to stay the same. He's a progressive, a go-getter. He wants to make new things happen. He's extroverted, energetic, upbeat, a charge-ahead, competitive kind of guy. He's a builder, a visionary, an entrepreneur. And yet he's still very much a salesman.

"What Aaron is selling is often more than just a tangible commodity. He's selling concepts, ideas, possibilities, *opportunities*," I said. "And he's been very successful—everything about his appearance and manner is intended to confirm that success for whomever he's dealing with. It's not so much a professional kind of image he projects, like Jennifer; it's a rich, affluent image. And there's nothing phony about it. Aaron is in this game to get rich—I should say rich*er* in his case—and, in the process, change the world."

"Not such a bad ambition," said Ann.

"No, not at all. Except that there are always people who don't want the world changed. At least not their part of it. And Aaron may have trouble relating to them," I said. "So we've got four people, four different personalities. And each of them, by the way, also has a different selling style than the others. Have you noticed?"

"I've noticed that—with the three working in my office, at least—they're not all good at selling the same kinds of products," said Ann.

"You're right. And what they're naturally better at selling has to do with their style of selling, which fits with their personalities, with what kind of people they are. Look at how Charlie Summers sells, for instance."

And I told her what I'd seen—Charlie with his hands-on style, handling the complexities for the customer so that the customer didn't have to worry about or deal with those complexities. Charlie's style included warm, personal contact with his customers. He took them to lunch, he dropped by, he stayed in touch. Inside Elemenco, he was like an advocate for the customer. He was sensitive to problems the customer was having; to him, a problem was an opportunity—as it had been when he'd cut through our internal bureaucratic crap to get the new software for Bob Lilly. Charlie brought in Haikkyu by nurturing the first fragile contacts, by getting them to trust him, by getting to know what they wanted, by proving that he could make *our* product meet *their* design requirements and deliver exactly what they wanted.

Charlie knew his stuff, but he was no technical wizard. Charlie brought in business because he paid attention, he was lovingly persistent, and he was responsive. He would walk the extra mile for his customers, and his customers would reward him with continuing business. There are a lot of companies selling computers and networks and cellular phones, but Charlie made ours stand out by adding his own special touch to the actual product, which added value and gave him—and us—an edge in the marketplace. And the key to it was Charlie's selling style, which was to build a *relationship* with the customer.

"Look at Kevin Duttz on the other hand, and you see someone selling in a very different fashion," I said to Ann.

Kevin, the work-a-day kind of guy, didn't bother with a special touch the way Charlie did. To Kevin, the desirable way to get business was to make the process easy for everybody— easy for him to sell and attractive for a lot of customers to buy. He believed in incentives and continual promotion and anything to make it convenient for the customer. If the market got tight, lower the price. To his credit, Kevin had an energy that enabled him to keep plowing ahead through a monotonous, basically boring routine and still keep it fresh.

"But don't ask Kevin any tough questions," I said to Ann, "because if it isn't in the catalog, he probably doesn't know and he's not about to go digging up the answer for you if he doesn't have to. In Kevin's mode of selling, the corporation is supposed to *display*—or promote—the product in the most attractive fashion possible, and have Kevin be the friendly guy who takes the order. Easy, convenient, simple."

"But Jennifer Hone doesn't mind complexity. Not at all. She even seems to enjoy it."

Jennifer was really in her element when she was juggling all the variables, managing every aspect of what we did for the customer, designing the perfect solution for each situation. Jennifer liked working with the higher-level managers. That was her world. That was where she wanted to be someday. She would not only hold hands, the way Charlie Summers did, she would offer expert advice.

"See, Charlie is no dummy, but he's no engineer either," I said to Ann. "But Jennifer *is*. She could walk out of sales tomorrow, go to our engineering and design department, sit down at a CAD terminal, and start doing productive work. Charlie couldn't create a design on his own. He's knowledgeable, but he doesn't have special technical expertise. That's one big difference between them."

Jennifer could meet with top managers and line managers, ask them smart questions, interpret what they really needed, and then oversee the execution start to finish.

"Ever notice how Jennifer is always asking questions?" I asked. "Why do you think she's doing that?"

"She's trying to get information, of course," said Ann.

"True, but it's more than that. It's because Jennifer has the extra duty of figuring out what is the right path to take. Most of Charlie's better customers already know which direction they want to take, because they know as much as Charlie, sometimes more. In fact, if Charlie tries to tell them what to do, they're going to resist and reject him. But Jennifer is at her best with customers like the MorrMart executives, who are relying on her to know what's best," I said.

Jennifer's way was to take the customer by the hand and say, come on, I'm going to lead you through the wilderness; I'm going to get you to the other side of the mountain. And if she does her job right, they do end up safely on the other side of the mountain. Her way of selling is to behave like a trusted *consultant.*

"And then there's Aaron Abbott, who's in a separate category altogether," I said. "Aaron is an expert in his own right who's got a reputation in the industry. He's got a recognized name not just because he glad-hands and shows up in the right places; he's a name because he has superior expertise to offer.

But, unlike Jennifer, who will nurture a project through to completion for a customer, Aaron is moving way too fast to hold hands with anybody. His style is to get the customer excited about possibilities, close the sale, and get on with it. Which is probably fine with most of his customers, who tend to be either executives—the money people—or sometimes expert users who can handle the technicalities on their own."

"Why do you call him a super-closer?" asked Ann.

"For one thing, because he's very good at that specific aspect of salesmanship."

"But every salesman has to do some closing," she said. "Kevin, Charlie, Jennifer—they all have to close in some fashion to get the sale."

"True. Aaron is a *super*-closer because closing is the primary focus of all his contacts with the customer. Once the deal has been closed, his relationship with the customer is usually ended, whereas with all the others it's often just beginning. Jennifer is going to stay with the customer until the project is over; Charlie and Kevin are going to try to build continuing business from the same customers."

"But what about Eddie Matt? Won't we continue working with him?"

"Elemenco will work with Diamond Skies, but Aaron won't work with Eddie Matt again unless there's another deal to be presented," I said. "That's why Aaron was dumping all the details in my lap this afternoon. That's not to say Aaron won't invest ten minutes in a phone call now and then, just to stay in touch. But I'll bet that's a lot less time than Charlie Summers gives to his accounts. For a major customer, in addition to plenty of phone calls, Charlie is going to be sitting down face to face at least once a month probably. And Jennifer at the height of getting a 720 Network installed might be talking to someone on the customer side every *day*. Am I right?"

"Yeah, you're right. I see what you mean," she said. "Which one of those styles do you think is best?"

"They all are."

"Wait a minute. They can't *all* be the best."

"Okay, let's say you're the customer. You tell *me* which one is best," I said.

I told her about going out with Kevin on his afternoon calls that day about two weeks before, the day we had gone to see Mr. Macy at Lakeside Electronic Controls. Macy was buying some AD510s, a standard product that's been around maybe eight or ten years (a very long time in this business) with only minor refinements in that time. Mr. Macy can buy these things from four or five other vendors; they all perform about the same. Kevin knows this and Mr. Macy knows this.

"Now does Mr. Macy need Jennifer Hone to come in and consult with him?" I asked her. "Does he need Jennifer to work on a custom design for him? Of course not. It's a mature product. Lakeside takes it out of the box, installs it in one of their own assemblies, and that's it. Does Macy need Charlie Summers to come in and build an in-depth relationship and try to understand his problems? Hell, no. Does he want Aaron Abbott coming in to get him excited about these AD510s? No, there's nothing about an AD510 to get excited about. Mr. Macy already has the administrative order from manufacturing or engineering to buy these things; he doesn't need a power close from Aaron for the emotional push to buy. The main issues important to Mr. Macy are price, convenience, and an efficient transaction. Kevin goes to see Macy and offers the best price and convenience; Kevin takes the order.

"A short while later, because Gene Cherson or Jim Woller or somebody drew a line on a map, here comes Kevin Duttz walking into Arnold Sternholtz's office at All-Points Express. Sternholtz has heard about these new satellite communications systems and he's mildly curious about one for his trucking fleet. And friendly, helpful Kevin is right there, pronto, ready to take his order. But, wait a minute, is this what Sternholtz needs? An order taker? These are complicated systems. The technology is new and evolving. There are no real industry standards. Each system we sell has to be customized. A lot of things can go wrong, and on a multimillion-dollar system, mistakes can be very expensive to everybody. Now, if you were Arnold Sternholtz, would you spend millions of dollars with a company that sent Kevin Duttz to see you?"

Ann laughed. She had a warm smile.

"No," she said. "If I were Sternholtz, I don't think I would."

"Yet Kevin is a really great salesman when his style matches the right kind of customer. For a display type of salesman, that's a customer whose company doesn't need us to supply hand holding or technical expertise—and won't pay for it either," I said.

"Which is Lakeside Electronic Controls, but not All-Points Express," said Ann.

"Exactly. What kind of technical experience does Sternholtz or his company have in satellite communications?"

"Little or none."

"Right. Kevin is no engineer, and he's not inclined to get deeply involved with his customers. So he's not the right one to help Sternholtz. And neither is Charlie Summers. Because even though Charlie would get involved and make sure all the details were tended to, he can't supply the sophisticated technical expertise to guide and educate the customer."

"But couldn't Charlie go get the answers from our engineers and explain them at the next meeting?" Ann argued.

"Yeah, but there are only so many times you can say, 'I'll get back to you on that.' Plus, you're relying on the customer to know which questions to ask. If it's new technology, the customer doesn't know what the right questions are. And, anyway, if you were Sternholtz, about to invest big money, wouldn't you want to be talking firsthand to someone who knew what was what?"

"Someone like Jennifer," said Ann.

"Exactly. You need a consultive type of salesperson like Jennifer. *Or,* because you're dealing with a company president who's going to be taking a pretty big risk committing the company to a new system, you need a super-closer like Aaron Abbott," I said. "Aaron would be the one who could deliver the emotional punch to get Sternholtz to make the commitment. Jennifer would be able to offer not only solid technical know-how, but also the patience and people skills to educate the customer and handle the complexity. But either of them would be more likely to be successful than Kevin, who's at the opposite end of the spectrum."

I turned around to the window. "How's the storm doing?"

"It's still coming down," she said.

Indeed it was, with a vengeance.

"Now look at this." I drew the map for her, organizing the marketing world by quadrants formed by the customers' needs for tech and touch.

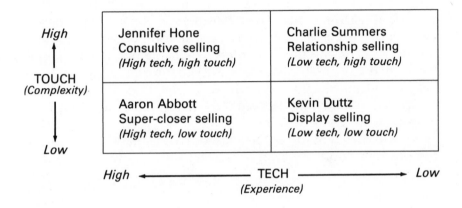

High ↑ | TOUCH *(Complexity)* | ↓ Low	Jennifer Hone Consultive selling *(High tech, high touch)*	Charlie Summers Relationship selling *(Low tech, high touch)*
	Aaron Abbott Super-closer selling *(High tech, low touch)*	Kevin Duttz Display selling *(Low tech, low touch)*

High ←————————— TECH ————————→ Low
(Experience)

I said, "Each of the selling styles—the super-closer, the consultant, the relationship builder, the friendly order taker—fits a specific corner of the market. And there isn't a customer, a product, a service, or a salesperson you can't place on that map somewhere. Not that I've encountered, there isn't."

She thought about that. "This really applies to all companies, to every kind of business?"

"Sure does," I said. "From aerospace to catering to stereos to ... I don't know, whatever industry is at the back of the alphabet."

"Xylophones," she suggested.

"Good enough," I said. "But there is something weird about Elemenco. Lots of companies have lots of products and lots of customers, but the majority of their customers will be in one or perhaps two *types* of markets. They'll be focused on, say, a relationship type of selling in a low-tech, high-touch market—even if the products are in slightly different industries. That's not the case with us. That's why I was lucky for working with Kevin, Jennifer, and Charlie."

"What do you mean?"

"I see now that we're in four different types of markets. And that's why I was lucky for having met those three—now four, including Aaron—because they all do different types of selling and they let me see what's happened to our marketing."

"What's that?"

"The reason Gene's Lean Mean Marketing Machine doesn't work is not because it's 'lean,' whatever that is, but because it assumes that every salesperson can be all things to every customer. It actually treats customers and salespeople as if they were a commodity, like interchangeable parts. Salespeople have been assigned customers and territories to make their field travel more efficient—which *is* a factor, but a small one compared to matching them to the types of customers they have to work with. Look at this."

On the lid of the pizza box, I started listing the customers, the products, and the kind of market they fell into.

Aaron Abbott

Diamond Skies	PowerSeat	Closing

Jennifer Hone

MorrMart	720 Network	Consultive
Midcontinent Warehouse Electronics	PCs, phones	Display
Bennet Insurance	Network	Relationship

Charlie Summers

Chicago and Midwest Railroad	Network	Relationship
Uniritz	Phones	Display
Haikkyu	Phones	Relationship
Santlinni	PCs	Display

Kevin Duttz

Urbana Systems	Cable	Display
Lakeside Electronic Controls	AD510s	Display
All-Points Express	Satellite system	Consultive

"You see," I said, "Jennifer Hone, the consultant, is not only supposed to sell to MorrMart, which is a good match, but also to Midcontinent, which is a display type of customer. She is totally mismatched with them. Midcontinent is the kind of customer you assign to Kevin Duttz. Meanwhile, Kevin is supposed to handle the lead for All-Points Express, but All-Points is really Jennifer's kind of customer. You find mismatches like that up and down the list. And this is only a fraction of our customers and salespeople. The same things have got to be happening not only elsewhere in your region, but in all the others coast to coast."

Ann said, "I knew there was something wrong with Gene's plan the day I heard about it. In fact, I was the one who stood up in the meeting where Gene and Jim announced their one-salesman-does-it-all idea. I was the one who said I had my doubts, but Gene Cherson put me down. He gave the line that a good salesman can sell anything."

"Well, you know it's actually true that a good salesman *can* sell anything—on a good day. The question is, for how long and how consistent can he be at it? It's a matter of odds for and against. It's not impossible for Kevin Duttz to sell a high-tech, low-touch product, but it's just not likely he'll be consistently successful at it. And Aaron Abbott *could* sell computer cable, or nuts and bolts, or insurance, or whatever. But a polished, charged-up guy like Aaron just isn't going to fit in with that variety of selling."

I drank some champagne. It wasn't great champagne, or even good champagne, but it was hitting the spot.

Ann examined the list and said, "I can see the answer to the original question—why we don't want a whole sales force made up of Aaron Abbotts. We don't have very much high tech, low touch business. So how would you organize it?"

"We need to organize so that the natural selling approach of the salesman complements the kind of product he's selling and fits with the customer's type of market," I said. "Or, in other words, we assign relationship accounts to salespeople like Charlie Summers. We move all the display customers to Kevin Duttz. And so on."

I took the pad of paper on which I'd drawn the quadrant grid and started writing in the names of the customers.

	High tech	Low tech
High (TOUCH / Complexity)	**Jennifer Hone** **Consultive selling** *(High tech, high touch)* • MorrMart • All-Points Express (Plus new business)	**Charlie Summers** **Relationship selling** *(Low tech, high touch)* • Chicago and Midwest RR • Haikkyu • Uniritz • Bennet Insurance (Plus developing relationship accounts)
Low (TOUCH / Complexity)	**Aaron Abbott** **Super-closer selling** *(High tech, low touch)* • Diamond Skies (Plus new business)	**Kevin Duttz** **Display selling** *(Low tech, low touch)* • Midcontinent • Lakeside Electronic • Santlinni • Urbana Systems (Plus maintaining telemarketing accounts)

TECH
(Experience)

"That's an idea of how we ought to be doing it," I said.

"Let's say most or all of our products were sold to customers who needed high tech, low touch," Ann said. "In that case, we *would* want a sales force of super-closers like Aaron Abbott, right?"

"Right, that's exactly it," I said. "If our customers were mostly low tech, high touch, then we'd want a sales force with a relationship selling style like Charlie Summers has. And so on. See, the companies that survive have been doing that for a long time, because matching your selling style to what your customers need is what works. If you have customers with low-tech, high-touch needs, you tend to hire relationship types of salespeople—because they're the ones who will fit in with the organization and that type of market. But Elemenco has customers and products in *every* type of market. That's very unusual."

"Is that good?" Ann asked.

"What's your guess?"

"More markets, more opportunities? Right?"

I glanced at the pizza boxes.

"Remember when we first talked about the four quadrants? Remember we discussed a hypothetical catering service and how it would be different in each type of market? Well, along the same lines, suppose you had a company that tried to be the best in frozen pizzas, a display market, while it tried to be successful in restaurant food supply, a relationship market—*plus* it tried to sell diet and exercise health programs to corporations for their employees, a consultive market, *and* market to doctors some kind of revolutionary food product that helps patients with heart problems. And to top it off, that company expected all of its salespeople to be equally good at selling all of its products and services. What are the odds that that company would be successful in all markets?"

Ann didn't answer.

"Those are roughly the same odds we're up against."

The pizzas were gone by now; some crusts and a single slice of mushroom and pepperoni neither of us could finish were all that was left. The snow was still coming down, but it was falling straight, not side to side. I went to the window and looked at the street. Absolutely nothing was moving down there.

"I've already made up my mind," said Ann. "I'm staying."

"I guess I will, too,"

We didn't talk any more business. In one of the cabinets, I found a little portable television. As I was setting it up, the cork from the second magnum of champagne bounced off the wall.

"Sorry," said Ann, bottle in hand. "Want some more?"

We turned on *Dallas*, but got bored and ended up talking instead. Talked and talked, past the news and weather reports advising everyone to stay put. The Carson show came on and we mostly talked through that and into Letterman. We stayed up and talked until past one. Somehow, it didn't feel like hardship, being there. It was like something you'd do with a college friend. It was fun.

"Well," I said, in the middle of a yawn. "I guess I'll leave you here and go down to my own office and try to improvise a bed."

A look crossed her face.

"You want me to stay here?"

"If you wouldn't mind," she said. "I mean, I don't want you to get the wrong idea or anything."

I knew what she meant.

I'm sure you're wondering, so I'll tell you. Nothing happened. She slept on the sofa. I took off my jacket and my tie and slept on the floor on some cushions from the upholstered chairs.

Around dawn I woke up. The snow had stopped. I got up and went to the window. I sensed someone beside me. It was Ann, standing in her stocking feet. She took my hand. I didn't know what to make of it.

"Beautiful, isn't it. So peaceful," she said.

Then she let go of my hand. "Too bad you're my boss."

She wandered back to the sofa.

Yeah, too bad.

I actually did get some sleep and woke up around eight o'clock. When I looked out this time, the streets were being cleared. Bleary-eyed, we went to the parking garage, got into our cars, and went home. I slept most of the afternoon.

People with new ideas tend to expect that all they have to do is announce those ideas to the world and everybody will immediately abandon the old ways and embrace the new with a great outpouring of money and love. It never works that way.

By Monday, the blizzard was a memory. Morrison was back in the office, having returned from Europe. Not wanting to waste any time, I scheduled a meeting with him in his office at two o'clock that afternoon. Right after I talked to Morrison, I hit the company's small internal art department with a rush order for some graphics. I'm sure they loved me for it, but it was just simple stuff, no talking dogs or prancing ponies. With that moving, I went over what I was going to tell Morrison. I'd come into the office on Sunday—had to work with my coat on because the building engineers had turned the heat down—and I had worked on a presentation. So I was already prepared for the most part.

The graphics were finished at one forty-five and at exactly two o'clock, I walked into Morrison's office. I had my presentation notes and my fold-up easel and my package of flip charts and my collapsible pointer, and I was ready to change the marketing policy of the whole company. Or I thought I was.

Jim Woller arrived right behind me; as I'd promised, I'd asked him to be there. Already seated in Morrison's office was Aaron Abbott. He had been talking to Morrison about the Diamond Skies deal, and Morrison had invited him to stay. I think that in the back of Morrison's mind, he imagined we were going to use Aaron as the kingpin around which all our sales efforts would revolve. Of course, what I proceeded to present did not exactly confirm that.

I set up the easel and went to it. Half an hour or so later, I turned from the last flip chart to three faces that looked as if I'd just explained quantum mechanics in Chinese. Woller's face was totally blank, as noncommittal as he could possibly make it. Abbott sat with his elbow on the arm of his chair, resting his chin in the palm of his hand, looking as though there might be something fascinating in what I'd said, but he couldn't figure out what it was. And Morrison seemed as if he just didn't get it, as if he wanted to be interested, but his mind was really on something else.

"Any questions?" I asked.

Nobody spoke for a moment, rarely a good sign.

"I have a question," said Aaron. "How do you know which product falls into what market?"

"It's a matter of what *customer* falls into what market, more than the product," I said. "Let's take PowerSeat as an example. Right now, PowerSeat is a high-tech product, because we're supplying a new application of a technology with which our one customer has no experience. Smart man though he is, what does Eddie Matt know about advanced telecommunications? Eddie Matt bought the concept, relying on *our* expertise, on Aaron's, not counting on his own or expecting his internal staff to tell us how to do it. Right?"

"Right," said Aaron.

"The way the deal is cast now, though," I said, "it's also low touch. We design it, we install it, and give them whatever technical assistance is required. But, after that, we hand over the service manual and they're on their own. They have to train their flight attendants and their maintenance people to handle product. If they want changes, it's up to their management to see the changes get made. So this is a high-tech, low-touch sale. But let's say PowerSeat continues to develop; what happens then?"

"We'll probably get some competition," said Aaron.

"Without a doubt," I said. "And in order to stay competitive, what do you think we'll have to do?"

"Lower the price," said Woller.

"That's true," I agreed, "but an emerging technology like this is still going to stay expensive for a while. As other companies get into the act, though, how are they going to compete with our mousetrap?"

"They're going to try to offer a better one," said Aaron.

"That's right. They'll come out with variations of Power-Seat that offer more features. They'll supply not only the technology, but the service as well. And the airlines that buy into the technology aren't going to be happy with modifying their planes to fit our product; they're going to want us to design the product around their planes. Which means?"

"Everything gets a lot more complicated," said Aaron.

"That's it. The complexity of the purchase will increase and we all know what's going to happen as a result. Our salespeople for PowerSeat are going to have to supply more and more support. There won't be just one or two meetings with the customer to get the sale. We'll have to sit down with the customer's managers and talk about the complexities. We'll have to custom design it to the fit the customer's exact needs. There will be a learning curve, and our salespeople will have a big role to play in educating the customer. Once we start doing those kinds of things, we're in a high-tech, high-touch market. Again time passes. What happens next?"

"Everybody on the customer side will be yelling about how there aren't enough standards," said Aaron. "They'll start wanting to mix components. They'll be wanting to use our transmitter, but somebody else's fax circuits. They'll be arguing over performance benchmarks."

"And the reason they'll be doing that?" I asked. "It's because the technology by then will be better understood, more widely accepted, and there will be people in the customers' organizations who know enough to be able to talk about the technicalities. Which means that PowerSeat will be moving into a low-tech market."

Morrison spoke up. "There will probably be a market shakeout, won't there?"

"Definitely at some point," I said. "If this system has the impact we think it will, *every* airline will want PowerSeat—or one of its imitators. Competition will increase and some producers will do a better job than others. Eventually, instead of having twenty-five manufacturers making twenty-five systems that are all differently designed and completely incompatible with each other, we'll end up with four manufacturers—let's hope Elemenco is still one of them—making systems with pretty much the same standard features. The product will be less exciting, but probably more reliable. Even so, PowerSeat will still be a complex purchase. But we'll no longer be designing it the way *we* alone think is best; we'll have to listen to the market and let the customer specify to us exactly what they want.

"That, in turn, means a change in the salespeople who sell PowerSeat. We now want good listeners, people who pay attention to the customer, people who don't make waves. We don't want revolutionaries or crusaders. We want solid, reliable salespeople who will form long-term, mutually nurturing relationships with the customers' managers and engineers, salespeople who will do whatever it takes to get the customers exactly what they want. With a standardized product, it's the loving attention to detail from the sales rep that helps add value and makes the difference in the market."

"Which, you're saying, has changed from consultive to relationship," said Aaron.

"Correct," I said. "That's probably where PowerSeat would remain for some extended period. But let's say still more time passes. What do we see happening? We see more than de facto standards; we see an industry council establishing legalistic rules. Like not only are transmission protocols all the same, but now maybe the controls are always the same size and in the same place on the seat, that sort of thing. PowerSeat is universally accepted. It's been engineered so that the only way it breaks is if the plane crashes. It's so reliable, there's virtually no maintenance. On the customer's side, an engineer doesn't even have to get involved any more. At this point, the salesperson doesn't need to spend that much time with the customer. Because now the average purchasing agent can handle the buy. So PowerSeat has moved finally into a commodity or display marketplace. And that's the market where PowerSeat will remain until either it's replaced by a new technology or we add value in some fashion to push it back to one of the previous markets."

"So it's like a product cycle," said Aaron. "Introduction, growth, maturity, and then it turns into a cash cow until it enters a gradual decline."

"You've got it," I said. "The development from market to market usually shadows the product cycle. But, in answer to your original question, about knowing what product goes into which market—you see, it's not just the product, but the relationship between the product and the customer. The technology of PowerSeat, or whatever the product is, might remain fundamentally the same all along, but we'd have to sell it in different ways according to what's going on inside the customer's head. Even when most customers are in, say, low tech, high touch, we might still have a few who require a consultive type of sale."

"Okay, okay," said Morrison. "Enough of the theory. What does all this mean to us?"

I thought the meaning to Elemenco was obvious. Obviously not.

"It means we're all over the map," I said. "It means we're not in just one type of market, or even two. We're in all four kinds of markets."

"What's wrong with that?" said Morrison. "We intend to be a diversified company. It seems to me that being in all markets means we're well-balanced."

"The problem is that each market requires its own distinct type of marketing and sales approach," I said. "Right now, we're trying to make a single, consolidated approach work in every situation. In fact, it's not really a single approach at all; it's a hodgepodge. And the results prove that it's *not* working."

Well, that was a tactical error, calling it a hodgepodge. Jim Woller jumped to the defense.

"How can you call our marketing organization a hodgepodge? It was very carefully conceived and implemented. Mr. Morrison here even approved the plan himself," said Woller.

"I don't mean you weren't careful," I said.

"Then you mean we deliberately created a hodgepodge?" said Woller. "As for it not working, I still say it's too early to tell yet."

"How long do you think we should wait?" I asked.

Morrison interceded then. "Dave, what are you saying that the company should do?"

"In my opinion, the first thing we need to do is take stock of ourselves and examine our priorities," I said. "We may want to pull out of some markets so that we can concentrate on others. I recommend a companywide audit to try to quantify how many customers we've got in each market and what they represent in terms of current sales and future opportunities. We also need to make some kind of assessment regarding our sales force: How many relationship-style salespeople do we have? How many consultive? How many in the display category? And how is our advertising skewed? Are our ads projecting a relationship image when what we really need is a consultive image? We need to answer those kinds of questions. Once we have that information, we can evaluate what we need to do, how we should reorganize, where to focus our resources—"

"Wait a minute. Are you saying you want us to do *another* reorganization?" asked Morrison. "Even after the one we've already been through?"

Woller immediately picked up the tone of Morrison's comment. "If we reorganize, what kind of signal are we going to be sending not only to our own people, but to our customers?" asked Woller. "It was hard enough, in a lot of cases, expecting them to cope with the changes we made last year. At the end of last year, Gene sent out a letter to every customer thanking them for their patience and telling them they could expect stability in the foreseeable future. Now we're going to start shifting accounts again?"

"We can't leave things the way they are," I said.

"What would you think about Elemenco if you were a customer?" asked Woller. "And how do you know it's going to be any better if we do reorganize?"

"Maybe we're not talking about a full reorganization," I said. "Maybe we just need a few salespeople to swap some accounts. But we need the audit to find out."

"All right, I have a suggestion," said Aaron. "Why swap accounts or reorganize? Why can't you just train a display guy to be like a closer when the situation calls for it?"

Woller nearly jumped to his feet. "That's a great idea, Aaron! You know, we could have some internal seminars—you teaching how to close a sale, for instance."

And Morrison said, "Yeah, Dave, how come we can't just have the salespeople recognize the situation and adapt themselves to what the customer needs—consulting, or low price, or whatever?"

Oh, great, I thought. *How do I get out of this one?* But I answered as honestly as I knew how. "Okay, it's true that on a short-term or occasional basis you get someone whose true calling is, say, consultive selling to act a little more like a super-closer or a relationship salesperson when the situation calls for it. But would you expect, let's say, a good shoe salesman to be just as good at selling corporate jets?"

"Maybe," said Woller. "With the right training, why not?"

"Because you've got some deep issues involved: personalities, training, experience," I said. "It's not going to work in the long run, if at all. By analogy, look at athletes. An athlete, even with coaching, isn't going to play all sports equally well. Once in a great while someone like Bo Jackson comes along and plays both baseball and football, but he's the exception, the one-in-a-thousand kind of phenomenon. Even within a sport, all football players are not going to be competent at all positions; great quarterbacks can't suddenly swap positions and become great defensive linemen. A lot of factors go into what type of athlete someone is going to be. The same with salespeople."

Morrison held up one of his meaty palms to end the discussion.

"All right, I hear what you're saying, Dave. But I think that Jim has made an excellent point. We can't risk alienating our customers just to prove a theory."

"I'm not just espousing a theory. Everything I've talked about, I've seen the evidence with my own eyes."

He held up a palm a second time and gave me a look. "I understand. And I think your explanation has merit. Now here's what I want us to do," said Morrison. "David, I want you to go ahead with your audit. Form a team to get the job done if you have to. Whatever you need I'll authorize. You put together a plan for what you want to do. Meanwhile, before we go risking our reputation, I want you to prove your theory in the Central Region first. They have the worst performance anyway, so if your ideas don't work . . . well, what have we got to lose? And since Central is based here in Chicago, we can keep closer tabs on what's happening. If we see significant improvements, then we'll talk about doing it companywide."

Morrison ended the meeting, but asked me to stay behind for a moment. The first thing he said was, "You've got to get us an increase in revenue."

"I'd like to, very much," I said.

"I don't know how much time we've got," he said.

"What do you mean by that?"

"I mean I need an increase in revenue. I need it soon."

He clearly didn't want to say any more than that.

"Well," I said, "I think the idea of starting with the Central Region is smart, but that means the other four-fifths of our sales won't be affected for some time. It's going to be tough to show an increase this year when we've got . . . well, as I put it earlier, such a hodgepodge approach."

"I could have kicked you for saying that," said Morrison. "I did approve Cherson's plan. I can't condemn it publicly. I even had the board of directors believing that move would help us. What am I saying? *I* believed it was the right thing to do. If we make changes now, we've got to make them quietly. Meanwhile, I need that increase in sales revenue—and income."

"Is something threatening you?"

He didn't say a word, but shook his head.

"You can't talk about it?"

Morrison nodded his head.

"I'll do my best," I said.

"Do better than that," said Morrison. "Get me a revenue increase for next quarter. If you can, I'll consider making your position permanent."

He wouldn't say more, but I knew something major was troubling him. By the end of the day, I'd heard what that something was. That afternoon, Elemenco released its fourth-quarter earnings report to stockholders. There were no earnings. We reported the worst quarterly loss in the history of the company.

I had Morrison's go-ahead to change the Central Region sales force, and I didn't waste any time. I got together with Ann Lansky later the same afternoon.

"The best part of it is that we have a free hand," I said. "We don't have to abide by Cherson's organization plan or policies. We just have to show results."

I noticed a slight raising of her chin as I said "we." She didn't seem to mind. It did feel as though we were a team.

"All right. Where do we start?" she asked.

"Let's make a distinction between current business and future business. I think that our first priority ought to be taking care of our current customers. We need to sort through the base of customers we already have and determine what type of market they're in and what type of salesperson each one needs."

"Okay, but how are we going to make that determination?" Ann asked. "We've got over five hundred customers in greater Chicago alone and five times that throughout the region. Are you going to have to meet personally with each one?"

"Obviously I can't do that. I wonder if we could get the salespeople themselves involved. Maybe they could help us out."

"That's a nice idea, but they're not going to know high tech from low tech unless you give them some instruction. Even then, who's to say it won't be a judgment call on their part?"

I thought for a minute. "Well," I said, "when in doubt, I believe in asking questions. What we can do is devise a set of general questions to tell us what kind of customer each is. With-

out getting into a lot of explanation, we'll distribute these questions to everyone in the sales force and have them fill out a
questionnaire—"

"Not for every customer, I hope," said Ann. "I want them
to have time for selling this month."

"Okay, we'll have them pick their top ten accounts and
maybe their top five or ten current new business prospects," I
said. "Then next month, they can give us the next ten or twenty
and so on. Meanwhile, we'll try to educate them gradually in
what this is all about. After a while, for the smart ones especially,
the questions will become second nature and they'll know what
to look for."

"What if they put down the wrong answers?" Ann asked.

I waved that aside. "All the answers won't be wrong, and
we won't expect perfection. At least this will get things moving in
the right direction. That's what's most important at this point."

I went home to the condo that evening and started draft-
ing a list of twenty true-or-false statements that would serve as
a litmus test to show who belonged where. Here's the list:

True or false:

1. This customer relies on our reputation for technical
   excellence, rather than on their own internal expertise for evaluating our products and services.
2. This customer recognizes that the quality of our technical assistance and followup is more important than
   price.
3. Price, to this customer, doesn't matter that much as
   long as the benefits we promise seem worthwhile.
4. What we're selling this customer has to be custom
   designed.
5. The product we sell to this customer is uniquely
   tailored to the customer's needs.
6. This customer has an established procedure for evaluating and purchasing our products.
7. This customer thinks they know as much as we do
   about what they're buying—or at least as much as
   they need to know.

8. The product or service we sell to this customer is so accepted and established that doing without it would be a major disruption.

9. There are three or more companies offering an equivalent kind of product or service as the one we sell to this customer.

10. This customer orders off-the-shelf products from us.

11. This customer expects regular contact, not just a phone call or meeting when you want to take their order.

12. It took a fairly long time for this customer to trust and depend on us.

13. This customer sometimes talks about business or personal matters not directly related to the immediate sale.

14. Personal service is more important to this customer than getting the lowest possible price.

15. This customer expects us to be aware of some detailed issues relating to them and to pay attention to those issues.

16. Except for small talk, conversations with this customer are focused on the product we're selling them.

17. If this customer is going to buy from us at all, they'll do it within one or two direct contacts with us.

18. This customer buys our product "as is" and does not expect us to install or customize the product specially for their needs.

19. Contact with this customer is mainly to make it more convenient and likely for this customer to place an order, rather than to discuss status or learn new information.

20. Once the order has been placed, this customer needs help from us only if there is a warranty problem.

Okay, now the first five, if they're answered as "true," tell us the customer is likely to be high tech; the second five, low tech. The next five indicate high touch; the final five statements, low touch. The true-or-false format would make it easier for us to set up a computer program to do the tabulations (how clever of us). I knew the questions were rather subjective and there could be problems with interpretation, but what the heck—we had to start somewhere.

The next day, I met with Ann. We had a secretary type up the questions with some blanks at the top for entering the customer's name, the name and job title of the main contact, and some other data. That afternoon we held a short meeting with everyone available in the Chicago office. Jennifer, Charlie, and Kevin were all there, along with the fifteen or so others. They filled a conference-room table and we had to steal chairs to seat them all. I think they knew something significant was up, but I didn't tell them very much to start. I explained that we were going to be making some changes and that we wanted their help.

"Obviously, you know your customers better than I do," I said, "because you work with them every day. This will help give us a sense of what kind of customer each one is."

I had each of them pick a customer at random and fill out a form in the meeting so they could ask questions about the questions. The rest of the forms they were to turn in the next day. It was a fairly easy assignment and most of them finished that afternoon.

If Elemenco hadn't had such a conglomeration of customers, we probably would not have had to do so many individual questionnaires to sort them out. But the exercise didn't hurt. It even got some of the salespeople to think about customers as individuals.

Ann and I, meanwhile, did our own survey, just for comparison. We went through the data base and sorted the accounts by size of sales revenue, then picked out the top 20 percent and started with the top 20 percent of those. I figured these accounts would have the most impact if something were wrong and we could get it to go right.

"What exactly are we looking for?" Ann asked me.

"One of the tipoffs to knowing what type of customer you've got is the job title of your main contact. If it's a closing sale, you're probably dealing with an owner or top-level executive, someone who makes economic decisions. If it's an *operating* manager, one who's not in our area of expertise, then it's probably consultive. On the other hand, if we're dealing with the data processing manager or one of the department staff—an *internal* expert—that's a clue it's relationship selling. And if it's a display sale, we're likely to be dealing with an administrator, like a purchasing agent, or an end user as the main contact."

Other evidence, of course, was the product itself. If the product at issue was a complex product that had to be customized, a 720 Network for instance, it was most likely consultive. If the product happened to be a standardized network board that the customer would install himself in his own PCs, it was display. And so on.

Sorting the salespeople was tougher than sorting the customers. You can tell somewhat by personality, education, and behavior who belongs where, but that can end up being quite subjective and inaccurate. Now, there are in fact scientific tests you can use to know who is a closer and who is a relationship type and so on, but with a whole office of salespeople and eventually a whole sales force to organize in a limited period of time, I had to settle for other measures.

What we did finally was work backward. Once we had the customers figured out, we took a look at who worked best with which types of accounts. Someone with a larger share of sales to low-tech, high-touch customers, like Charlie, was likely to be a relationship salesperson—and should be given more of those types of accounts. Someone with a high ratio of sales to customers like MorrMart probably had a consultive selling style and should get more high-tech, high-touch prospects. For better or worse, that was how we got it done.

Each market reveals itself through its own distinguishing characteristics. For instance, take a closer's high-tech, low-touch market. Any customer in this market is going to be buying on speculation, often accepting a higher degree of risk in exchange for one hell of an improvement or gain. What these buyers want much of the time is a new or unique product that is simple to install and use, yet gives them a pride of ownership or a performance edge tied to the product's specialness. If you want to identify products that fit into that kind of market, you look for those qualities: new, unique, owner pride, edge, performance.

Exotic sports cars, power boats, high-stakes commercial real estate, the first of any really new invention—these are sales material for the super-closer. But then so are those special kitchen implements you see demonstrated to crowds at county fairs. Moving those slicer-dicer gizmos takes a closer kind of sell. It's the kind of sell that supplies an emotional push to get people to do what they ordinarily would not, a push to make you charge through the fear of risk and embrace the promise of the improvement.

At the time Aaron Abbott joined the company, Elemenco had only a couple of products that were truly high tech, low touch. PowerSeat was one in that category, but just barely, because it was so complex you needed someone to work with the airline operations and maintenance management to get it installed and functioning properly. It would quickly become high tech, high touch.

PowerCase, the briefcase communications system, was definitely a super-closer's product. The customer relied on Elemenco's technical support for the system to function, yet the complexity of the purchase was fairly simple. There was only one model of PowerCase. It was unique. At that time, there were portable computers and laptops on the market, but nobody (except maybe the CIA or the KGB, who weren't marketing their developments) had integrated so many functions into a single, lightweight, portable transmitter-receiver. VLSI circuitry built into a composite materials case, proprietary error checking on transmission and reception, a featherweight printer—this was sophisticated stuff. But nothing about PowerCase was custom designed for an individual user. For technical questions, we had a hotline number, but aside from that the customer was on his own. If the customer bought it, he had to load his own software into its computer and invest some time learning how to use the thing. Those aspects made PowerCase a low-touch sale.

On Thursday, as we'd planned, Aaron Abbott and I went out to Elemenco's R&D center in Oak Forest. I was looking for innovations that would help us in any of our markets. Aaron was looking to see if we had anything that might qualify as The Next Big Thing to come along.

I drove us there in one of the company cars, which seemed to make Aaron uncomfortable. I don't know if it was my driving—whether too fast or too slow—or that he wasn't in control, or what it was. But he fidgeted the whole way. To keep him occupied, I asked about his weekend in Palm Beach. Turns out his flight to Florida was cancelled, but the son of a gun was able to get himself on the last plane to fly out of O'Hare that night, which got him to Atlanta, where he was able to make a connection.

When we got to Oak Forest, the head of research gave us the grand tour. Most of the work there had to do with refinements to existing products and creating new versions of them. The first thing we saw was the 486 computer Elemenco was developing, basically a more powerful new generation of the same technology that was already on the market. Aaron was bored by it. But down the hall, we found a project that got him very excited.

The cause of his excitement was something that looked like a tiny piece of glass. Actually it was a new type of artificial crystal. I could barely see it down among the apparatus. Why was this exciting? Because this tiny crystal, with more development, could become to *optical* computing what the transistor was to electronic computing back in the 1950s. Indeed, the crystal might turn out to be more valuable than diamonds—or as worthless as a splinter of glass the same size. Nobody would know for several years at least.

For now, we had a piece of equipment the engineers called MAXADIL, an acronym derived from words I never committed to memory. But this was a basic "engine" that would enable a system to let people call up from home at any time of day, dial in a code, and get any movie on the system they wanted to watch. MAXADIL could simultaneously broadcast 512 movies from laser disk, handling as many as 32,700 individual subscribers on a pay-per-view basis, and for greater capacity you could daisy-chain a series of MAXADIL units together.

"It wouldn't have to be a movie, would it?" asked Aaron.

"No," said the lead engineer. "It could be any kind of programming. It could be videotext. Legal, technical, educational programming, whatever. But movies are the biggest draw, as we see it."

"So as a customer, if I suddenly develop an intense desire to watch *Casablanca* at two in the morning, all I do is punch in the code and there it is on my TV?" Aaron asked.

"Sure, as long as it's on the system," said the engineer. "You can watch as many movies as you like, and you don't have to return any videocassettes the next day."

"Very interesting," said Aaron. "Very interesting indeed."

He paced in front of the MAXADIL test unit, a battleship-gray box roughly the size of a refrigerator and every bit as unexciting to look at.

"This has possibilities," Aaron said to me.

"How soon can we start marketing this?" I asked the engineer.

"This part is basically functional now," he said. "We're in the process of doing the final testing. I'd say we need a few more weeks at least."

"Weeks? Did you say *weeks*?" said Aaron. "Well, let's get going! Let's sell some!"

"Well, to develop the whole system though—"

"Why waste time developing the whole system?" asked Aaron. "We own the key ingredient. Let's get it on the market, let somebody else take the risk of developing the whole package, maybe learn from their mistakes and come out with our own version in a year or two. Or not at all, depending on the market."

"There's risk either way," I said.

"Our company needs sales *now*," said Aaron.

"True," I said.

He was elated as we left the R&D center, his hands gesturing wildly as we walked to the car.

"I'll tell you, PowerCase is a good product, but it's small potatoes compared to some of the things we could be getting into," said Aaron. "Dave, if we want this company to grow, the thing to do is to spin off stuff like the cable and the connectors, the personal computer line, even the cellular phones. Dump it.

That's all yesterday's technology. Sell it now and put the capital into *emerging* technology like MAXADIL."

That was about what I expected him to say. If Elemenco had been his company, I'm sure that's what he would have done. But a closer's market is often only 1 or 2 percent of the total potential. I was not at all sure a market that small would support a company of our size. Besides, there were three other markets to think about.

The other markets have their own characteristics. To find a consultive market, look for buyers of complex products for which there is little or no internal expertise. A typical product for high tech, high touch is likely to be an advanced system often of many components (as opposed to a simple, single product) offering flexibility, expandability, and a custom design. Sometimes, too, in high tech, high touch, you'll be offering an improvement to an existing system. Professional installation and customer training are part of the sale.

Consultive buyers are inexperienced but real users. They're going to be people like Fred Carver, the vice-president of store operations for MorrMart, a line manager. Fred and the people who work for him will be using our 720 Network on a daily basis.

For Elemenco, the 720 Network and our Apogee System satellite communications were in a high-tech, high-touch market. PowerSeat, if it became more complex, would also ease toward this market. But some of our low-tech products could also be high tech, high touch for customers who were inexperienced.

The motives of an individual customer to buy from you depend on a couple of issues that split along the high-tech–low-tech division. In high tech, the buyers will want growth and improvement. The ones who don't buy, in high tech, will be confident or sometimes overconfident in their present way of doing business.

In low tech, buyers typically want to solve a problem. Those who don't buy usually want to maintain stability and stick with existing methods; they'll reject you in favor of their current supplier.

To find a relationship market, look for buyers purchasing a product that is complex but has been around for a while and has been forced by market pressures toward standardization. In low tech, high touch, the customers are looking for these qualities: a widely accepted product or service, flexibility in features and options, a match with existing quality specifications, on-time delivery to specific schedules, cost savings, repeatable performance, an understood technology.

These buyers are both experienced and real users of the product and they're the experts, or they have access to internal expertise. On the seller's side, you've got the benefit of widespread acceptance, but also more competition. You distinguish yourself by doing special things for each customer while delivering the expected standard.

Display selling may sound as though it lacks status, but a mature market does provide the largest numbers of buyers. Low-tech, low-touch customers are buying products or commodities that are standardized, easily replaceable, low cost, and readily available when needed. The uses of the products are commonplace and well understood. To stand out in this market, either you offer a lower price or you offer more convenience. Or you do both, if your costs allow.

Late on an afternoon, I was leaving Ann Lansky's office and ran into Charlie Summers near the main door. We said hello to each other and stopped to shoot the breeze for a minute. While we were standing there, Kevin Duttz came by.

Charlie had some wiring diagrams in his hand. I asked him what the diagrams were in reference to. He said he had just sold 250 of our 386 work stations, but each unit had to be specially configured, and he was going to go home that night and mark the customer's specifications on the diagrams so the service technicians would be able to do the setup right.

"That's all? Only 250?" said Kevin. "I just got off the phone with a wholesaler in Minneapolis, and I sold him a thousand units of that very same work station."

"Who's going to set them up for the customer?" asked Charlie.

"Nobody," said Kevin. "They're plain vanilla. Standard. They're going from our plant to his warehouse, no additional service, no cost to us. Which is *better* than your deal."

"Kevin, you can't sell work stations like they were pork bellies or sides of beef!" Charlie said.

As they were arguing about who had landed the superior sale, Jennifer Hone came through the door.

"How are things at MorrMart?" I asked her.

"Fine. In fact, that's where I was this afternoon and I've got great news," she said. "I just sold one of Fred Carver's managers a complete departmental system with fifteen work stations."

"That's great news?" asked Kevin. "Only fifteen work stations? I just sold a thousand!"

"What's great about it is these fifteen are going to be like no other work stations on the market. They're going to have specially designed motherboards and a custom interface card." She went into some of the technical details. "They'll be ten times more powerful than the current design," she concluded. "It'll be like giving each user a minicomputer."

"Are you sure that's the best solution to their problem?" asked Charlie. "You're going to have to deviate from the standard bus to do that, aren't you?

"I decided they should do it this way, because it's the way to give them *optimum* performance," said Jennifer.

That's where I left it.

You see? The same type of work station, but three different types of sales.

One morning Ann Lansky asked me, "Have you heard about the rumor that's going around?"

"About what?"

"About us."

"About *us*? As in you and me? What kind of rumor?"

"They think we're having an affair," she said.

"Well, they think wrong," I said.

"I *know* that, obviously," Ann said. "But the truth hasn't stopped the tongues out there from wagging."

"Why would anyone think we're having . . . whatever?"

"I guess it's because we're spending a lot of time with each other."

"What's wrong with that? We're working on an important project."

"And because we spent that Friday night together in Gene Cherson's office."

That stunned me. "How did anyone find out about that? I never told anyone. It was nobody's business."

Ann looked away. "It's my fault," she said. "I told Jim Woller."

"Why would you tell him?"

"Because he asked me how I got home in the storm. He said it took him four hours to get home and he asked how long it took me. I told him how we were stranded here and didn't make it home until the next morning. And Woller said, 'Aha!

So that explains the pizza boxes and the empty champagne bottles in Gene's office.' "

I let out a sigh.

"I didn't have anything to hide!" she said defensively. "I told him the whole story. He made a few smart remarks, the way he usually does, but I thought that was the end of it."

"I'm not angry at you," I said. "What do you want to do about this?"

"What *can* we do?"

I pretended to think for a minute and said, "We could rent a motel room."

Before she could say anything, I hastily added that I was just kidding. Neither of us said a word for a minute or more.

"Well, why don't we just watch our step in the future and quietly spread the word that there's nothing going on," I said.

"Right, good idea," said Ann. "Okay, what do we do now that we've sorted the larger accounts?"

We got down to business.

Basically what we did was divide Ann's sales force into three teams. Jennifer Hone headed the consultive team. We didn't call it that; we called it the New Systems Team. Charlie Summers was appointed leader of the relationship team, which we called the Key Accounts Team. And Kevin Duttz became leader of the display team, which we called the V Team. Some thought the *V* stood for victory; actually it referred to *volume*. Those three were natural picks not just because I'd worked with them, but because each one had the best performance with the types of customers they'd be serving.

Kevin and the V Team had the most: eight out of the nineteen people in the office. The relationship team was the next largest with seven, and the consultive team had four. We split them that way because that was how many of each type we had in the Chicago office. Which didn't surprise me. Among salespeople overall, super-closers are relatively rare and consultive people, though more numerous, are still fairly few. The majority of salespeople are best at relationship or display selling.

Ann and I met with each team, assigned them their accounts, and told them the focus of their responsibilities—what kinds of customers they would be working with, what to do with leads for other markets, what kinds of products would be their specialty. Then we charged each team with coming up with its own business plan. Rather than tell them what to do, I decided that they should tell us. I had a strong hunch that they would tell us pretty much what I wanted to hear.

Then we kept an eye on what they were doing, and we waited.

Sometime later that week, I had a chance to confront Jim Woller with the suspicion he had been the root of the rumor. Of course he denied saying anything to anyone. He claimed that someone else had found the pizza boxes and the empty champagne bottles and that that someone had started the rumor. Not good ole Jim Woller, no sir.

I got a call from Reed Morrison one day.

"Do you know Jack Dorfin?" he asked.

Dorfin was president of DigitLand, a national office and computer equipment chain and the largest distributor of our desktop systems.

"What about him?"

"He's upset about one of our ads," said Morrison. "Would you please give him a call and try to straighten things out."

Sure, I love doing things like that. Dorfin had received an advance copy of one of our new ads. Our policy was to mail advance copies to important customers, dealers, and distributors, not for their approval, but to get some extra mileage out of the ad and to alert them that our ad would appear in such-and-such magazines. Dorfin had received one of these and he apparently didn't like what he saw.

"Which ad is it?" I asked him.

"The one with the mouth," he said.

I told him to hang on for a moment. Behind my desk was a binder with all our ads. I opened it up and found the one he was referring to.

It was a full-page, full-color ad. The main graphic was a closeup profile of a mouth, wide open and shouting into a nearby ear. The headline read, "You Talk . . . Elemenco Listens!" Below that was a small, inset photograph of one of our desktop computers with a price: "$4,998!"

The body copy claimed that our customers were screaming for lower prices so Elemenco was slashing them. Then it talked about the technical superiority of the computer featured in the inset. Finally, there was a subhead that read, "Announcing Elemenco's Direct Order Hotline!" The copy said that customers who wanted to order direct from Elemenco could now do so by calling our order line. Then at the bottom was an 800 number, plus the emblems for Visa and MasterCard.

"What don't you like about it?" I asked Dorfin.

"I don't like anything about it," he said.

"Could you be more specific?"

"First of all, you don't know the price of corn," said Dorfin. "A system comparable to the one you're showing there typically lists for at least $1,000 below what you claim is a reduced price. You're not going to build my traffic with a price like that."

That wasn't the only thing he didn't like. In fact, that was just the beginning.

"You've already got your own sales force calling on the corporate accounts, which effectively cuts us out. Now you're going direct to the smaller business accounts, which frankly you don't understand anyway. And furthermore I hate the mouth!" said Dorfin. "It's vulgar and stupid."

He threatened to drop our entire product line if we didn't pull the ad, but after we had talked for some time, I got him calmed down some. I did what the ad implied; I listened to him.

"What bothers me the most," he said just before we hung up, "is this ad tells me that you guys just don't seem to know what you're about."

The real benefit of Dorfin's call was that it got me to think about what kind of image we were projecting in our advertising. I'd had too many other things to worry about to this point, but now I sat back and flipped through the other ads in the binder.

Aesthetically, the ads were perfectly acceptable. Pristine photography, clear and sometimes clever copy, clean design. But I saw in our ads a problem even deeper than the issue of angering one (or more) of our distributors through direct response.

The mouth ad was not typical. Most of our recent advertising was vague and rather pointless. Many of the ads said in effect how Elemenco did this and did this and this and this, and, oh, yeah, we also do *that*. I could sense the stamp of Gene Cherson again. Our motto in these ads should have been, "Elemenco: We Do Something for Everybody."

But the mouth ad seemed to be taking us down a path I wasn't sure we should follow. I went down the hall to see Nick Dominica, our advertising manager. I told him about Jack Dorfin.

"At least somebody called," said Nick.

"What do you mean by that?" I asked.

"Most of our advertising doesn't get any reaction at all," said Nick. "I think that's our real problem."

"You may be right," I said.

"I personally liked the ad," he said. "It wasn't going to win a Clio, I grant you, but at least it had something definite to say. Right or wrong, it seemed to make a stand."

"Isn't this the first time we've had credit cards in our advertising?"

"Yes it is."

"Why did we go with this approach?"

"Partly because that's what the research told us to do," said Nick. "And partly it was to take advantage of the telemarketing technology that Gene was so hot to install."

He told me that the ad had been in the works for a long time. They had developed the concept the year before, but it had been put on hold.

"One of the things that held us up was that we were going to offer a really low price in the ad, but that got everybody upset," said Nick. "Gene finally gave the go-ahead last December. I don't know, maybe because everything was looking so bleak. In the meantime, prices have dipped again and what would have been a competitive price last year is now pretty high."

"Okay, then, let's pull the ad and run something else," I said.

"What do you want to run instead?"

"You pick it. But no credit cards, no prices, and no encouragement of direct response," I said. "Aside from that, there are some factors related to what we're doing in sales that everybody ought to be thinking about. I want to hold a special meeting with our advertising account team."

There are a number of good agencies in Chicago, but ours was in New York. Don't ask me why. I wanted anybody who had anything to do with the account to be in the same room, hearing the same information. Robb Jamison is a decent enough account manager, but what I wanted, what I thought we had to have, was complicated and I couldn't count on the message to make it through many translations without getting garbled. So rather than bring the agency to Chicago, Nick and his assistants and I flew to New York.

As promised, Robb Jamison brought in the whole account team: the creative director, the copywriters, the artists, the media buyer, and the market research director, plus the head of the agency's New York office, Joe Willis. We even agreed to pay everybody on the agency side an hourly rate just to have them sit there, listen, take notes, and try to understand. I went to the front of the room, which felt like role reversal; normally the agency people would be the ones presenting.

After I'd explained the quadrant, I said, "What Elemenco needs from you are four distinctly different campaigns tied to four distinctly different markets. I'm not about to tell you what the ads should look like or how the copy should read. That's your job; that's where we want your help. I'm simply going to give you the image we want to project and the focus of our efforts in each market."

I began with the image likely to be successful in closing: innovative, modern, unique, advancing new technological opportunities. We wanted people to perceive us as serving exclusive customers.

"That's what we want for PowerCase, PowerSeat, and perhaps for a new product or two we may be introducing later this year," I told them.

Next was the image we wanted for consultive: expert, competent, professional, state of the art.

"We want to look contemporary, but not radical or daring. We want to appear smart and sensible, yet progressive," I told them. "And in this market, we want to be perceived as serving leading customers, not exclusive customers."

The 720 Network and the Apogee System were the key products here, plus some of our smaller networks and desktop computers for less experienced customers.

For relationship, where we would be selling a number of products ranging from local-area networks to desktop PCs, we wanted to project an image that we were caring, friendly, loyal, dependable, nonbureaucratic. We wanted to be perceived as offering personalized service to established customers.

"If the image of high tech, low touch is the effect of a shot of adrenalin," I said, "then low tech, high touch by comparison is the market where we want the image to generate the warm, fuzzy feeling."

I talked finally about display, the market where we would find most of the customers for our 100 percent compatible PCs, our computer cable and connectors, our modems, our off-the-shelf software, our standard cellular telephones, and a number of other products.

In a low-touch, low-tech market, the image we wanted was that Elemenco was a traditional, long-standing company that observed the standards and offered convenience, the right price, and an abundant supply of whatever product we had to offer. If possible, we also wanted to be seen as the dominant supplier of the product, not filling a niche in the market, something more desirable for low tech, high touch.

"We are no longer serving exclusive customers, or leading customers, or established customers," I said. "In a low-tech, low-touch market, we are serving customers everywhere."

At the end of all this, I opened the meeting for questions. The first to speak was the creative director, a guy named Ted.

"I think I understand the theory, and I think it's very interesting," he said. "My problem is with how this affects the kind of advertising we develop for you."

"As I explained, we need four different kinds of approaches to match the quadrants of the marketplace."

"No, that's not the problem I see," said Ted. "Let's say we come up with these four distinctly different images for Elemenco and we create advertising based on what you've told us. Who's going to believe you?"

"I don't understand what you mean," I said.

"It's difficult enough to get *one* market to know who you are. Based on what you've told us, we're now going to have to do that four times in four different ways," said Ted.

The art director, a woman named Frieda, added, "With this, it's like you're telling one market, 'Look at us, we're red!' Then you're telling the next market, 'Look at us, we're green!' And the next one, 'Don't worry, our true color is purple!' And so on."

"That's why I can see problems with believability," said Ted. "I mean, isn't there going to be some overlap between these markets? What happens if the customers get together and compare notes? Can you say that you're one type of company to one customer, and then go down the road and convince another customer you're really a completely different type of company?"

Robb Jamison, probably trying to assert control over the discussion, the way a proper account manager should, said, "I think maybe that's why we've sought in the past to give a unifying voice to your advertising."

"I have something for you to consider," said Joe Willis. "I know this is outside of your jurisdiction somewhat. But are you sure Elemenco should even *be* in all four of these markets?"

I paced in front of the room, feeling the gathering resistance from them, worried that everything I'd said would now be disregarded. I couldn't let that happen.

"All your points are well taken. And all I can say is that for the time being our company president, Reed Morrison, wants Elemenco to pursue all four types of markets," I said.

"Oh, I see," said Joe Willis, as if that explained everything.

"Therefore, we need the four different images I've described. This is the best direction I can give you. It will be a major part of how we evaluate your performance as an agency. Now it's up to you, as our account team, to deliver."

It was an authoritarian response and I don't think they liked it, but I didn't know what else to say.

"I'd like to make one more comment," said Ted.

"Go ahead."

"You understand that just because we successfully create the image you want doesn't mean the customer will agree with it," he said.

"I understand that," I said, "and it's our job to make sure the images you create bear some semblance to reality, that our performance agrees with the image and the expectations the customer has of us. But the types of images we're seeking have to be based on what I described to you."

And that was that. No more debate. We spent the rest of the time at the agency talking about implementation.

We had a few hours to socialize after the meeting before heading to La Guardia. Our group split up, Nick's assistants going off with the account executives, while Robb Jamison took Nick and me for an early dinner at a restaurant where I had no intentions of even pretending to reach for the check. The creative director, Ted, and Joe Willis came with our group.

Sitting in upholstered chairs and having a drink before dinner, we were still talking about the meeting and about business. Joe Willis was particularly curious about the quadrant theory I'd described.

"Tell me, that grid or quadrant or whatever it is, do you think that might be applicable for other companies?"

"Absolutely it is," I told him. "Everything I've described has implications not just for Elemenco, but other companies and other industries. You may find it useful in serving your other clients as well."

We all sipped our drinks on that.

Then Robb said, "Just for the sake of asking, where does the advertising industry fit in all this?"

"It's mostly consultive, isn't it?" said Joe Willis.

Rather than just giving him an answer, I said, "Look at the evidence.

"Most companies of any size have someone like Nick: an internal expert who is supposed to manage the advertising function, which means that there are established procedures for buying advertising services. Then there's the personal aspect. If an account manager changes agencies, it's not uncommon for clients to follow that person to the new agency. Advertising is well established and an accepted part of doing business; it's low tech. Yet complexity is high. Every ad and every campaign is virtually handmade. And this is one of the things that differentiates one agency from the many others filling the Yellow Pages: the level of service and attention the client gets.

"You put together all those aspects and a number of others," I said, "and you see that most ad agencies are in a low-tech, high-touch market. Doing well in the business requires a relationship type of selling."

"Sure, but doesn't advertising have its consultive aspects?" Willis asked.

I got the impression that Willis thought "consultive selling" sounded more prestigious than "relationship selling," even though it's wrong to attach more status to one than another.

"It depends. If you're dealing with a small, growing, young company and your contact is the owner or a manager rather than an internal specialist, then it might be a consultive sale if your agency is involved in developing their market strategy."

Joe Willis looked at Robb Jamison and said, "Maybe we ought to be more consultive."

"You have to sell the way your customer thinks is appropriate," I argued. "Look at related kinds of business communications. If you were selling professional fund raising, for instance, you'd probably be in a high-tech, low-touch market and you'd need a closing style. Or look at public relations. If you're a PR agency that sells coaching to help executives cope with news media interviews, that's a consultive type of sale. If on the other hand you're selling a program to the company's internal PR department, that's going to be more of a relationship type of sale. Likewise, general advertising most of the time will tend to be in the relationship category."

To make Willis feel better, I added that the majority of business-to-business and industrial sales are in the relationship category, so he had a lot of friends. We all did. Most consumer products are in display markets and the selling is of the friendly-order-taker variety.

"What about financial services?" Robb asked me.

"Again, it depends on what you're talking about. If you're talking about an established Wall Street stock brokerage, that's probably a relationship sale. A discount brokerage, on the other hand, may be selling a display service. If you specialize in venture capital or junk bonds, you're probably in a closing market and if you're good you're probably a super-closer. If you're into some kind of turnkey investment management, that's a consultive market," I said.

Ted was stroking his beard. "Let's take something basic like cars," he said. "Where do car salesmen fit into this picture?"

"It depends on the car, the customer, and who's selling," I said. "If you're in fleet sales, that often takes a relationship approach."

"No, I mean the normal car dealership out there in normal America," said Ted. "Where do their salespeople stand on the quadrant?"

"If it's the kind of salesperson who builds a personal clientele, who gets the same customers coming back every couple of years, who works to get each customer a car with exactly the options wanted, handles the interface with the service department after the sale—that's a relationship salesperson. That approach will work better with an upscale car like a Porsche or a Mercedes-Benz," I said. "On the other hand, if it's a high-volume dealership, then it's a low-tech, low-touch sale—"

"And you're dealing with order takers," Ted said, finishing the thought. "You think about all those used-car salesmen out there, the kind with the high-pressure closes. They don't seem to fit the kind of market or image you were talking about."

"An emotional closing approach can be very effective, especially with young, first-time buyers. But just because a certain kind of selling goes on doesn't mean it's appropriate," I said. "Some companies and some salespeople don't know what market they're in. Some salespeople shouldn't even be in the profession, and a lot of others are not very well trained. The way they sell may be driving away more customers than they bring in. And in fairness to the sales reps, some sales managers don't encourage their people to do what's best for the customer."

"Do you think too many dealerships have concentrated on price as the focus of the sale?" Robb asked.

"Well, automobiles are not my industry," I said. "The point is, you use whatever approach is appropriate to your customer. If your market is resisting you, then you'd better try something else. Which is what we're trying to do at Elemenco."

We went from talking about the dealers to the auto manufacturers and their suppliers, and from there to industry overall. To prove to them that there was an aspect of all four types of markets in nearly every industry, I requested a supply of cocktail napkins from the waiter and drew the quadrant for a couple of industries.

Modular Auto Components

Electronic airbag safety devices	Steering systems
Navigational radar	Engine mounts Standard shock absorbers

Manufacturing

Flexible robotics systems	Numerically controlled machining systems
New robotically controlled laser equipment	"Shoot and ship" Plastic moldings

By the time the maître d' told us our table was ready, I was glad to get off the subject. We started telling jokes and stories and generally had a good time. Later, outside the restaurant, Joe Willis shook my hand while Robb Jamison hailed a cab for us.

"A very productive day, I thought," he said. "I learned a lot myself. I think everybody did."

I wondered how much would sink in. It can be a long time before a new idea takes root. On the plane back to Chicago that night, Nick sat next to me.

"How well do you think they'll do?" I asked him.

"I don't know. Sometimes with Robb, it's like he's psychic, like he can read your mind," said Nick. "And sometimes you couldn't get his attention if you hit him over the head with a two-by-four."

"My guess," I told him, "is that they will be closer to the mark in one or two of the markets, but not all four. I'm not saying that's guaranteed, just a guess. Meanwhile, why don't we start quietly gathering samples and portfolios of other agencies, so we're ready to talk if they're way off target."

"You mean you'll fire them?"

"I hope not," I said. "But we may have to split the account by market, and I just want to be ready."

Nick seemed to have concerns about that. "Gene was adamant last year about consolidating everything with one agency."

"Well," I said, "Gene isn't running things now."

15

The weeks went by. I did some traveling, talked to some customers, tended to my normal duties, but still kept close tabs on how things were coming along downstairs in Ann's office. If more gossip circulated about my supposed affair with Ann, it didn't reach my ears.

At the end of March, I flew to San Francisco. My house in San Jose had sold. I went to the closing, then stayed an extra couple of days to meet some of our sales reps on the West Coast. One of the things I did while I was out there was to get a firsthand look at our retail chain, which was continuing to lose money.

The Elemenco store I visited was in a shopping plaza near Sunnyvale. On one side was a wallpaper outlet; on the other was an ice cream parlor. I walked in just as the lone salesman was stifling a yawn.

"May I help you?" he asked.

"In a minute."

I wanted to look around first. I wandered past the various computers and printers. It was a normal, boring computer store. One small difference between this one and every other normal, boring computer store was a display in the center of the floor with backlit color photographs depicting Elemenco's satellite dishes and corporate networks.

"What's this here for?" I asked the salesman.

"I don't know," he said. "I guess they think it'll remind people of Elemenco's other fine products."

I asked to see the manager. I'd called ahead, so he was expecting me, and he came out of his office to talk to me. His name was Harvey Salter.

"It's been very quiet since last fall," Harvey told me. "Not much traffic."

"Any particular reason you can think of?"

He pointed through the window. "You can see one right there."

Across the plaza, I could see another computer store, one of our competitors. In its front window was a hugh banner that read, "All Prices Half Off List!"

"Let's take a look," I suggested.

Harvey and I walked across the plaza to the other store. Just inside the door was a line of shopping carts. I mean, really, *shopping carts*. That's what decades of technical evolution have yielded: a computer you buy in a store with shopping carts. It was self-service. All the merchandise was in cartons on well-stocked shelves. Floor samples were there so people could play with the machines, and this store, unlike ours, had people in it. While the Elemenco store promoted our own line, this store offered hardware from all manufacturers.

"Look at this," said Harvey. "We offer basically the same system, but they've got it for 25 percent less than we do."

"Why can't we promote better service to justify our higher price?"

Harvey laughed. "I think better service is part of our problem."

"What do you mean?"

"Our store has a technician in the back who fixes machines that break. This store doesn't have a technician. If you buy a system from Elemenco and something breaks, we try to fix it. If you buy something from this store and it breaks, you just bring it back and they give you a new one. They even let you return software."

"How come we're not doing the same thing?"

"I'd like to, but it's against policy. I'm told we'd lose money," said Harvey. "These guys don't have the overhead of an Elemenco. They can run on slimmer margins and make it up on volume. And, anyway, how are we ever going to compete being a me-too kind of operation?"

We didn't linger long. Outside, I said good-bye to Harvey and wished him luck. I had a hunch he'd probably be looking for a new job before the year was out.

The retail chain was a small part of Elemenco's total operations, yet it was significant. More than anything else that spring, my visit to the store in Sunnyvale drove home the notion that Elemenco didn't belong in a display market.

I was back in the office on the first of April, but came in late that morning. When I got there, the whole office seemed empty. None of the secretaries were at their desks. The offices were vacant.

Then Nick passed me, and I asked him, "Where is everybody?"

"You don't know?"

"Know what?"

"He's b-a-c-k."

"Who's back?"

"Gene Cherson."

Then I remembered what day it was.

"Yeah, right, April Fools," I said.

"No, really. Cherson is back."

"He can't be. He's only been gone, what, two months? Two and a half?"

"Well, he's in his office now. Came in this morning while you were out. Everybody is in there with him."

Indeed, they were, his whole staff—*my* whole staff—and most of the secretaries. They stood in a large semicircle around his desk, while he stood behind it and told war stories about his recovery.

"Look at this," he said as he opened his suit jacket. "Had to buy all new suits. The old ones fit me like a tent. I'm a changed man."

In appearance, he obviously was. The fat, most of it, was gone. He'd lost probably twenty pounds. His face seemed narrower, looser. He now had a waist. His skin was pasty, but otherwise he seemed fine.

"And you quit cold turkey?" someone asked him.

"Given the alternative . . . " Gene said.

Laughs and chuckles from the audience.

"No, seriously, there are times when I still want a cigarette. There are times when I still want a drink, but I guess those days are past me now," he said.

"We all missed you," said one of the secretaries. (She was probably up for a raise.) "You'll be back full time with us?"

"In spirit if not in flesh. Miraculous recovery or not, the doctors tell me I should just work half days for a while, but we'll see. I'll be counting on all you staff people to help me out a little more than usual. And the first thing you can do is tell me something I want to know."

He began looking face to face around the office.

"Who the hell drank all my champagne?!"

Lots of laughs on that one. When they quieted down, I spoke up.

"It must have been Goldilocks," I said.

Well, that broke up the party. Sensing tension, they began to filter out. I stayed and waited until they were gone.

"Welcome back," I said, offering a hand.

He shook it.

"I understand you've been filling in for me," said Gene.

"Reed Morrison asked if I'd step in. Have you talked to him yet?"

"Talked to him late yesterday. He knows I'm here, if that's what you're asking."

"I just wondered what your plans are."

"My plans are to come back to work and start doing my job again," he said. "Close the door, will you."

I did, and when I turned around, I asked Gene, "Do you want a full briefing on what's been going on?"

"No, I don't need that," said Gene. "Jim Woller and I have been talking over the past few weeks, and I think I have a handle on what's been going on. I understand you've been—what's the word I want to use—coveting my position."

He tapped the top of his desk.

"This position is filled," he said. "And, God willing, it will be so for some time to come. I also hear you've been mucking around with our sales organization in Ann Lansky's region."

A dirty little smile crossed his face, then disappeared.

"Well," he said, "that's going to stop."

"No, it's not," I said.

"We need a unified, national policy—"

I cut him off. "Reed gave his personal approval. The changes are underway now and I suggest you wait and see what happens before you pass judgment."

He didn't push it. Instead, he asked, "And what's this about selling PowerSeat to Diamond Skies?"

"What about it?"

"That's the dumbest deal I've ever seen. Diamond Skies has only got about thirty planes total. We should have held out until one of the big airlines bought it."

"The big airlines probably will buy it after it's been proven as a viable concept," I argued. "In that kind of high-tech sale, you need a gateswinger to lead the way."

"A *what* kind of sale?"

I didn't bother explaining.

"I'm going to ask our legal department if we can get out of that contract," said Cherson. "At least the exclusive clause."

This time, *I* didn't push it. PowerSeat was outside our main business and if he wanted to win that round, let him.

"Well, I'm sure you have obligations to attend to in your area of product development," he said. "Thank you for, ah, covering for me. If I need to know anything else, I'll call you."

I went back to my office and got on the phone to Reed Morrison to find out what my true status was, but he wasn't taking any calls. In fact, I tried again several times, but it was late the next day before Morrison called me back.

"What is it?" Morrison asked me. "I've a lot of things cooking up here."

When I asked about Gene Cherson and who would head marketing, he said, "David, I had to give him his job back. I mean, he was on medical leave. It's *his* job. He's been with the company for . . . I don't know, a long time. Look, try to work with him. That's why I brought you in."

"But he's already threatening to undo everything I've set up on the Central Region," I said.

"All right, I'll tell him hands off. Anything else?"

"To be perfectly honest, I don't know how much good I'll be able to do with Gene back in his corner office," I said. "I think he's going to try to sabotage me."

I heard Morrison sigh on the other end of the line.

"Don't worry, you're protected," he said. "Okay, I've got to go. I've got some other calls to make."

16

"He says we're protected," I told Ann. "Let's keep going with what we're doing."

"What does Gene's coming back mean for you?"

"Gene and I may never be pals, but as long as Morrison is chief executive, and as long as we show an increase in sales for your region, everything should be fine. All I can do is concentrate on our project and on what I was hired to do, product development. I may even need to work a few less hours than I have been," I said, and, looking around at the mess strewn about the bedroom, added, "Maybe I'll even have time to pick up this place once in a while."

I was calling her at home from the company condo, which remained my place of residence and after-hours office.

Ann said, "Are you still house hunting?"

"Yes and no. Yes, I want to buy a house. And, no, I'm not because I haven't had any time to go look for one. Why do you ask?"

"A very nice townhouse is for sale in my neighborhood. Do you like townhouses?"

"Well, I'm pretty sure I don't want a suburban ranch. I'd have to hire a gardener to take care of the yard or the neighbors would run me out of the city. How do you know about this place?"

"It's just around the corner from me. I'm friends with the owner," she said. "She's being transferred to Denver. I'll set it up so you can see the place if you'd like."

"Sure. Why not."

"If you buy it, we can carpool together," she said.

"You know how to keep the rumor mills busy, don't you?"

Maybe I touched a nerve; she didn't say anything. I changed the subject.

"So how are the teams coming on those business plans they were supposed to develop?"

"I don't think they've taken them very seriously," she said.

"Well, let's schedule some meetings so that they do start taking them seriously."

We talked a while longer about nothing in particular, then said goodnight. I went into the kitchenette to find whatever was in the freezer that I could microwave.

Aaron Abbott stopped by my office. Aaron was on the road much of the time, so it was unusual to see him. But it wasn't wholly unexpected. True to his word, Gene Cherson was agitating to have the Diamond Skies contract renegotiated. As soon as I saw Aaron, I figured that his visit had something to do with that. My defenses went up immediately, because I had every intention of staying out of that one.

"Jim Woller and I are going to lunch today," Aaron said. "Why don't you join us?"

I was ready to say I was busy, but the fact that Woller was going along made me hesitate. I decided to be direct.

"Does this have anything to do with Diamond Skies?"

Aaron laughed and said, "No, no, I've got that under control. I want to talk to the two of you about some new business."

"What kind of new business?"

"Well, come with us and you'll find out," he said. And when I still hesitated, he said, "Come on, come on! I promise it'll be worth your while."

He came around the side of my desk, grabbed my hand, and yanked me to my feet.

"It'll do you good to get out of the city for a few hours," he said.

"Out of the city?"

He told me where we were going. It was some country club that had reciprocal privileges with his own club back in New England, but I knew it was way the hell up by Lake Forest.

"That's a long drive, isn't it?"

"Don't worry. It'll be productive time," he said. "I want to show you something."

"But what is it?"

"A surprise."

Woller joined us in the hall and we left. In the elevator, Aaron announced that he would drive. We walked with him to his car in the building garage. I was expecting one of our usual company sedans, but instead we headed for a black Audi V8 Quattro, about $50,000 worth of automobile.

"Yours?" asked Woller.

"Ours," he said.

"Are all the salespeople going to get one of these?" I asked.

Aaron seemed to read my mind. "No, but don't worry. I talked to Morrison about it. He approved it. I told him I thought we needed something with a bit more panache than your average company car as our selling platform."

"What do you mean?"

"This is our show car. Come on, hop in."

Jim Woller got in back and I slipped into the passenger seat. After Aaron was behind the wheel, he pointed out the goodies inside. Aaron had had our development engineers rework the car's dashboard. The conventional glove box was gone, replaced by a locking compartment in the driver's side door. Cut into the dashboard on the passenger's side was a tray with a couple of connectors at the back. This was where Aaron put his PowerCase unit, sliding it back carefully so that power and data connections were made.

"Watch this," said Aaron, pointing to a small joystick next to the radio.

As soon as he touched it, the tray began to move. Motors, which sounded like the ones in power seats, positioned the PowerCase so that Aaron could use it as he drove. For the passenger—me, in this case—it was a tight fit. I had to keep my legs out straight or my knees would bump the tray.

"You see? It's a complete traveling executive office," Aaron claimed. "As soon as I saw PowerCase and heard about PowerSeat, I knew that all we would have to do is adapt the technology to a car and we would open a new gold mine."

As we left the parking garage, Aaron was still explaining the features. Outside, it was a raw and rainy April day. On the freeway, I found my right hand instinctively gripping the door handle. He was an aggressive driver, using the car's power and superior handling to slalom through traffic on the wet pavement.

As soon as traffic gave him half a chance, Aaron began using the phone—one of ours, which he'd had converted to a speaker phone with voice recognition that allowed hands-free dialing—first to make reservations at the club where we were going, then to get some actual work done. I was less curious about the technology than in how he was using it to sell.

I listened as he tried to line up appointments on the East Coast for the following week. On one of the calls, the woman he was talking to cut him off rather rudely and hung up.

"Does that bother you?" I asked him.

"Not usually," Aaron said. "I think of myself as a Babe Ruth kind of hitter as far as my batting average in sales. When Babe Ruth came to bat, he generally either struck out or he hit a home run."

"No kidding. Is that right?"

"Well, so I'm told," said Aaron. "The Babe was before my time, you know. Anyway, the point is that's how I see myself as a salesman. I either hit a home run or I strike out. Fortunately, people don't remember all the times I struck out. They remember all the home runs I hit."

He made, I gathered, a large percentage of cold calls, contacting people he'd never met before, though Aaron knew quite a few people through his high-level networking. He used his name to advantage—and ours as well. If someone recognized either his name or ours, it bought Aaron a couple of minutes to find out if he had an opportunity there.

He was smooth. He could qualify the person on the other end in one or two questions, finding out if the person or the company had the resources to buy from us and if we had anything that would justify his time to try selling it to them. I heard him use a handful of phrases, each adjusted to the context of the conversation, that would both test and entice the potential buyer.

At one point, he said to the person on the phone, "Tell me, what was it you originally liked about the system you have now?"

The answer was the proven technology and affordability of the current system. One more question indicated that he was satisfied with its performance and expected three or four more years of service from it, and shortly after that Aaron gracefully ended the call.

"How come you didn't push to get in to see that guy?" I asked him.

"First of all, I never push anybody," he said. "I draw them to the sale, but I never push. From what that guy said, I knew he'd never buy anything that would justify the time to go see him. Why waste his time and mine? When I'm working, I go all out from morning until . . . well, sometimes nine, ten o'clock at night if I have a dinner meeting with people. Everyone I call on the phone, I ask myself the question, is this person going to be worth the investment of my time? If not, I move on right away."

And with that Aaron picked out the number of a new prospect, one who, as it happened, mentioned that he was upset that his company was unable to stay in touch with people on the road between the company's various offices. Aaron made an appointment to see him later in the week.

Meanwhile, Aaron was using this luncheon outing as an internal sell to Jim and me. "You see, even while the three of us are going to lunch, we can be in touch. We can run numbers in a spreadsheet. We can send and receive documents, right here in the car. Let me show you. Give me something we can fax."

He was reaching for a piece of paper, just as we were passing a big truck.

"That's okay, Aaron," I said, watching the big wheels spinning next to us. "I believe you. I've seen fax machines work before."

"Here, Jim, try the phone," said Aaron. "Call in and check your voice mail."

As Jim was doing that, Aaron was saying, "You know, this is going to be *it*. I'm serious. I just have a feeling in my bones that the traveling office is the next big thing."

"What exactly do you want to sell?" Jim asked him.

"The whole package," said Aaron. "All we need is a patent on the tray mechanism, and we can start selling these the next day to any dealership that sells luxury cars."

Half of me had doubts; half wanted to go with it.

"Jim, what do you think?" I asked.

"I think it has potential."

Finally, I said, "All right, let me get someone to do a breakeven analysis of this, and we'll see what we can do about getting this on the market."

We reached the country club, which of course was not in the country but in the suburbs, and ordered lunch. I asked for grilled salmon, sat back, and hoped I could relax and enjoy it. However, there was more on Aaron's agenda than show cars and selling our version of the traveling office.

Jim Woller excused himself to go to the men's room, and as soon as he did, Aaron asked me point blank, "Do you have any idea why Gene Cherson is screwing around with the Diamond Skies contract?"

"I thought you said you had that under control."

"I do. I was just wondering what might have caused him to start arguing with success."

"You ought to ask Jim Woller," I said. "He works more closely with Gene than I do."

I really didn't want to get involved.

"But I thought you might have a more objective outlook," said Aaron.

I put down my salad fork. "All right, if you want my opinion, I'd say Gene feels he's lost control. I think he's just trying to reassert his influence."

"Well, he picked a crazy way to go about it," said Aaron. "Do you realize what percentage of the market at this point in time is likely to go for an idea like PowerSeat? About 2 percent.

That's my guess—2 percent if we're lucky. And he wants to throw it away because the deal isn't big enough!"

"I know," I said. "I understand."

"I knew you would, because you approved when I first told you about the arrangement," said Aaron. "So here's what I'd like to do. I'd like for us to work together on this. I happen to know Morrison has granted you immunity, so to speak, for Central Region from Gene's organization plan. I know that because Morrison himself suggested I talk to you. Why don't we suggest to Eddie Matt or his technical people that they insist the contract be serviced out of Chicago. Which is probably where it belongs anyway. That way we can say this is part of your experiment. The deal stays intact, everybody wins."

I was getting involved whether I wanted to or not.

"All right, fine," I said. "I know we need the business."

"And there's no need to say anything to Jim about this right now, is there?"

I didn't even respond because Woller walked into earshot just then.

As soon as we got into the Audi after lunch, Aaron checked his own voice mail. There was a call from Sheldon Hurley of Hurley Commercial Services, which happened to be on the way back downtown. Aaron called him back right away, got through, and two minutes later had an appointment.

"This is perfect," said Aaron. "Absolutely perfect. I've been missing this guy for weeks. Do you mind? It won't take more than an hour. But if you need to get back to the office, I'll loan you the car and I'll get a cab back downtown."

Both Jim and I declined. Jim called in to let the office know where we were, and off we went to see Hurley. When we got there, Aaron asked one of us to stay in the car and make a phone call in exactly five minutes. Jim volunteered and Aaron wrote down the number for him to call.

"And if you don't get an answer," said Aaron, "press this button here, and it will automatically redial in one-minute intervals."

Aaron grabbed a second sample of PowerCase out of the trunk and the two of us went inside. On the way in, Aaron said to me, "I could have programmed it to make the call without Jim, but three of us in there at the same time might be, you know, a little much for Sheldon. Even two is a lot, so let me do the talking after the introductions. Okay?"

No problem, I told him.

From the reception area, Aaron led the way to a corridor whose decor signaled we were in top-management territory. We reached an office with a brass nameplate on the wall outside: "S. T. Hurley."

Sheldon Hurley himself came out and welcomed us, took us into his office, and gestured to some chairs while he sat behind his desk. Aaron and Sheldon took a few minutes to get caught up on each other while the secretary brought coffee. Almost effortlessly, Aaron eased into a concise description of Elemenco that made us sound like the grand wizards of the electronic age. As he was talking, his briefcase—our PowerCase unit—on the floor next to his chair began to beep.

"Excuse me, Sheldon," Aaron said. "I should take this."

Sheldon seemed at first irritated by the interruption, but then became fascinated as Aaron opened up his briefcase and picked up the telephone receiver, which was thin and light-weight, no thicker than a fountain pen. Aaron was listening for a few seconds, but his eyes were on Sheldon, watching his reactions.

"Uh-huh, uh-huh. Thanks, Jim, but I'm in the middle of an important meeting right now, " Aaron said. "Let me get back to you after we're finished here. Right. Yeah, just stay put. Thanks for calling."

He hung up, but left the PowerCase sitting open on his lap.

"What's this, your new toy?" Sheldon asked.

"Sheldon, this is the Rolls-Royce of executive briefcases," said Aaron. "It's actually one of the key reasons why I decided to join Elemenco. Now I'll be perfectly honest with you. The call I just took was from one of my associates. We arranged that call in order to show you that with PowerCase you can be any place in America and still be in touch with anyone who needs to reach you. I'm anxious to show this to you, because you'll be interested."

With that he came around the desk and put the Power-Case in front of Sheldon.

"Right now, at this very moment," said Aaron, "not one in a hundred business executives—in your industry, probably not one in a thousand—has anything like this. Feel how light-weight it is."

He had Sheldon pick it up to see for himself.

"That's about as light as a normal briefcase, yet it has a personal computer, a printer, a telephone, and a fax capability all built in. The reason it's so lightweight is that most of the electronic circuitry is sandwiched in the walls of the briefcase itself, made possible by a revolutionary technology. Here, take the wheel, so to speak. Anybody can use this, it's so easy," said Aaron.

"Well, I'm not much up on computers," said Sheldon.

Aaron extended his right index finger and made a point-ing gesture. "Can you do that?"

"Sure."

"Then you are the *master* of this machine," said Aaron.

He showed Sheldon how to manipulate the track ball that moved the pointer around the screen in the lid of the case.

"Here, try the phone," said Aaron. "Try calling your secretary."

After he had Sheldon chuckling over the call to his secre-tary, who was just outside, Aaron got him to try the fax machine, sending a letter that was on his desk to a company fax machine down the hall. Then Aaron got me into the act; he had me go down the hall with Sheldon's secretary and send the same letter back to the briefcase. Great fun.

Aaron kept him "at the wheel," and with every passing minute, I could actually see Sheldon behaving more and more like an owner of the machine.

"I'm sure you travel a lot, don't you, Sheldon?" Aaron asked him. "How long did it take the two of us to connect with each other?"

"You're right. I'm probably out of the office more than I'm in. We have twenty-seven offices around the country, and overseas as well, and I'm constantly on the road."

"Really? How many decisions involving a million dollars or more would a man in your position have to make in an average month?"

"It's hard to say. Quite a few," said Sheldon.

"If you're out of the office and a decision needs to be made, how much might that cost you?"

"Well, I know what you're trying to say, but I'm never that far from a phone," said Sheldon.

"How many telephones have a built-in fax machine so you can send and receive contracts on the fly? How many telephones have a built-in computer to let you analyze profit potential and call up information?"

Sheldon was getting the message. "I grant you it would be nice to have all those together. But something like this I'm sure costs a bundle, and—"

"The real question," said Aaron, "is not about price. The real question is, what does it cost you not to own one compared to how it will enhance your decision-making performance if you do own it? PowerCase is a $19,000 investment. As soon as it has enabled you to approve even *one* of those million-dollar decisions before your competitor, this investment starts making money for you."

Sheldon put a hand to his chin. He knew, I'm sure, that he was being sold, yet he seemed now to want this gadget.

"Now think for a moment," Aaron said. "If a machine like this could make your own day more productive, think of how that could be multiplied if everyone who traveled for Hurley had access to PowerCase. Think about it! Speed and precision add up to your competitive edge."

He began working that angle. At first, I thought to myself, no, there's no way; Sheldon is never going to go for this. But the more I listened to Aaron, the more I began to disbelieve my own conclusions. He was weaving a spell, mesmerizing Sheldon more with every phrase, magically binding the man and the product together.

"An executive in your position deserves the most powerful tools available," he was saying. "Just as your people, too, deserve tools to let them be more productive."

Sheldon voiced an objection. "Well, I still don't know. I've been doing business for many years without one of these things, and you are talking a lot of money."

"Absolutely it's a lot of money," said Aaron. "Which is why I said *investment*. Sheldon, I have a personal goal—that everyone who spends money to buy PowerCase will *make* money with PowerCase. Now as a businessman, you know that cost means little if the return on investment is large enough. You know that, don't you?"

"Sure."

"Frankly, I wouldn't want you to own a PowerCase unless you were getting a return on your investment," said Aaron. "Sheldon, how many people in your company travel on a regular basis and are out of the office more than three days a month?"

"Maybe two dozen," said Sheldon.

"So twenty-four, plus yourself," added Aaron. "Now, I want you to know, this is not an offer I make every day. And I make this offer to you today and today only. Invest in twenty-five units of PowerCase today and I will let you try them at no obligation. Try them for ninety days and if you're not using them productively to help you boost your profitability, I will buy them back from you. This is a no-lose proposition for you."

"What about setting them up?" asked Sheldon.

"I fully expect you will have no problems whatsoever," said Aaron. "PowerCase is specifically designed for simplicity. Our documentation has been praised by every customer I've talked to, plus there is a technical hotline for your secretary to call, if you do have a question or two. Plus you have my offer to repurchase. Sheldon, you absolutely cannot lose on this. I'm serious! Now, would a delivery on the first of the month be good for you, or do you need them sooner than that?"

A pause. Not a word from Aaron. Sheldon again rubbed his chin. "I'd like them sooner, if we can get them," he said finally.

"Let me check on delivery," said Aaron.

I had to make a conscious effort to keep my jaw from falling open. *He was going for it!* Quick math in my head: $19,000 times 25 is $475,000. Half a million, or close to it, from stopping by to see Sheldon after lunch.

By hitting one key, Aaron had PowerCase printing out a sales agreement, which impressed Sheldon all the more and convinced him that he'd made the right decision.

"All I need is your signature right here," said Aaron.

And we were out of there. Jim was waiting in the car. Proving, I guess, that our products did have merit, he was even getting some work done using the phone.

Aaron dropped Jim and me back downtown and took off in a hurry to meet another prospect.

As we walked into the building together, Jim said, "You know, I wasn't crazy about the phone call that set up his pitch."

"I wasn't either."

"It was too dramatic," said Jim. "Not Elemenco's style."

"I agree, but that's a closer for you."

He walked three, maybe four steps before he said anything. "You really think you've got him pegged."

I walked two or three steps before I answered him. "Everybody is an individual," I said. "But it doesn't hurt to categorize if it helps us understand something. After a while, when you see a pattern that is demonstrated time and again . . ."

"What do you mean?"

"A sense of drama is very often a part of making a closing type of sale," I said. "You can almost count on it. That's part of the selling style of a super-closer: theatrical, enthusiastic, confident. All through the presentation, Aaron threw out phrases like 'you deserve this.' He was giving the customer permission to buy. That's another earmark of a closing type of sale."

As we got on the elevator, a thought occurred to me.

"Next week, Ann Lansky's sales teams are going to present how they plan to approach their respective segments of the market. Why don't you join us? I think you'll see how each approach can be valid, yet be very different from the others. And afterward I'll show you how they all differ from what Aaron does so well."

I half expected Woller to have some excuse not to come, but he accepted right away. "Okay, I'll be there."

He even seemed interested.

17

Just for the record, I invited Gene to attend those meetings where the sales teams made their presentations, but with his half-day work schedule, he couldn't be there. Woller came with me, though. In the first meeting, the consultive team offered a plan for developing its market.

Jennifer Hone and the three others—all men, all with engineering backgrounds—opened by talking about new business. Jennifer explained what had been happening with Arnold Sternholtz at All-Points. She had reopened the door there and had met with Arnold and a few of his line managers a couple of times.

She said, "After I ran the clock on him—"

"Excuse me," said Jim Woller, "but after you did *what?*"

"Ran the clock on him," she said. "That's a phrase I use. It's how I visualize my way of getting information. I see it as a clock, like a stopwatch. With new customers, I start at zero, not knowing very much about them. By the end of the conversation, I want to be as close to sixty—which is knowing everything I need to know about them—as possible and being ready to set up a selling opportunity. With each tick of the clock, I want to be gaining new information that tells me who they are and what benefits we could provide them. The first few ticks, we're maybe just talking casually about the weather. The next few ticks, I try to find out what their business is about, how technically advanced they are, and so on. By eight or nine on the clock, I want to know things like what their budget is, names of the key managers, and things like that."

"I see," said Jim.

"Anyway, I ran the clock on Arnold," she continued, "and based on what he told me, I see them as a hot prospect."

And that was fine. It was great news. She had a heavy-duty presentation scheduled with them in another week, and if it went well, All-Points would become a customer. But this wasn't what I wanted to know. Ten minutes after they started, I knew the whole exercise had been a waste of time. Their presentation was a status report on specific products and individual customers. They weren't giving me the overall strategy. In fact, I was embarrassed that their focus was so low, so near-sighted on the little pieces, when I wanted them to stand back and see what they were all about. It wasn't their fault. It was all mine. They just didn't understand what I really expected.

So I let them finish, and sit down around the table, then I tried another tack.

"What I want to know is *how* you intend to sell from start to finish," I said.

They turned and exchanged looks with each other.

"In order to get sales, certain things have to happen in certain ways," I said, trying to drop a hint. "A sequence of events has to take place."

Not a glimmer.

"Think in basic terms. What are we trying to do when we sell?" I asked.

Jennifer volunteered an answer, saying, "We're trying to get someone with purchasing power to say yes to us."

"Right. But before we get to yes—or no—a number of things have to happen first," I said. "Do you just walk in and hand the potential customer a pen to sign the contract?"

They laughed at that.

"Sure would be nice if it happened that way," one of the guys said.

"But it doesn't. Seriously, how many times does a stranger come to you on the street and just hand you money?"

That didn't need an answer. I got up from the table and went to a chalkboard at the front of the room.

"To make a sale, what's the very first thing you've got to do?" I asked them.

"You've got to let them know who you are and that you've got something worthwhile to offer," said Jennifer.

"Okay. Or in other words, you've got to create and shape their impression of who we are. You've got to build our image in their minds. Let's say that's where it begins, with building an image to attract the attention of potential customers and get them to take us seriously," I said. "After that, what happens?"

"You've got to call on the prospect and make a presentation," someone else said.

"Wait a minute. How do you know who to call on?" I asked.

"We need some leads."

"That's it. We've got to generate some leads," I said. "And how do you know if it's a good lead or a bad lead?"

"You've got to qualify the prospect."

I began writing these down: *image building, lead generation, qualifying*.

"Now we're ready to go for the sale," I said. "We've decided we have something to offer them for our mutual advantage. What happens next?"

"We make a presentation."

"Right. A *presentation*." I added that to the list on the board. "And after you've given your spiel?"

"Most of the time, they'll have questions and doubts."

"Exactly. They'll have *objections*. But let's say we satisfy those. What next?"

"Ask for their business."

"You *close* the sale in some fashion," I said, writing that down.

Nobody said anything more. I turned to them.

"Well? Is that it?

One or two nods around the table.

"You just take the money and run?" I asked.

"No, of course, not," Jennifer said. "We've obviously got to deliver what we've promised. We've got to give them service. We've got to try to build additional business and so on."

"Which implies some kind of continuing relationship with the customer, at least on some types of sales," I said, "because you want them to buy from you again and again."

I wrote down *customer relations, customer service,* and *resale (or repeat business).*

"So as you can see," I said, "there are nine different steps in the selling process. Each step has to be successfully completed in series for the total sale to be successful."

1. Image building
2. Lead generation } Presale
3. Qualifying

4. Presentation
5. Answering objections } Sale
6. Closing

7. Customer relations
8. Customer service } Continuing Sale or
9. Resale (repeat business) Postsale

"Now there are a lot of different ways to go about accomplishing each of those nine steps," I said. "There are any number of images we might project and many ways to go about building them. There are a variety of strategies we could use to generate leads. There are various methods and issues with respect to qualifying . . . and so on through all nine. What you have to decide is what are the most *appropriate* ways in your particular mode of selling."

By now, I had met and talked with the salespeople enough so that they understood something about the quadrants and why they were on different teams. So I said, "Let me give you an example. You all know of Aaron Abbott. If I were a super-closer like Aaron, I would want to build an image of my product as innovative and unique. To generate leads, I might want to hire a PR firm to create a media event at which I would demonstrate my product in a theatrical light. . . ."

And I went through all nine steps the way a super-closer would approach them. In the end, we had quite a list:

Closer Selling

1. *Image building*
   - Project and demonstrate high performance, uniqueness, innovation.
   - Make use of high-profile individuals.
   - Show state-of-the-art technical savvy.

2. *Lead generation*
   - Create demonstration events (media/PR events).
   - Offer free product trials.

3. *Qualifying*
   - Most of the prospects question the basic need or benefit of the product (cold market).
   - Seek the gateswinger open to risk, excited by the vision of big opportunity.
   - The ultimate decision maker will have total budget control to commit to sale.

4. *Presentation*
   - Is usually one-on-one.
   - Should be theatrical, exciting.
   - Demonstrate the product.
   - Show off product's uniqueness.
   - Help the prospects to picture themselves enjoying the benefits (that is, build the dream).

   - Presentation bottom line: The benefit is really worthwhile.

5. *Answering objections*
   - Objection: Customers question need for the product.

- Response: Closers demonstrate opportunity and return on investment, and give the prospects "permission to buy."

6. *Closing*

- Make an immediate request for the order.
- Offer limited time period to buy (emphasize risk of losing the opportunity).
- Note the restricted availability.

7. *Customer relations*

- This is seldom a continuing relationship.

8. *Customer service*

- Refund money, replace product if customer is dissatisfied.

9. *Resale (repeat business)*

- Usually none.

"That's how a successful super-closer would deal with the nine steps," I said. "What I'd like to know is how you and your team might approach them."

The initial reaction from the group was slow. While waiting for someone to speak up, I saw Jim Woller in the back of the room. He was rubbing his chin thoughtfully.

Finally one of the salesmen said, "I don't know that there's much I would change."

To my surprise, Jim Woller was the one who spoke up. "Really? You'd sell the same way as Aaron? Isn't it obvious that the last three steps would be far less important for Aaron than they would be for you?"

"It's a project-oriented sale when we install something like a 720 Network," the salesman argued. "How many other 720 Networks are we going to sell to the same customer?"

"But in order to do the installation and complete the sale, you certainly have to be concerned about customer relations,"

Jim said. "After Aaron closes, he moves on. But you're going to be dealing with that same customer at least for the duration of the project."

"And even if we can't sell the customer another 720," said Jennifer, "we can sell system improvements and other things down the road."

"Or you might sell the same product to a different division in the same company," added Jim.

"I can see a lot of other differences between our approach and the closer's, too," said Jennifer. "Lead generation, for instance. We need credibility more than flash. So we might want to have our PR people place some case histories and bylined professional articles for us."

Someone else on the team thought that he might prefer to do a free seminar as an event rather than a glitzy demonstration. Well, they were getting the hang of it. I started making a list for them as they talked:

Consultive Selling

1. *Image building*

    - Use a high-level team approach.
    - Be professional, expert, competent.
    - Build technical credibility.

2. *Lead generation*

    - Give away free educational information.
    - Place bylined articles in professional journals.
    - Schedule speaking engagements.
    - Offer information booklets, seminars, and how-to manuals.

3. *Qualifying*

    - Most of the prospects are lukewarm (that is, they believe in the benefits of better information and communication, but are not sure our technology is the best way to achieve it).

• Prospects at least need to be open to new methods of accomplishing promised benefits.

4. *Presentation*

  • Demonstrate the initial concept to high-level decision makers.
  • Educate the customer in the basic concepts.
  • Offer case history support.
  • Provide a team to design a solution tailored to fit the prospect.

  • Presentation bottom line: Our methods really produce benefits/results.

5. *Answering objections*

  • Objection: Customers (line managers especially) will worry about interruption of operations.
  • Response: Must convince them of long-term improvement that will be more than worth the trouble of interruptions.

6. *Closing*

  • Agree on a concept or pilot test.
  • Sign letters of agreement.
  • Develop project schedules that customer agrees to.

7. *Customer relations*

  • Conduct continuing, patient one-on-one education.
  • Produce information mailings.
  • Ensure guaranteed responsiveness.
  • Document and communicate constantly—keep the customer involved and aware of our attention and progress.

8. *Customer service*

  • Design and install the system.
  • Train the customer's users.

- Provide followup system maintenance.
- Track benefits to demonstrate the wisdom of the customer's decision, and find areas for further improvement.

9. *Resale (repeat business)*

- Consultive sales tend to be project-oriented, so there is often little chance to sell same product to same customer.
- Maintain contact to sell new products or to expand the sale to additional divisions or functions.
- Eventually switch to relationship selling for continuing business.

When we were done, I asked them which of the steps they thought were most important to a consultive style of selling. After some discussion the team decided four were key: image building, presenting, answering objections, and customer relations.

For the rest of the meeting we worked on ways they could be the best in those four critical steps. Jennifer, it was decided, would talk to Brian in public relations about measures for better image building and improved information mailings. Others in the team would make arrangements to get more training to improve their skills in presenting and answering objections. And customer relations would be a steady, day-by-day effort to stay on top of what was happening.

The next day, we met with Charlie Summers and the Key Accounts sales team and went through the same basic process. Here is what the relationship salespeople came up with:

Relationship Selling

1. *Image building*

- Project our dependability, loyalty to established customers.
- Emphasize nonbureaucratic, personal service.

- Show we are caring and friendly, and that we understand "they want to know how much we care before they care how much we know."
- Demonstrate knowledge of product, customer, market.

2. *Lead generation*

- Offer a free service (an audit, analysis, evaluation, check-up, etc.).
- Treat prospects like customers until they are customers.

3. *Qualifying*

- Most of the prospects believe in the products, but aren't sure we are the best providers (warm market).
- Most of the prospects will question our ability or commitment to provide the extra service.

4. *Presentation*

- Show capabilities.
- Build personal relationships.
- Demonstrate personal as well as company commitments.
- Offer other client relationships as supporting evidence.

Presentation bottom line: We are the best provider.

5. *Answering objections*

- Objection: Customer is likely to invoke not-invented-here objection.
- Response: Convince customer of superior delivery and added-value advantages of doing business with us.

6. *Closing*

- Acceptable closing technique: a handshake.

- One-on-one development of personal relationships.
- Specification bid.
- Quick response to customer need.

7. *Customer relations*

- Regular personal contact by account manager.
- Tours of our facilities.
- Entertainment.
- Trade shows.

8. *Customer service*

- Top-level service delivery skills.
- Emphasis on accessibility to key account managers.
- Hotlines and internal systems for quick response.

9. *Resale (repeat business)*

- Expand product or service purchases from same user.
- Solicit referral sales to other users in the same company, other companies.
- Perform annual relationship audits.

After we had the list, Charlie Summers said, "I can't see that the first few steps are as important to us as the later ones. A lot of times, we know the customers long before they actually become customers."

"What we need," said another of the Key Accounts people, "are ways to stay close to the prospect on a regular basis. Then, whenever opportunity finally knocks, we've got to be ready at the door."

They were right. The really important steps to winning in a relationship market are in the latter part of the nine. Relationship salespeople have to be very good at answering objections, closing, customer relations, customer service, and getting repeat sales. Steps such as image building and lead generation often happen over an extended period of time.

"I'd like to see us revive the Elemenco golf tournament," said Charlie. "It was done away with in the name of efficiency and cost cutting, but in years past I know at least half my customers were sure to show up."

The rest of the team thought that was a great idea, too. Jim Woller was swayed. He even agreed to authorize the funding out of his own budgets. On the more serious side, from my point of view, they talked about quick response procedures—being able to do the kind of thing Charlie had done when Bob Lilly had his software problem.

At one point, Charlie said, "On our side of the market, it's as much or more a battle of hearts as it is a battle of minds."

The following afternoon, we met with the V Team and talked about display selling through the same nine steps. I had to help them out more than the other groups, because even though the company had been moving toward a display style in many respects, we didn't have some of the key things that would make us strong in that type of market—like an image of being a dominant supplier and a standard-bearer, pricing that would make us appear to be the best buy, and brand loyalty. The list we came up with was more a list of goals than anything else:

Display Selling

1. *Image building*

   - Be perceived as dominant supplier.
   - Observe the standards: dependable, acceptable quality.
   - Provide good price and convenience.

2. *Lead generation*

   - Maintain brand awareness through advertising.
   - Offer buying convenience and price advantage.
   - Use purchase-convenience tools and incentives (mail-order catalogs, 800 numbers, discount coupons, and special promotions).

3. *Qualifying*

- The customers know they want or need the product (hot market).
- Market will question a supplier's features and options.
- Convince customers we offer the best fulfillment of their needs.

4. *Presentation*

- Stress flexible feature and option packaging.
- Include catalogs and point-of-purchase displays.
- Emphasize ease or convenience of purchase and delivery as well as price advantage.

- Presentation bottom line: We offer the best buy.

5. *Answering objections*

- Objection: Buyers, who are often entrenched in established habits, may say, "That's not the way we've always done things."
- Response: Convince customer we offer the better buy, and make the buyer look good in his or her organization for giving us the order.

6. *Closing*

- Offer sales promotions.
- Provide telephone-ordering service.
- Hold annual contract negotiations.
- Accept credit cards or offer convenient terms.

7. *Customer relations*

- Annual organization-to-organization meetings.
- Surveys of customer satisfaction.

8. *Customer service*

- Accept returns, provide substitution.

- Automate delivery tracking, share information.
- Do joint-usage forecasting.

9. *Resale (repeat business)*

- Emphasize inventory restocking.
- Offer special discounts, incentives.
- Provide special financing.
- Promote brand loyalty.

"What do you think are the keys to a display market?" I asked them.

"Repeat business," Kevin Duttz suggested.

"Customer relations and customer service," said someone else.

"You're right," I said. "In a high-volume market, you know you've got a lot of prospects. You don't have to spend as much time qualifying, and you don't want to waste too much time on a single prospect in presenting or overcoming objections. The selling has to be nonconfrontational with the customer and systematized for efficiency."

"Keep 'em coming back for more," said Kevin.

"Exactly," I said. "The main draws are price and convenience. Given the company's current financial status, there isn't much we can work with on price. So excellent customer service is the only real tool we've got that will make a difference."

They spent the rest of the meeting talking about ways we could make doing business with the customer more convenient. They talked about ideas such as inventory stocking programs. One sales rep suggested working out a just-in-time program. Someone else recommended product-of-the-week promotions. Still someone else wanted us to develop a quick approval procedure for customer credit. It was great to watch them get involved and come up with the ideas.

By the end of it all, I was feeling good about a number of things. The teams were focused on exactly the kind of selling that would make each of them successful. We had given them guidelines, but had left it to them to use their own creativity in supplying the specific measures. Much of the rest was really a matter of letting each team do what its members were already inclined to do—what many of them had been doing individually for a long time.

Jim Woller had participated in all of it. I got the sense that he seemed to understand what I had been trying to get across to him for a couple of months. He came up to me before he left and said, "It all makes sense now."

That was enough for me. It was the best thing he could have said.

I also talked with Ann after the meeting.

"I really get the idea things are shaping up," I said to her. "We really seem to be on the right track."

It was the end of the day; I had my feet on an empty chair and was sitting back with my hands clasped behind my head. Ann was in a similar attitude; she was leaning back, her shoes kicked off.

"And it hasn't been that long," she said.

"Well, it will be months before we see major results," I said. "It can take a long while for a change like this to mature and deliver big time. But I think we're definitely headed in the right direction."

"Do you think we'll see anything by next quarter?" she asked.

"Right. Well, we might. We might," I said. "In fact, I'd bet we'll see some good signs."

She put her hands behind her head, the way I was holding mine, and something about the way she was sitting made her look especially attractive just then. Which made me uncomfortable.

I sat forward.

"What's the matter?" she asked.

"Nothing," I said. "Nothing at all."

"Your face changed."

I stood up. I glanced toward the door. No one. We were alone.

"Nothing. You just look good," I told her.

"Thank you," she said.

"Are you okay with me saying something like that?" I asked her.

"Yeah," she said. "It's fine. From you."

I turned to get my briefcase and I heard her say something, but I couldn't make it out.

"What did you say?" I asked her.

"I said you look pretty good yourself."

I laughed. I said, "Thanks. Let's get out of here."

She put her shoes on, and we gathered our stuff and walked out together. Even though nothing could happen between us, I had another reason to feel good.

When I lived in California, I owned a Porsche. I was driving into the mountains on a four-lane highway, going faster than necessary, but in no particular hurry. I passed some guy in one of the older Vettes, the kind that was all engine, and was about to ease right when I saw from the edge of my eye that the Vette was still beside me. The jerk was making a race of it and up ahead, with gorge on one side and mountain on the other, the four lanes narrowed down to two.

Riding the bus to work in Chicago one morning after Ann and I had set up the sales teams, I remembered that experience while thinking about Gene Cherson. Funny how the mind works.

No one ever directly said so, but there was a race between us. The race was Ann Lansky and I with the Central Region against Gene Cherson and Jim Woller with all the other domestic regions. I could sense it; I believe everybody in marketing could. I say that Jim Woller was on Cherson's side because he still was. Woller may have understood and even believed in what I was trying to do, but Cherson was still his boss and he was still obliged to manage sales Cherson's way.

Our internal competition was quiet. After the initial confrontation when he came back, Cherson and I seldom dealt face-to-face. He would invite me to meetings only when product development, still my official area of responsibility, was specifically involved. From time to time, I attempted to make some peace by stopping by his office to explain how Ann and her people were doing, but he seemed to resent this. I sent him copies of key reports and memos, but he never responded. Like the guy in the Vette, he seemed determined to prove that his machine had horsepower.

Winter warmed toward spring and the first quarter closed. In Ann's region, we had a modest gain over the fourth quarter, and a thin increase in sales over the first quarter of the previous year, but nothing remarkable, nothing decisive. Which was about as I expected; it would take time for the salespeople to get around to all the customers and for things to develop.

In the other four regions, performance was not terrible, but also mediocre. A few victories—a 720 Network in the Northeast, a couple of large contracts for work stations in the Southwest—offset the disgruntled customers who withdrew their business. The second quarter, I expected, was when we'd see the first true signs of success or failure in the Central Region. On the books we started the period more or less even with the other regions.

While we waited for results, we all had plenty to do. When I wasn't minding product development, I spent a great deal of time on the road, some of it with Ann, meeting with the other salespeople in the Central Region and arranging the kind of matching we had done in the Chicago office.

I invested many hours in dialogue with everyone from office managers to the salespeople to customers to service technicians. On a good day, in the course of one of those dialogues, a face or two in the room would become enlivened and I would know I had broken through. Much of the time, though, the expressions ranged from indifferent to unreadable. It would have been nice if everyone I talked to had jumped to their feet and shouted, "Yes, yes, that's it! Now it all makes sense! You've saved my career!" But that doesn't happen. Most people who stand to benefit from a new idea are noncommittal or at best passively intrigued when they first hear about it. I knew that and I was prepared to endure the slow process of acceptance.

Meanwhile, back in greater Chicago, early words and signs began to trickle in. Jennifer Hone's dealing with All-Points Express were successful; Arnold Sternholtz signed up for an Apogee System based on the design configuration she supervised. Another member of the consultive team, a young guy named Ron Ferris, who was just a couple of years out of Carnegie-Mellon, brought in a contract for a 720 Network for a bank in Milwaukee.

Charlie Summers personally introduced another member of the relationship team to Bob Lilly of the Chicago and Midwest Railroad, and even stayed involved until Bob was comfortable with the new guy. Ann told me that Charlie was spending significant time taking care of Haikkyu, and he had won a small contract for manufacturing a circuit to calculate and give a digital readout of fuel mileage. It was clearly a test for us, and it might lead to a full-production contract later this year or early in the next. He also got an unexpected call from hardened bargain-hunter Petrina Yarkovic of that restaurant service company called Santlinni. Martha Beckley had made Petrina call; Midcontinent had delivered the Mitsugami equipment, which worked fine, but they had totally botched the setup and service end of the sale. Small victories are sometimes the sweetest.

As for Kevin Duttz and the V Team, they mostly kept close to the phones and the fax machines. From the looks of what control records Ann and I could bring up on our computer screens, they were indeed making a lot of sales on the products they were assigned.

News on Aaron Abbott was mixed. He was out of town most of the time, working on a national basis and selling significant numbers of PowerCase. I heard that he had lined up at least one car dealership in Los Angeles for the traveling-office concept. Gene had finally dropped his objections to our one PowerSeat sale. That order was installed on a couple of Diamond Skies' planes and Brian generated some nice publicity on it. When they both were in town at the same time, Aaron was working on Reed to put some capital into developing MAXA-DIL. But Morrison was loath to take a risk like that while the company was bouncing between losing money and breaking even.

On his own, Aaron was doing fine—a great job for as much as one man could do. But I happened to be in Cherson's office when a call came in from a customer in Philadelphia. Aaron had sold them some PowerCases that were supposed to integrate with the network that we'd sold them. Well, it was one of our older networks and the new machines didn't integrate. The Philadelphia customer was upset.

Cherson right away called Aaron, put him on the speaker phone, and asked him about handling the problem.

"They've got a money-back guarantee," said Aaron. "Have them return the units, and I'll resell them."

"Money back like hell! We need the sale!" said Gene. "So let's fix their problem for them."

"Well, why didn't you have technical service people take care of it?" Aaron asked.

"Because you sold them the PowerCases," said Gene.

"Look, Gene, I am currently in Denver; tonight I will be in Phoenix; the problem is in Philadelphia. I can't personally follow up on these kinds of sales. It may be three or four months before I'm back in Philadelphia again, and anyway I don't see that as my responsibility," Aaron said. "If you want followup, then get me an assistant. Or do I have to pay for that out of my own pocket, too?"

Gene shook his head, which of course Aaron couldn't see, and said, "All right, all right. You go on to Phoenix. We'll take care of it."

After he hung up, Gene began to complain to me. Since he wasn't sharing much of anything with me these days, I saw it as an extraordinary slip of the tongue.

"All Abbott wants is his commission," said Gene. "After the sale, he doesn't care."

"I don't think Aaron is being insensitive," I said. "He just can't take care of it."

Gene stood up and flung his arms out in frustration, a common gesture for him in those days. "You were here when Morrison brought him in. What was it that Morrison thought was so wonderful about him? Abbott is smooth, I'll grant you that. He had his own little $50 million company, but big deal!"

Frustration vented, Gene sat down again. "Abbott won't last with us," he continued. "He just doesn't fit into this company."

"You may be right," I said. "As for the problem in Phila-delphia, you may want one of our consultive types in that region to go in and talk to them."

"*What* kind of types?"

While I worded an answer in my mind, Gene looked at me coldly and, as if telling me this was none of my concern, said, "I'll have Woller look into it."

So much for that.

As spring grew on, Gene went from working partial days to full days. He delegated more responsibility than he used to, but everyone was worried he would keel over again with another heart attack. Gene was confounding his own doctors, who would have had him using a walker to get around by now. While I understood his drive, I couldn't understand where he got his energy. Compared to the man who had been rushed to the hospital a few months before, Gene Cherson in all public appearances was Hercules.

He began traveling to the other regions "to motivate them." Word came back that on more than one occasion these motivational visits had turned into shouting matches. The regional managers probably *wished* he would have another heart attack.

Word began to get around on other topics as well. SAMMY, that program Jim Woller had developed to sell more of everything to everybody, was a total flop. Woller himself now disowned it as much as he possibly could. And from a couple of sources in the other regions, Ann pieced together bits of news to form an interesting conclusion: In order to survive, nobody was totally abiding by Gene Cherson's original plan. When cus-tomers complained that they didn't like the sales rep they had been assigned, the sales managers, on the sly, had been swapping accounts, matching the salespeople with market and customer on an informal basis. Without knowing it, they were actually using the quadrant system, but they had no pure strategy. They were just reacting to whatever storms of discontent blew in.

For me, days in this period blended together, but a num-ber of little things happened in my own small sphere. I tried at one point to have my job title changed from "product develop-ment" to "market development," which really fit better with what I was doing, but Cherson blocked it. I also bought that townhouse near Ann, just because it was a decent place and I needed somewhere to live. Ann and I got to be better friends. We had cause, after all; we were in this together, this race, not that either of us wanted it. But we stayed just friends.

On those trips we made to the nether Midwest reaches of her region, we typically would spend the day with the salespeople, usually go out to dinner with them, and retire, the two of us, to separate rooms at the Holiday Inn or wherever.

One time, on an odd evening with nothing to do in Iowa City, we went to the movies together. Afterward, she joined me for a drink in the motel lounge where a kid in a cowboy hat sang songs by Neil Diamond while his synthesizer, pretending to be his band, went "shickey-boom, shickey-boom" beside him. It was too loud to talk, so we danced. Later that same night, I stared at the concrete block wall, painted high-gloss white, that separated our two rooms and wondered what Ann was doing on the other side. Was she staring at the wall and wondering what I was doing? I almost went and knocked on her door to find out, but I didn't. Sometime very late, I decided this was stupid and crazy, that I was too focused on Ann because I was too focused on work, and that when I got back to Chicago, the hell with it, I would have to meet some new women. I spent the summer going out with schoolteachers who still lived with their mothers and cosmetologists who thought I was wonderful because I wore a suit, while Ann and I stayed just friends.

As the second quarter came to a close, I tried to find out the numbers for the company in general and the Central Region in particular. Just about everything I'd been gleaning from Ann indicated a good quarter for us. But my few buddies in the controller's office were reluctant to give me any raw figures, so I had to wait like everyone else.

In the middle of an afternoon, Morrison's secretary called and asked me to come to Reed's office right away. She didn't say why. At the elevator, I ran into Gene Cherson and Jim Woller, who had just pressed the "up" button. Cherson stared at me and said nothing. Woller looked down at his shoes.

We got on the elevator together, we got off together, and we all walked into Reed's office together. He was in his shirt sleeves, computer printouts covering his desk. Through the window, Lake Michigan was shimmering blue and the sky was sunny. The only cloud was the one that seemed to cover Reed's face.

"Gentlemen," he said, "I thought you might like to have a peek at the financial summaries for the second quarter. I know you've all been anxious to find out how we've been doing. Unfortunately, I think, you'll be disappointed. I know I was."

Reed doesn't lose his temper very often, but he lost it that day.

"Dammit, Gene, you've been promising me a turnaround for months. Where the hell is it? Just look at these numbers! What am I supposed to tell the board? How could we possibly be doing this badly?"

Jim Woller was examining one of the printouts—probably trying to avoid eye contact with Reed.

"The picture isn't totally bleak," Woller said after Reed quieted down. "Look here . . . we had a 32 percent sales *increase* in one region."

"Which region was that?" Gene asked.

"The ah, let's see . . . the Central Region," said Woller.

As if he didn't believe it, Gene took the printout from Jim and read it himself.

"That's right," said Reed. "The Central Region. Which I happen to know has been applying that quadrant idea that David brought in. Do you see that, Gene? A 32 percent increase in sales. And after you give me your best explanation on why the other four regions did so poorly, we are all going down to see Ann Lansky and personally congratulate not only her, but her entire staff."

Which was what we did. Morrison called first to make sure she'd be there, then the four of us went down to the conference room on her floor, where Ann and every salesperson in the office had gathered. Morrison had brought with him 32 long-stemmed roses, one for each percentage point of increase, presented them to Ann, and shook her hand.

"You kept an open mind. You had the guts to try something new. You and everybody in this room worked hard. And it paid off," said Morrison.

His words were pointed, I think, as much at Gene Cherson as they were to Ann.

"I give you my very best," Morrison continued. "And though I won't quote a figure here and now, I'll tell you that you can all expect something a little extra when the next checks come out. When you do something right at Elemenco, you hear about it with more than just words. Keep up the good work."

Gene was a good actor and did his best to echo Morrison's sentiments. So did Woller. And so finally did I. By the time I was pumping Ann's hand, she was beaming and all but blinking back tears. I was glad for her.

But a 32 percent gain in one region was not going to save the whole company.

19

One morning back in May, long before the second quarter closed, I had an interesting conversation with Nick Dominica and Robb Jamison. I was on my way to get a cup of coffee, and when I reached the alcove where the pots were stationed, I found Nick playing the gracious host by pouring coffee into Robb's cup.

"What brings you to Chicago?" I asked Robb.

"We're going to present the new campaign," he said.

"Really? The one we talked about with the four different images and thrusts?" I asked.

"Well . . ." Robb looked at Nick to try to see what he could safely say. "No, not based on that."

Advertising, of course, ceased to be under my influence as soon as Gene came back. Having many other things to concern me, I hadn't bothered to stay on top of developments in that sphere.

"We had to scrap that," said Nick.

"Because of Gene?" I asked.

Nick looked over his shoulder to see who was listening. Then, in a lower voice, he said, "Yeah, it was Gene who canceled it. But mostly we stopped because it just wasn't going to work."

"How do you know it wasn't?'"

"We did research," said Robb. "It turned out that Ted, the creative director on your account, was right. Each of the ads worked individually and tested well. But as a total package, they provoked mass confusion. Nobody understood what kind of company Elemenco was supposed to be. Which, by the way, pretty much agrees with market research of your own about how customers perceive you now."

"So we canceled the four-way approach and went with an umbrella theme," said Nick.

They took me back to Nick's office and showed me artwork for the ads. Most of them had images that would work best in a display market. I didn't interfere. I had other things to worry about.

As I say, that happened back in May. By now the ads were appearing. But in the meantime, I had done quite a bit of thinking and analysis.

Soon after the books for the third quarter started, Morrison called a big meeting on cash flow. The head of operations was there, along with his heads of inventory control and production planning. They were on one side of the table, while Gene Cherson, Jim Woller, and I were on the other. Reed Morrison and our chief financial officer sat at opposite heads of the table.

The main issue had to do with the unsold inventory sitting in warehouses around the country. It seemed that, in every product and component category, portions of the inventory were turning over rapidly while other portions were getting a bit dusty. Some components were back-ordered, which meant lost or delayed sales; others wouldn't sell even with a substantial discount.

After we listened to a litany of inventory levels, Morrison took over. "Okay, Gene, as I recall, you said last year something about getting it right, about *listening* to our customers, and producing exactly what the market wanted. So what happened? How come we've got some product that's nearly impossible to unload, and other product that we can't make fast enough?"

"Well," said Gene, "last year, as you pointed out, we wanted to do things right. We did a survey of our customers. We asked what they wanted. And we planned out production accordingly, based on what they told us. My guess—and I must admit that it is only a guess—is that in the intervening time, our customers' needs changed. What they thought they needed turned out not to be the case."

"I can't believe I'm hearing this!" Morrison said. "We damn near bet the company on the idea that production based on market research and a new sales organization would save the day. Now you're blaming the customer! Well, Gene, you said the customer would buy all this stuff. I want to know why you haven't sold it."

Gene began turning red. "Well, obviously we didn't get the mix right," he said. "Perhaps production planning misread our projections—"

The head of operations jumped on that excuse, arguing that everyone had sat down in a number of meetings the previous year to hash this out, and everyone had signed off on the production levels.

It got quiet in the room.

Then I heard my own voice saying, "I think I can explain."

It was a planned move on my part. I had started preparing for this as soon as I heard what the meeting was going to be about.

"I think we fell into a trap that many companies before us have fallen into, and probably many others after us as well," I said. "The problem is not really that our customers' needs changed. Needs do change, sometimes rapidly, but that's not the particular snake that bit us this time. And it's not that we didn't plan thoroughly, because certainly enough effort and care went into that."

"Then why do we have these inventory problems?" Morrison asked.

"Because customers lie," I said.

A few nervous chuckles followed that remark.

"That's the plain truth of the matter," I said. "Customers lie. They don't know they're lying. It's not a deliberate attempt to screw us up or cause us problems. But we all know that every customer has a wish list. They wish we'd do this, they wish we'd make that. It's smart for us to talk to the customers and find out what they want. Only we should never count on them telling us the absolute truth. Just because we produce what they *say* they want doesn't mean the customer will actually *buy* a product with all these options and features if we produce it for them."

By now, a number of people in the room were familiar with the quadrant I used to explain markets and development. I got to my feet and found an easel and drawing paper at the corner of the room. With a red marker, I showed that as products and services develop, they tend to follow a rather predictable pattern:

Simple (High tech, low touch)
↓
Complex (High tech, high touch)
↓
Standard (Low tech, high touch)
↓
Commodity (Low tech, low touch)

I reminded Reed of our discussion a few months before on PowerSeat. When a new technology comes along, the products created by it start out having one application, one shape, limited features. As time passes, and the customers begin to accept the product, they begin to demand more. So the product becomes more and more complex. Other companies get into the act. Finally, though, the market demands order and an end to incompatibility, and forces the producers to standardize. Rather than promoting more variety, though, increasing demand often causes more and more product parity. Finally, what most of the market demands enters the status of being a commodity.

"Most options and features go through an evolution similar to the product itself," I said.

I drew this out for them:

Luxury model option
↓
Luxury model standard
↓
Standard model option
↓
Standard model standard

"We might want to look at what happened in the American automobile market in the 1970s and 1980s," I said.

When the Japanese began to become significant competition to the domestic car makers, the American companies were offering a tremendous range of options—many of which the buyers either didn't care about or didn't want to pay extra to get. This bewildering range of options offered by American automakers was actually a huge tracking and control problem and to some degree a waste of money, because the marketplace didn't care about a lot of the options.

Enter the Japanese automakers. They reduced the range of options *and* made more options into standard features. This not only reduced the manufacturing and inventory complexities, which saved somewhat on costs, but it also pleased car buyers, who perceived this as higher value.

In our case, I explained, there were a number of things we could do in each market. Working backward through the markets, on products in a display market, for instance, we might standardize all features and restrict the number of models. On products in a relationship market, we probably would want to seek market niches and offer a variety of standard options. In a consultive market, we might want to leave things open and allow the designers freedom to bring in whatever features and options the customer required. In a closer market, the problem is greatly reduced, because the product is so young—and often so simple—that there aren't any options; it's a take-it-or-leave-it proposition.

"But there are many, many factors that figure into the equation," I said. "For instance, as we go from new high technology and on through the cycle to commodity products, we all know there is a dynamic relationship between volume and profit margin. On a commodity, you have a slim margin, but you make your money on volume. On high technology, volume is small, so you keep your margin high. Partly to help justify your price in a consultive market, you want to bundle together value-added services with your product at what seems to be more than worth the price. To gain an advantage in a display market, you want to show the lowest possible price, so you unbundle and charge extra for special services. Do you see what I mean? It's all very complex."

"Yeah, well, that's all very interesting, professor," said Morrison, "but what are we going to do to solve our inventory problems?"

I gestured with my marker.

"Don't you see?" I asked them. "The very complexity makes it virtually impossible for us to pursue the strategy we've attempted for the past few years. We have tried to pursue every market and every opportunity."

"And what is wrong with that?" asked Gene.

"Nothing, in an ideal world," I said. "But we work in the real world where there are real limits. Every company, as we all know, has an internal culture, and part of the function of that culture is to set limits on what is acceptable and unacceptable, possible and impossible. A culture that makes it right to be a crusader for new technology makes it wrong to go with the flow and abide by standards on an old technology—and vice versa. A culture that makes it right to customize service to individual customers in high-touch markets doesn't permit you the simplicity and efficiency you need to survive in low-touch markets."

Gene was glaring at me, but every other face in the room was receptive.

"Several months ago, our ad agency tried to come up with a campaign that tried to define an image for us in all four markets," I said. "Today, I've got to thank Gene Cherson for canceling that campaign, because it was wrong. It would have been a disaster if we'd gone ahead with it."

That remark softened Gene's glare, but didn't eliminate it.

"It was wrong for the same reason our whole strategy has been wrong," I said. "As this meeting proves, just like last quarter's performance proved, we can no longer afford to try to be all things to all markets. It just doesn't work. We have to decide where to focus our efforts."

At the easel, I flipped to a new page and began to make some lists. Here's the first one:

High-tech, low-touch company focus
High-profile individuals
Emphasis on research and development

Theatrical airs
Optimism and excitement
Crusading efforts

"Now I ask you, is that Elemenco? I don't think so," I said. "Yet we're trying to compete in that market with PowerCase and PowerSeat—even while we need a different kind of focus with our Apogee System and 720 Network in a consultive market."

High-tech, high-touch company focus

Orient ourselves to market needs
Nurture a corporate image
Do conceptual selling
Take total responsibility for benefit
Have a team focus
Emphasize design
Stress training and education

"Now, is *that* Elemenco?" I asked. "I think that fits us better, but you tell me. Is that the best company we can be? Look at another type."

Low-tech, high-touch company focus

Dominate market niches
Develop specialty product or service images
Have a network orientation
Emphasize customer satisfaction
Strive for sales and service leadership
Have comprehensive production capacities

"What about that for our company focus? Should we try to be that kind of company? If we want to do well with low-tech, high-touch products, like our less advanced networks and work stations, we have to try. But not only are we already being pulled in three directions, we also have products in a fourth market, which means we need a fourth type of focus."

Low-tech, low-touch company focus

Brand awareness and loyalty
Being cost-competitive
Sales promotion
Mass media advertising
Distribution ownership
Distributor support

"What I'm telling you is that Elemenco doesn't *have* a focus. We're an *un*focused company," I argued. "And that is the root of most of our problems. Now we could try to find the right balance—in design, marketing, sales, production—for every product we offer. But to try to do that, I believe, would be a lost cause. I believe that the inventory problem we're facing is just another symptom of the overall misconception that Elemenco can be all things to all customers. Before we go any further, we need to answer for ourselves a much more fundamental question: who are we? We have to decide what kind of company Elemenco should become."

Heads now turned to Morrison, who was drinking all this in, and who finally said, "I think I understand what you're saying, David."

Then, to my surprise, he adjourned the meeting—for everyone except me, Gene, and Jim. When the room emptied out, Morrison asked me to close the door so that we would have privacy.

"We're entering into some strategic discussions, and I didn't want word of this to be circulating prematurely," said Morrison. "I want to discuss this confidentially with just the three of you. All right, David. You have the floor again. What exactly are you recommending?"

"I have a specific plan with four steps," I said.

"Which are?"

"First, we continue the approach we've taken in the Central Region and expand it nationally to cover the other regions," I said.

"Good. What else?"

"Based on an analysis I've done to find out where we're really making our net income and where we're not," I said, "the second step would be to focus on customers in the consultive and relationship markets. I have some numbers to show you that will back me up. But in principle, we need to apply our resources in a way that will make us the best in our industry along the high-touch axis."

"Okay. I'm not saying I agree or disagree," said Morrison. "But keep going."

"Third, I suggest we spin off PowerCase and possibly even related products like PowerSeat into a separate company," I said. "The only salesperson we've got who is successful at selling these products is Aaron Abbott. And we've only got one of him. Let's put those products into the kind of entrepreneurial company that can be successful with them."

"And the fourth step?"

I said, "We are not making money in the display market. Our retail chain is the clearest example of that. But look at our other display-category products. You'll see we're making lots of *sales,* but we're not making money. Oddly enough, this is where the telemarketing and efficiency measures we've implemented are strongest. They're just not doing us much good. I think we need to sell off the retail chain as well as our computer cable line, our low-end personal computers, and all other products that fall into commodity status. The exceptions would be products we can add value to and sell successfully in a relationship market. Everything else should go to companies that operate well in display markets, and we should put the money from those divestitures toward improving our positions in consultive and relationship markets."

"What happens to salespeople like Kevin Duttz and the V Team?" asked Jim Woller.

I suggested packaging the sale so that the sales teams for the display market went with those products. Otherwise, we could train a few of those salespeople to be a little bit more like Charlie Summers and the relationship people. In any case, good salespeople were always in demand, whatever the type of market; anyone who was not a misfit in the sales profession would not have to wait in the unemployment line very long even if we had to lay off a few of them.

"But one thing is clear," I said. "We can't stay in all four markets, or even in three. At the very most, we can be in two markets. I think the consultive-relationship combination is the best one for Elemenco. But whether it's a closer-consultive axis, a consultive-relationship axis, or a relationship-display axis, we've got to choose."

Morrison nodded, seeming to agree. I sat down. Then Morrison turned to Gene.

"Okay, you've heard all this, Gene," said Morrison. "Does David's plan have your endorsement?"

"No, it does not have my endorsement," said Gene. "Last year, we made a commitment to a strategy which said we would serve every one of our customers as best we possibly could. I think it would be a major mistake to back away from that strategy now just because of a few mistakes in planning and some setbacks in the marketplace. It's just a question of time."

Morrison looked at Jim Woller. "What do you say, Jim?"

Jim took about ten seconds before he opened his mouth.

"I believe the Central Region proves David's quadrant idea works," he said finally. "And what the hell. It just plain puts it all together in a way that makes sense. I think we ought to try it."

Gene's expression said he felt betrayed.

"Sorry, Gene, but we're out of time," said Jim.

"I agree," said Morrison. "David, we're going to give you your chance. I want your first priority to be drawing up a formal proposal for what you've outlined here. I'll review it quickly with my staff and with the board, and if no flaws are apparent, we'll go with it. Give yourself a new title in the proposal. Make yourself special coordinator of—what should we call it? Let's call it the Quadrant Project."

"Now, Reed, I think you should hold on for a minute," Gene argued. "You're talking about a major shift in strategy and throwing away a lot of good effort and investment. Do you realize that?"

Morrison nodded to Woller and me in a way that indicated we should leave. On my way out, I could hear Gene still protesting over my shoulder.

"Reed, I'm telling you that if you're just going to ignore everything I've worked so hard to set up, I've got to consider it a vote of no confidence," said Gene. "Now is that the way I should take it or not?"

"Well, Gene, I'd say that if that's the interpretation you want to give it, that's up to you," said Morrison. "And if that's the way you feel . . ."

That was all I heard, because the door closed. I went back to my office tense, but elated. About fifteen minutes later, my phone rang. It was Morrison.

"Forget about being special project manager," said Morrison.

My stomach sank. My first thought was that Gene had said some magic words to convince Morrison that my plan was no good.

But Morrison said, "Gene is going to take an early retirement, effective at the end of the week. Consider yourself our new vice-president of marketing and sales."

Epilogue

At five-thirty, the sky was darkening and the sun was a red dot about to sink beneath the orangish plains. Charcoal-gray clouds directly over the city promised snow that night. We had a window table in that restaurant at the top of the John Hancock Building. Ann sat across from me, and Jim Woller sat beside her. I was looking out at the orderly grid of streetlights, bright against the dark blocks of Chicago, and the channeled chaos of traffic streaming along.

"What are you smiling about?" Ann asked me.

"Nothing important," I said. "I was remembering a time in California when I was driving on a highway in the mountains. I was trying to pass this guy and he decided to race me. I couldn't ignore him because the road was narrowing from four lanes down to two."

"What happened?"

"I backed off," I said. "I hit the brakes and fell in behind him."

"That was smart, but why does it make you smile?"

"Well, after the road narrowed, it got more and more twisty as we got higher into the mountains. The guy who wanted the race had to slow down. Couldn't handle the turns. I knew the road and waited for the right chance, passed him on an inside bend where I could see no one was coming, and went on my own merry way. The other guy didn't even try to keep up."

"What made you think of that?" Woller asked me.

I shrugged my shoulders. "Who knows? Like I said, it's not important. Anyway, when this is wrapped up, I'd like it if you'd both stay for a little while. I'm going to buy a bottle or two of champagne."

Both of them seemed pleased by that proposition. We were currently all nursing glasses of club soda and cups of coffee.

"You don't want to start now?" asked Ann. "It could make our answers a lot more interesting."

"Believe me, with this woman, you need all your senses," I said.

I looked toward the elevators. "Here they come."

Brian was leading Lynne Welsey toward our table. We'd arranged to make the interview over dinner, partly for cordiality and partly for convenience. Ann and Jim had just returned from a road trip and had come straight from the airport to be here. I introduced Lynne.

"I'd like you to meet Jim Woller, our executive national sales manager in charge of corporate accounts"—our own lingo meaning he managed relationship sales—"and Ann Lansky, national sales manager for new systems"—which meant she managed the consultive teams.

Lynne shook hands and, after she sat down, the first thing she said to me was "Congratulations."

"Thanks, but why?"

"Well, two reasons," Lynne said. "First, I understand you've had a promotion since the last time we talked."

"That's true."

"And I just finished talking to Reed Morrison," she said, "who gave you a lot of the credit for Elemenco's turnaround late in the year."

"That's generous of him," I said. "But I really think that Ann and Jim, as well as the salespeople who are out there dealing with our customers every day, deserve more of the credit than I do."

"Considering you started the year with two consecutive quarters of losses, Elemenco did extremely well to turn in a $75 million net income," she said.

"Thanks," I said. "Of course, as we've reported, a large portion of that came from our spinoff of PowerComm."

At the end of the year, we had finished setting up the new company and sold a 75 percent interest to Aaron Abbott and some other investors. That gave us a $40 million nonrecurring gain. By keeping a 25 percent share, Elemenco would stay in touch with any new technology that PowerComm developed on its own, and we might purchase some of that technology as it matured into a consultive market. Meanwhile, Elemenco would continue providing key components to existing products like PowerCase, which gave us a small source of ongoing revenue. We had also sold off the cable line for a rather small amount, though that would be on the current year's books, and we had another company interested in buying our retail chain and low-end personal computer products.

"But the other $35 million was made the old-fashioned way, wasn't it?" Lynne asked.

"Very much so," I said.

"Mr. Morrison said it was all in the marketing. How did you manage it?"

"Basically we found a way to enable our salespeople to work with the types of customers they would be most effective with," I said. "After we focused our marketing and began using the right approach, matched with what the customer in each market needed, most of our salespeople became much more successful."

"Can you be more specific?"

"Instead of a salesperson having a 46 percent success rate," I said, "our rate of successful sales shot up to around 82 percent. And we're just beginning to reap the benefits of that. This year I expect to see tremendous growth, and within the next two years, I wouldn't be surprised to see us top $1.5 billion in sales and keep on going."

The waiter brought menus. As we ate dinner, I turned the talking more and more over to Ann and Jim, and let them explain the specifics in greater detail. I also got in a few plugs about some of the new products we had coming—an 840 Network, which would do everything the 720 did but would also have the communication features of our Apogee System; a new standardized office network that was likely to keep the relationship market happy for some time; plus an advanced network based on the forthcoming 486 machine.

As the waiter cleared the plates, Lynne said, "One last question: do you still expect to help build the great company you talked about last January?"

"Absolutely I do," I said.

"Even with selling off much of the product line and pulling back from a sizable portion of the market?"

"The best way to build a great company is to build on its strengths," I said. "Which is exactly what we're doing. We could never have got there trying to be everybody's electronics and computer company. This way, focusing on types of markets where we have an edge in our sales approach, the odds are much more with us."

"I'll say this: you've come a long way in a year," Lynne said.

"Come back again next year, and I think you'll see we've done even better," I offered.

Lynne insisted on paying for her own dinner, though Brian made every attempt to take care of it for her. As she stood up to leave, she put out her hand.

"Good luck to you," she said. "Good luck to all of you." I let go a sigh of relief as she and Brian left.

"That was a hell of a lot better interview than the last one we had with her," I said.

"Yeah, and you didn't even have to throw out any of that blue sky crap," said Woller.

I laughed at first, but then I was puzzled.

"How did you know that's what Gene asked me to do?"

"That's what Gene always called it," said Woller.

I waved for the waiter, and on a separate check ordered the champagne I'd promised.

"This is on me," I said. "It's my personal thanks to both of you for your hard work and support."

We drank some champagne and talked a bit of business. Though the year had ended well, there was still a lot of work to be done. With sales taking off, we would eventually need to add more salespeople and we had to work on our recruiting process to know how to select these individuals. We still needed to deal with compensation issues so that we could keep the star performers and avoid the turnover problems that were still with us to some extent. We had to develop an incentive system that would really work. And we had to develop new customer service functions geared to our chosen markets. Anyway, we talked a while and then Woller left. Ann and I sat there and finished the bottle.

"So how's your love life?" she asked as the business conversation tailed off. "Are you still dating the nurse? Or is it the airport car-rental agent? Or all of the above?"

"None of the above."

"Really? How come?"

"I don't know. A lot of reasons," I said. "Some of them don't want to put up with the hours I put in. With most of them I can't talk about work, which is important to me. They don't understand it or they're not interested. And they don't interest me." I looked at Ann. "Not the way you do."

She seemed shocked. She didn't say anything, but under the tablecloth, I felt her hand touch mine, hold on for a few moments, then squeeze my fingers and let go. Outside, white flakes of snow began to fly past the window.

"We'd better not stay too long," said Ann. "I remember another night of drinking champagne while it snowed outside."

"At least the food tonight was better," I said.

"Oh, I thought my pizza that night was pretty good, especially considering the alternative."

We shared a cab to Lincoln Park. The snow was a few inches deep in the street. When we got to Ann's place, I paid the fare and got out with her. My own place was just around the corner; I could walk. Ann went to the top of her porch steps. When I finished with the cab, I joined her there.

"I'd ask you in," she said, "but it's kind of late."

"You're right," I admitted.

She stood there silently for a second.

"You know, in the last year I've really come to like you a lot," she said. "I've learned new things from you, I tried new things at work because of you, it's paid off, and I've grown a lot in my job. You're not really a boss to me. You're a good friend. And yet I wish it could be more than that."

She put a hand on my arm and leaned forward, I think to kiss me on the cheek, but instead my lips went to hers and stayed there. The kiss went on and on, good and long, but it did end and when it was over she pushed herself away even as she clung with both hands, as if off balance, to the sleeves of my topcoat.

"That didn't happen," she said when she caught her breath. "And it can't happen again."

She unlocked her front door. I thought she was going to go inside without saying goodnight. Instead, she turned on the doorstep and poked my chest with her finger.

"But, mister, if you ever change jobs . . ." she said with a laugh.

"Yeah, well, I don't think that's going to happen," I said, "not any time soon. And—"

"And whose fault is that?" she said.

"What?"

"Whose fault is that, smart guy?" she asked. She was smiling at me. "You know, if you'd just let Gene Cherson run things *his* way, we wouldn't have this little problem. Elemenco would have gone belly-up and we'd both be working for different companies or we'd be out of work and I could invite you in and in the morning we'd go blow our unemployment checks on brunch. But, no, you had to come in and save the company! You had to make Elemenco profitable again!"

I felt my own sad smile curling up.

"I'm still not taking all the blame for that," I said. "In fact, you had something to do with it, as I recall."

"And now look at us," she said. She sighed and then opened her door and stepped inside. "Well, see you tomorrow."

Afterword

The Quadrant Solution is a novel, of course. Elemenco is not a real company, and the characters and situations in the book are fictional. However, the underlying principles of the story are based on actual research. The principles that David Kepler applied to Elemenco affect every type of business and every company in a free-market economy. In fact, if you work in marketing or sales, you can identify the market quadrant(s) of your own sales force and company products.

For a better understanding of the characteristics and ideal criteria of the sales personality types represented in *The Quadrant Solution* by Aaron Abbott, Jennifer Hone, Charlie Summers, and Kevin Duttz, see the Appendix. A checklist that will help you make a rough determination of the quadrants your own company and sales force need to penetrate in your marketplace is available (at no charge) by writing to AMACOM Books.

The quadrant concept was developed by The H. R. Chally Group, a Dayton, Ohio, firm that offers professional selection and market- and customer-assessment services. Chally first developed its selection-validation technology for the United States Justice Department in the mid-1970s through a data-based statistical methodology. The concept of the market quadrant was derived from selection-validation research involving the sales forces of major corporations.

The validation research that confirmed the market quadrant theory involved well over 250 companies in a multitude of industries, but Chally is continually adding to its data base. To date, the firm has tested more than 150,000 individual sales and management candidates, validated success profiles for more than 200 corporate sales forces, and collected quantitative performance ratings and purchasing data from more than 7,000 corporate customers throughout the English-speaking world.

The companies in the Chally data base range from business service companies (Saatchi & Saatchi Advertising, Inc.; United States Cellular; and ADT Security Systems, Inc.) to industrial companies (Monsanto; Zellerbach; and Weyerhaeuser Company) to computers and electronics corporations (TRW, Inc.; Reynolds & Reynolds; NCR Canada; and Delco Electronics) to financial service companies (The Frank Russell Companies; New York Life Insurance Company; American Capital Management & Research, Inc.; and GMAC).

To translate the ideas and the work of The H. R. Chally Group into the story that became *The Quadrant Solution,* business novelist Jeff Cox joined forces with Chally chairman Howard Stevens. Over the course of a year, they worked together, reviewing the concepts and practical applications of the Chally System. Their collaboration included meetings with Chally staff, clients, and colleagues. Jeff Cox created the novel that brought to life the concept of the market quadrant.

What you read about in *The Quadrant Solution,* therefore, is based on hard evidence. One caveat: As you know, a life insurance company can accurately predict life expectancy for groups of men and women, but will not make the same prediction for any *individual* man or woman. Chally's research is more specific because, for practical reasons, companies must make decisions about individual salespeople. While the concepts in this book are statistically valid and appropriate in the general sense for all to apply, companies may wish to develop unique selection profiles that provide precise criteria for their own sales forces.

As mentioned above, you can obtain a free booklet with

a quick checklist that will enable you to determine roughly which quadrants your own company and salespeople need to penetrate in your marketplace. For a copy, write to the publisher:

☐ Please send me the free *Quadrant Solution* booklet.

AMACOM Books
Editorial Department
135 West 50th Street
New York, NY 10020

Remember to include your name, title, and business address.

Appendix

A Closer Look at the Quadrant Solution—Salespeople and Customer Types

Which selling and marketing approach best describes you (or your business)?

Super-Closer Selling
High-Tech/Low-Touch Marketing

High-Tech/Low-Touch Customers:

Are buying on speculation
Often accept a higher degree of risk
Need the salesperson to supply extra emotional push

The Super-Closer Sales Personality:

Extroverted
Energetic
Optimistic
Competitive
Strong work ethic
Success image, but not necessarily frugal
Positive mental attitude
Highly self-confident

Most Important Selling Skills:

Qualifying
Presenting
Answering objections
Closing

Focus of Closing-Style Selling:

Demonstrating the product or service
Interesting the prospect

Selling Style:

Theatrical
Confident

Values Super-Closers Provide:

Concept and vision
Enthusiam
Permission to buy

Technical savvy, especially on a broad-concept level
Opportunity
Sense of urgency

Company Image:

Opportunistic
Innovative
Modern
Unique
Serving *exclusive* customers

Company Focus:

Use high-profile individuals (rainmakers)
Emphasize innovative/breakthrough research and
    development
Generate optimism and excitement
Engage in crusading efforts

Key Marketing Efforts:

Lead generation

Customers Want:

A new or unique product offering:

A novel or revolutionary design
Simple installation and use
Ego enhancement for the buyer
A performance increase tied to uniqueness
A competitive edge

Best Lead Generation Methods:

Plan demonstration "events"
Offer free product-demonstration trials

Qualifying:

A cold market; most prospects question the product's
    basic need or benefit

Gateswingers or trailblazers excited by vision of big
opportunity

New Business Presentations:

Are usually one-on-one
Are theatrical and exciting
Demonstrate the product
Show uniqueness and newness
Help prospects visualize themselves enjoying the benefits
Build the dream

Presentation bottom line: The benefit is really
worthwhile

Answering Objections:

Objection: Customers will question need for the product
Response: Demonstrate opportunity and return on
investment, and give the prospect "permission to buy"

Acceptable Closing Procedures:

Make an immediate request for the order
Offer limited time period to buy
Emphasize risk of losing the opportunity
Note the restricted availability

Customer Relations:

Seldom a continuing relationship after the sale

Customer Service:

When customer is dissatisfied:

Refund the money
Replace the product/service

Resale Strategy (Repeat Business):

Little or no repeat business of same product to same
customer

Consultive Selling
High-Tech/High-Touch Marketing

High-Tech/High-Touch Customers:

> Are buying complex systems
> Have little or no internal expertise
> Need a knowledgeable, patient salesperson

The Consultive Sales Personality:

> Career-oriented, especially toward management
> Status- and image-conscious
> More academically inclined
> Independent and self-developmental
> Team-oriented
> Self-confident
> Nonimpulsive, patient
> Against extreme risk-taking

Most Important Selling Skills:

> Image building
> Presenting
> Answering objections
> Promoting good customer relations

Focus of Consultive Selling:

> Educating and training prospects and customers
> Supervising implementation after the sale

Selling Style:

> Expert
> Competent

Values Consultive Salespeople Provide:

> High-level concept approach
> Professional image
> Technical credibility

Patient teaching
People skills
Service excellence
Team building

Company Image:

Expert
Competent
High tech
State of the art
Serving *leading* customers

Company Focus:

Promote a respectable corporate image
Take total responsibility for benefit
Use team-oriented approach
Emphasize design excellence
Educate the customer in concepts and applications

Key Marketing Efforts:

Image building
Lead generation
Qualifying
Presentation

Customers Want:

An advanced system offering:

A custom design
Flexibility in features/options
Expandability
A performance improvement over standard systems
Installation, training, and service bundled with the
sale

Best Lead Generation Methods:

Give away free educational information

Place bylined articles in professional journals
Offer booklets, seminars, and how-to manuals

Qualifying:

Prospects open to supplier's method of accomplishing
the benefit

New Business Presentations:

Demonstrate the initial concept to high-level decision
maker
Educate the customer in the basic concepts
Offer case history support
Provide a team to design a tailored solution

Presentation bottom line: Our methods really produce
benefits/results

Answering Objections:

Objection: Customers will worry about interruption of
operations
Response: Convince customer that long-term
improvement will be more than worth the trouble of
interruptions

Acceptable Closing Procedures:

Agree on a concept or pilot test
Sign letters of agreement
Develop project schedules that customer agrees to

Customer Relations:

Continuing, patient one-on-one education
Information mailings

Customer Service:

Design and install the system
Train the customer's users

Provide followup system maintenance

Track benefits to demonstrate wisdom of the customer's decision

Find areas for further improvement

Resale Strategy (Repeat Business):

Consultive sales tend to be project-oriented, so there is often little chance to sell same product or service to same customer

Must sell new products or additional services

Expand sale of same products or services to other divisions

Eventually change to relationship selling for continuing business as internal expertise develops

Relationship Selling
Low-Tech/High-Touch Marketing

Low-Tech/High-Touch Customers:

Are buying complex but standardized products/services
Have internal expertise, need less from supplier
Still need dependable purchase and delivery support

The Relationship Sales Personality:

Strong work ethic
Guilt feelings when not doing something
Self-sufficient, independent
Unhappy when bossed around
Cooperative
Loyal
Traditional, even rigid values
Conservative
Resistant to administrative details or paperwork

Most Important Selling Skills:

Answering objections
Closing
Promoting good customer relations
Ensuring customer service
Promoting repeat sales

Focus of Relationship Selling:

Providing customer service
Establishing good feeling

Selling Style:

Dependable
Loyal to the customer

Values Relationship Salespeople Provide:

Practical experience
Customer knowledge

Product knowledge
Top-level service delivery skills
Customer-comes-first advocacy
Reliability and accessibility

Company Image:

Caring
Friendly
Loyal, dependable
Personal, nonbureaucratic service
Serving *established* customers

Company Focus:

Dominate market niches
Develop specialty product/service images
Emphasize customer satisfaction
Strive for sales and service leadership
Have comprehensive production capability

Key Marketing Efforts:

Lead generation
Qualifying
Presentation

Customers Want:

A widely accepted product/service offering:

A standard design with flexibility in features/options
A match with existing quality specifications
On-time delivery according to specific schedules
Some cost savings
Repeatable performance
Understandable technology

Best Lead Generation Methods:

Offer a free service (an audit, analysis, evaluation, etc.)
Seek opportunities to develop relationships
Treat prospects like customers until they are customers

Qualifying:

> Prospects who:
>
>> Want or need the product
>> Are looking for the best provider
>> Question seller's ability or commitment to provide extra service

New Business Presentations:

> Show capabilities
> Build personal relationships
> Demonstrate personal and company commitments
> Offer other client relationships as supporting evidence
>
> Presentation bottom line: We are the best provider

Answering Objections:

> Objection: Customer is likely to invoke not-invented-here objection
> Response: Convince customer of superior delivery and added-value advantages

Acceptable Closing Procedures:

> A handshake
> One-on-one development of personal relationships
> Specification bid
> Quick response to customer need

Customer Relations:

> Regular personal contact by account manager
> Tours of facilities
> Entertainment
> Trade shows

Customer Service:

> Provide top-level service delivery:
>
>> Emphasize accessibility to key account managers
>> Install hotlines and internal systems for instant response

Provide on-site seller representative:

Improve facility-to-facility adjacency
Vary inventory/delivery options
Automate and share production tracking

Resale Strategy (Repeat Business):

Expand product or service purchases from same user
Solicit referral sales to other users in the same company
Perform annual relationship audits

Display Selling
Low-Tech/Low-Touch Marketing

Low-Tech/Low-Touch Customers:

Are buying standardized products and services
Major variables are price and convenience

The Display Sales Personality:

An enjoyer of people
Impulsive
High physical energy level
Easily bored; happier when there are things to do
Low career-advancement ambition
Work secondary to home and personal goals

Most Important Selling Skills:

Ensuring customer service skills
Encouraging repeat business

Focus of Display Selling:

Communicating product availability
Responding to the customer

Selling Style:

Nonconfrontive
Systematized

Values Display Salespeople Provide:

Price and delivery knowledge
Basic product information
Consistently friendly service

Company Image:

The dominant supplier
Is the standard or observes the standard

Convenient location, service
Attractive prices
Available when needed
Well-established
Serving customers *everywhere*

Company Focus:

Develop brand awareness and loyalty
Be relentlessly cost-competitive
Provide continuous sales promotion
Emphasize mass media advertising
Provide distribution ownership or close distributor
   support

Key Marketing Efforts:

Presentation
Closing
Resale

Customers Want:

Standard products and commodities offering:

Low cost
Easy replacement
Ready availability when needed

Best Lead Generation Methods:

Maintain brand awareness through advertising
Offer buying convenience and price advantage
Use convenience tools and incentives (mail-order
   catalogs, 800 numbers, discount coupons, and special
   promotions)

Customers Are:

Administrators
Consumers

Qualifying:

>A hot market; an abundance of customers who know
>they want or need the product or service
>Prospects who question a supplier's price, features, and
>options

New Business Presentations:

>Stress flexible feature and option packaging
>Include catalogs and point-of-purchase displays
>Emphasize ease of convenience of purchase and delivery
>Show price advantage
>
>Presentation bottom line: We offer the best buy

Answering Objections:

>Objection: Buyers, who are often entrenched in
>established habits, may say, "That's not the way we've
>always done things"
>Response: Convince customers that seller offers the
>better buy, and make customers look good in their
>organization for giving seller the order

Acceptable Closing Procedures:

>Offer sales promotions
>Provide telephone-ordering service
>Hold annual contract negotiations
>Accept credit cards or offer convenient terms

Customer Relations:

>Annual high-level supplier-customer review meetings
>Surveys of customer satisfaction

Customer Service:

>Accept returns, provide substitutions

Automate delivery tracking, share information
Do joint-usage forecasting

Resale Strategy (Repeat Business):

Emphasize inventory restocking
Offer special discounts, incentives
Provide special financing
Promote brand loyalty